# The Keeper

# The Keeper

## Paul Cockburn

*Virgin*

*With thanks to Danny and Jack Shreeve and the boys of Remove B, plus Mr Ryecroft and Mr Owen, The Mall School, Twickenham, for invaluable market research.*

First published in Great Britain in 1996 by
Virgin Books
an imprint of Virgin Publishing Ltd
332 Ladbroke Grove
London W10 5AH

A catalogue record for this book is available from the
British Library.

ISBN 0 7535 0085 X

Typeset by Galleon Typesetting, Ipswich
Printed and bound by
BPC Paperbacks Ltd, Aylesbury

*For Robert James – dynamic goalkeeper and now hard-tackling midfielder. Not to mention future England batsman.*

# One

—⚽—

They ran across the darkened car park, following a line of low plants. The taller one kept his eyes up, watching the security camera on the corner of the roof. It was still sweeping the other side of the building; they still just had time to reach the blind spot in the shelter of the generator building.

The smaller figure – a good foot shorter than his colleague – led the way, running quickly even though he was crouched low to make the most of what little cover the newly planted bushes offered. It wasn't much. Not only were the plants several seasons short of maturity, but it was late autumn and the branches were quite bare of the foliage the architects had planned. If the camera turned towards them, there was very little the two figures could do but trust the darkness.

They were both dressed entirely in black. The taller one was a man of about eighteen or twenty, and wore black Levis and a short leather blouson jacket. His pale face was shaded by a baseball cap. His companion was at least five years younger, and his jeans were frayed and patched, more dark grey than black, and his coat was a long, baggy affair that reached below his knees. He had nothing to cover his head but a shaggy mop of dark brown hair.

Their feet scratched through loose stones as they came to a halt beside the generator building. The taller one grinned.

'That's got us past the cameras,' he said, with a sly wink. 'I told you we could make it.'

The other one nodded, breathing steadily. He watched his mate's breath clouding in the cool night air. 'What next?'

'Up.'

There was a metal ladder attached to the side of the small, square building. They both climbed up, cautious now, trying

1

hard to minimise the noise. On the top, they were in plain sight once more, but the security cameras on the clothing superstore were angled down to the ground. They were practically invisible up on the roof.

The generator building had a back-up power supply which was connected to the superstore – and all the other warehouse-sized shops around the new retail park – by thick wires carried at roof level on metal gantries. These frames were light and flimsy. The younger of the two looked at the nearest one and shivered.

'OK,' said his companion urgently. 'Over you go.'

'That'll never take my weight . . .' the other one whined.

'Sure it will! Those cables help hold it up, don't they?' The boy crept to the edge of the roof and placed a little weight on the gantry. It didn't collapse under him. Not then, at least. 'See?' The boy looked back and nodded. 'Remember. Walk lightly over the roof and no-one will hear you. Use the ruler to jemmy the lock on the air conditioning vent. You go down, you go round. It'll come out in the store rooms. Go over to the loading bay door. Use the key I gave you in the alarm. Open the box, throw switch thirteen, close the box and switch the alarm back on.'

'I remember.'

'Make sure that you do.'

The smaller figure peered over the edge once more. 'What if there's a security guard?'

'I told you; it might say twenty-four hour security on the signs, but three nights in four there's nobody there. And if we get unlucky tonight, it'll be that cold in the store room that your man will never venture out of his cosy little office. He'll sit there watching the CCTV, or more likely he'll be fast asleep. Now go!'

There was no point denying it any longer. The younger of the two crept out on to the gantry and started to edge along it on his hands and knees.

At first – and he was mightily relieved about this – the gantry felt as solid as a rock. But by the time he reached the middle, he could feel it sagging under his weight and shifting slightly in the cold, raw wind that whistled up the side of the building. It made an ominous creaking sound.

He looked back. His companion had disappeared. Common sense told the boy to turn back, but common sense wasn't his strong point. He went on, even more slowly than before. His hands were turning blue with the cold, and his teeth were chattering.

When he reached the largest building, he breathed a long sigh of relief. He felt like he needed to pee. There was no time though, and he wanted to get off this roof and into a little shelter at least.

Just as planned, he managed to prise off the grille on the face of one of the large square boxes dotted over the roof. There was a mounting just inside the hatch for an extractor fan, but that hadn't been fitted. It was when his fellow thief had heard how some of the fans were faulty and removed for repair that the plan had been born.

The boy slid into the narrow tube. Almost at once he felt his shoulders stick. There was a terrifying moment when he thought he was going to be jammed in there, but he managed to fight his way back out. He removed his coat, stuffed it into the tube in front of him, and climbed in again.

This time he had that extra little bit of room that his bulky coat had denied him. He wriggled forward and made his way along the pipe, letting gravity take him down inside the building, and then crawled along the vent to where it emerged from the high ceiling of the store room. He levered the mesh off that end of the duct and tied some string to it so he could lower it silently. There was a pile of boxes directly below; the mesh made a metallic clattering sound as he allowed it to lie flat.

The boy followed, dropping his coat and then falling the three or four metres on to the pile himself. He landed awkwardly, almost pitching off the side of the stack, but managed to hang on. One of the boxes on the top layer fell off the palette and landed with a noisy clatter on the floor below.

He spent the next few minutes dreading the sudden glare of lights and the sound of people approaching to investigate. Nothing happened. He got up and crawled to the edge of the stack. There was another, lower stack beside it. He dropped down on to that, and then slid down its face to the cold stone floor.

Quickly pulling on his coat, the boy ran to the delivery bay door. He was eager now to get to the end of this, to get the job done. He found the alarm, turned it off with the stolen key, quickly flicked Switch 13 to OFF, and reset the alarm. Then he tapped on the inside of the loading bay door.

At once, he heard a key turn in the lock of the smaller man-sized door set into the huge entrance to the bay. His companion slipped in from outside, looking stern.

'What took you so long?' he hissed threateningly. The boy cowered. At once, the taller man's face split in a wide grin, his eyes narrowing. 'Never mind. Let's do what we came here to do. We want Predator boots, Jordans, that kind of thing. We can't carry a lot, so we'll go for the best. Pull this off, and maybe we'll come back next week, eh?'

The man pointed him towards a stack of trainers off to the left. The boy turned and went where he was told.

In that corner of the stock room, he found Reeboks and Nikes. The boy used his steel ruler to slit the shrink wrap on the stack, then removed a dozen pairs of the Air Lites, spilling them from their boxes into a bag he had produced from his coat pocket.

He was just turning away to rejoin the other when he saw something along the aisle that snatched at his attention. It was a rack of Umbro jerseys, the dazzling multi-coloured ones that goalkeepers wear. The boy couldn't help staring at them. He had taken five or six steps before he even realised he was walking towards them.

'Hey!' A sharp voice. A woman's, but sharp and challenging. A torch beam hit him in the face. 'What are you doing here?'

He knew she didn't really want an answer to that question. Though dazzled by the light, he caught glimpses of her dark grey uniform and the bright shiny peak on her cap.

He was on the point of turning and running for the door when he heard the scuff of someone moving quickly, and the torch beam suddenly spun crazily up into the air. The boy heard something go smack. It reminded him of hearing a wet fish hit the draining board in his mother's kitchen.

It took his eyes a while to readjust to the darkness.

His companion was standing over the fallen woman, making sure she was down. He had a long tube of cloth in his hand –

the boy knew it was a thick woollen sock, loaded with pebbles. The woman groaned very softly. There was blood seeping through her pale hair in front of her ear.

The man was grinning. 'It's just as well I never let you out of my sight,' he whispered triumphantly. 'Never!'

'What do we do now?' the younger one asked.

'Too much to hope they'd leave a woman on her own in here,' his smiling companion replied. 'Otherwise we could get the truck and load up –'

Light flooded the room as all the overheads went on at once. They both saw the man over by the doors at the same moment. His eyes were fixed on them too, and on the shape slumped on the floor.

'Hold it right there!' he yelled.

After that, everything fell into confusion. The boy heard his mate yell 'Run!' and the two thieves made a break for the door. The older one crashed into the male guard, and they fell to the floor, punching and kicking at each other. The boy hesitated, then went out through the door at top speed. Somewhere along the way, he lost his grip on the bag, and the boots were gone. He kept running. Home was several long miles away, but he didn't stop until he got there and could fall on to his bed, fighting back the tears.

'Just like I said,' came a familiar voice from the darkness in the corner. 'I'm always there to keep an eye on you.'

# TWO

It was so cold that November that every step Russell took across the field made the grass crack. His breath hung like mist about his face, making him look even paler. He hugged his arms closer to his chest, feeling the chill wind bite through three T-shirts, his hooded jacket and the long coat he wore over the top. He hurried over into the shelter of the low building in the corner of the field.

It was still too early for anyone to be around, but Russell took a while to check the place out anyway. It was perfectly quiet. There was a light in one of the houses that backed on to the small, square playing field, but no other sign of life. By moving round to the far side of the single-storey building, Russell knew he would be out of sight from the houses and yet still able to hear when the first cars drove up the shingle road.

Russell scratched his head through the jacket's hood and his thick mop of copper hair. It was so cold that even his hair ached, and his ears stung with a sharp, raw pain. Standing beside the wall of the building, he blew on his hands and looked around once more. Still all was silence. He reached into his pocket and pulled out a slender metal rule, slipping it into the gap between the window and the frame. The faulty catch quickly fell open.

He levered the narrow window open and climbed up and through, using some beer crates stacked conveniently by the back door. It was a tight squeeze, but Russell was both slender and agile. Within moments, he was able to drop down on to the clubhouse floor.

The dim light of dawn barely penetrated through the curtains of the rooms inside, and Russell moved slowly from the loo and into the bar. It smelled of stale cigarette smoke, flat beer and some other stuff Russell didn't care to imagine. The counter was sealed off behind steel shutters. Russell weaved his way around the small round tables, each piled with four metal and plastic chairs, and went through the doors at the far side into a short passage. The club-house's main doors stood closed and locked one way, while the other led into the changing rooms. At the back of the building, there was a locked store cupboard, but Russell knew the key was always left on a locker in the changing room. He reached up and found it, then unlocked the store.

Inside, he scarcely found room to stand. There was cleaning equipment in one corner — mops, brooms and buckets and piles of old rag — and in another corner there was a huge net filled with footballs, some of them looking almost prehistoric. The whole of the longest wall was taken up with shelves, on which were stacked tins of paint, creosote and line white, along with some white spirit and embrocation. Under the shelves, two bags contained goal nets, neatly folded, on which were piled five-a-side goalposts and two crossbars, a stack of about ten traffic cones, some painted tyres and some low hurdles. The room smelled of liniment and unwashed socks, and of much else beside that wasn't all so savoury.

Finally, there were two wardrobes side by side; one relatively new and large, the other tatty, old and narrow. When he had first seen them, with their iron bars and padlocks across the doors, Russell had wondered what treasures they contained, and how he might find out. It had taken him several weeks to realise that the older wardrobe had no back — he could drag it forward and reach everything inside.

What he discovered had given him a secret pleasure. Thirteen shirts hung on wire hangers from a rusty old rail; one bright yellow, with a pattern of black slashes across it, the other twelve red and white striped with blue numbers, and the words 'Moss Car Hire' stencilled on the front.

Russell took the thick, golden goalkeeper's jersey from the wardrobe, removed his coat and sweatshirt and pulled it on. Down on the floor he found a pair of gloves, and he picked them up as well.

He paused, listening, to make sure all remained quiet, then

selected the topmost ball from the large net. He gave it a squeeze, then bounced it twice on the concrete floor. It was too soft. He tried another and found it much harder. He tucked the second ball under his arm, grabbed his gear, and returned the way he had entered.

Clambering back out into the raw, cold air, Russell quickly made his way to the corner of the field, down by the fence overlooking the HGV depot and the by-pass. Some time ago, someone had dumped a pile of broken paving slabs there. Russell had salvaged the best and stood them in a row, leaning against the chain-link fence.

He faced them now, dropping his coat to act as one goalpost, about six metres from where an iron fence post had been driven into the ground.

Having marked the goal, Russell set himself and drove the ball against the row of paving slabs. The ball hit one of the slabs in the centre, and rebounded chest-high into Russell's hands. He dropped it and hit another hard drive. The ball came back at him a little lower this time, and he dropped to his knees to gather it.

Because the broken slabs overlapped each other in a crazy paving pattern, the bounce was wholly unpredictable. Over the next hour, several of Russell's straight drives went back flying wide to his left or right, sometimes spinning wildly. A few flew high, and he had to take off quickly to reach them.

Shot after shot, as quickly as he could line them up. Each time he hit the ball, Russell had to rebalance himself quickly, to be ready for whatever trick the paving slabs delivered. He was forced to dive full length several times, or fling himself up to flick a high ball over the imaginary bar. The cold ground jarred his bones, and he felt his flesh bruise. No matter how much it hurt, though, he kept the drill going, until the morning light had brightened a little further and the mist on the low ground around the by-pass had lifted.

Breathing hard, Russell picked himself off the floor for the last time. There wasn't time to rest just yet. He kicked the ball ahead and raced back to the clubhouse. It took him another five minutes to put everything back the way he had found it. He was just slipping out through the window when he heard the first car creeping along the stony road.

He used the ruler to tap the catch back into place, then trotted away to the hole in the fence over by the line of tall trees that partially screened the field from the houses. He dropped down an embankment, through a drainage culvert, and reappeared out on the back road that led to the field. A few other cars were winding their way down towards the stone-strewn path and through the gates with their fading, wooden sign: 'PROPERTY OF STONEBRIDGE FC. PRIVATE. KEEP OUT.'

Russell sat down on a bench at the edge of the black square of cinders that served as a car park, and watched the two teams emerge from the changing rooms, thumping balls out in front of them as they ran out on to the pitch. It had warmed up somewhat since dawn, but they were all muttering and cursing about the chill air. One figure, dressed in yellow and black, complained more than most.

'Coach! It's happened again! Look at this shirt!' The boy tugged at the grubby sleeve, pointing out the grassy smudges to a man of about 40, who though he was wearing a thick coat over a track suit, was still shivering. 'Why can't Mrs Stewart wash my shirt like she does the others?' the boy moaned. 'It's filthy!'

'I'll have words, honest I will,' said the man, smirking slightly. 'But don't worry about it now. We've got a game to win.'

The boy didn't appear to be able to forget the state of his jersey that easily. He rubbed at the marks on his breast, and Russell could still hear him whining when he took up position in goal.

The team coach ignored him, clapping his hands together as he tried to encourage his players to warm up and get ready for the game. They went through their routines unenthusiastically.

Russell took a look at the opposition, clad in red and blue, like Oldcester United or Crystal Palace. Unlike the red and whites, this lot looked sharp even before the kick-off. A blondish kid hit shots at goal with both feet, while a tall, broad-boned red-headed boy practised heading the crosses fed to him by an energetic Asian boy. They looked a pretty good outfit in Russell's opinion – not that he had a lot to go

9

on, other than watching the various senior and junior sides that turned up to use this small pitch.

He was a little surprised by their goalkeeper. Alone among his shouting, clapping, eager team mates, this one seemed a little subdued. Russell also noticed how short he was. There wasn't another lad on the pitch who didn't have three or four inches over him. He was a good keeper – very quick on his feet and agile – but it was clear that he didn't like anything driven too high over his head.

The referee dragged himself away from his Thermos and his car, and settled the toss. He waved the teams to change ends, looking irritable when they didn't move quickly enough. Half of them weren't ready when he waved his arms to start the game, adding a loud blast from his whistle.

It was a strange game to watch. Russell wrapped himself as deeply as he could in his baggy coat, and watched as the red and blue uniformed visitors quickly overwhelmed the home side. The ball hardly ever entered their half. Even when the local coach urged his team to just hoof it upfield, the ball was quickly returned into their territory. The red and blues played the ball quickly along the ground, pushing passes behind the opposition's sluggish back four, where they were snapped up by the blond lad and the Asian kid. It was 2–0 at half-time, and it might have been 7–0.

The short goalkeeper had touched the ball twice. Two back passes.

He looked thoroughly dejected as he followed his team mates to the next bench along from Russell, where their manager, a smart young man in a hooded sweatshirt, jeans and trainers, handed out drinks and bananas from the back of his care-worn old car.

'You all right, Mac?' he asked the keeper.

'No, I'm not all right. I'm freezing!' The boy had a strange, rolling accent. His thin, pale face was almost blue with cold. Russell knew how he felt, and he at least had a coat on.

The manager gave him a hot drink from his vacuum flask, and rubbed a little warmth back into his shoulders.

'Just don't lose concentration,' the man said. 'I think we've got this game under control, but it only takes a couple of lucky breaks to bring a team like this back into contention.'

Russell knew that it wasn't likely that a couple of lucky breaks could bring Stonebridge FC's youth team back into anything. There were sixteen teams in the League they were part of, and they were lucky to be as high as sixteenth. Russell had seen them cave in 8–2 just two weeks before.

The blond kid went over and tried to cheer up his keeper with some joke about an incident at school. A car alarm had gone off and everyone had thought it was a fire drill; something like that. Mac smiled briefly but then the ref called a premature end to half-time, and the blond-haired manager sent them back out for the second half.

'You'll be all right, Mac,' the manager said. 'That first half was only about forty minutes. I think the ref wants this to be over even more than you do.'

Mac's face looked strained with bitter disappointment as he walked slowly back out on to the pitch. 'I hate being in goal!' he snapped as he left.

Russell's frozen ears caught every word.

He watched the second half even more closely than the first. The red and blues completed their demolition of Stonebridge FC. Once the score reached 6–0, he turned his attention to the lonely, unrequired figure in the visitors' goal. He kept a close watch on Mac for perhaps ten minutes, ignoring everything else – even two more goals – until the referee decided the frozen massacre might just as well be over, and called time after no more than about 30 or 35 minutes. He was the first one off the pitch, climbing straight into his car and driving away before some of the players had reached the touchline.

Russell remained huddled where he was, listening to the bright chatter of the red and blues as they headed over to the side, to be greeted with plastic cups of hot soup and the warmer congratulations of their team boss.

'Nice win, lads, keeps us top no matter what Parkside or Gainsbury have done today. Now, the Stonebridge manager tells me that their showers don't have any hot water, so I suggest we call it a day and go home.' There was a chorus of agreement. 'Training Wednesday as usual. Don't forget to bring your kit back, washed and ready for next week. Go on, then, beat it.'

The boys began to move off in small groups towards the cars parked behind Russell. Frozen parents emerged from behind their Sunday papers to congratulate them on a great win, and to urge them to hurry.

One of the fathers caught Russell's eye. He had stepped out of an expensive German (as far as Russell could tell) car, and was making his way over towards the red and blues' manager. The small goalkeeper had already retreated into the car's warm depths. Russell listened closely.

'Iain Walsh?' the smartly dressed father asked.

The coach turned round and smiled back. 'Yes, hi. You must be Mac's father . . . Mr MacIntyre?'

'That's right, yes, I'm Donald's father.' Russell noticed he had an exaggerated version of his son's heavy accent. 'Have you got a moment?'

Walsh said he had, and finished packing away his gear into the boot of the old Honda. The taller man waited, the breeze barely stirring his wavy brown hair. Russell waited too.

'I just wanted to have a talk with you about Donald,' he began once Walsh was ready. 'Don't get me wrong about this, because we're delighted he's been selected for the Colts, but he really isn't happy playing in goal.'

Walsh uttered a short, dry laugh. 'He's said so. I'm keeping an eye out for someone, but –'

'But?'

Walsh straightened. He was a fair bit taller than the dark man with the strong, rolling accent, and he was much beefier. When he came up to his full height, as he did now, he seemed to take up a lot of space.

'The truth is, Mac's a good goalkeeper, but a bit of an unknown quantity anywhere else.'

'He'll stay an "unknown quantity" if you don't give him a chance!'

Walsh acknowledged that this was true, and thought hard before he continued. 'The fact is, though, Mr MacIntyre, I think Mac will struggle to get into the team in any other position. We've said for a while now that we'd welcome someone with a bit more weight at the back, but apart from that there aren't any real openings. If Mac doesn't play in goal, I feel he might end up dropping out of the Colts altogether.'

Mr MacIntyre took a moment to consider this. 'I see. So you don't see a role for Donald in midfield, say?'

Walsh shook his head. The two men stood still for a few moments, clouds of vapour gathering around them like a fog bank.

'I'm sorry,' said Walsh at last. 'If we find another keeper, I'm prepared to let Mac try out for one of the other places, but until then –'

'Yes, yes, I understand,' the other man replied quickly, and then he went back to his car. Russell heard the boy asking questions as the door opened, but they were cut off as it shut with a dull 'clunk'. Moments later, the engine turned over first time, and the sleek blue car backed out and nosed its way along the black path, its tyres crunching the loose stones and cinders.

The Honda followed a few minutes later, then the last few cars pulled away. Soon, the only one left was a red Fiat with a Sheffield United scarf in the back window. The home team manager had gone back into the clubhouse.

Russell trotted over to the double doors, swung one back and went through the small doorway to his left, into the bar. The manager was lifting chairs down from the tables, glancing at his watch. Russell looked up at the clock above the bar – it was close to midday.

The man noticed him. He jumped in surprise, clearly not having heard a sound as Russell entered the room.

'Hey! You're not supposed to be in here! Clear off!'

'Who was playing today?'

'You what?' queried the man, his voice squeaky and high. He waved a hand at Russell, his face creased by a deep frown. 'Go on, get out of here!' Russell remained still, stubbornly waiting for his answer. The man glowered at him for a moment longer, than sighed in frustration. 'Stonebridge Town Youth "A",' he replied, gracelessly.

'I know that,' said Russell, evenly. 'The other team.'

'Riverside Colts. Happy now? Go on, get out of here.'

'Where do they play at home?'

The man stopped what he was doing and stared more intently at Russell. 'Don't I know you?' he asked, trying to get a good look at Russell's face in the dim light of the bar. Russell was still wearing his hood up.

13

'Where do they play at home?'

The man narrowed his eyes, obviously trying to remember something. He lifted down another couple of chairs. 'Over the river, near Spirebrook. You know where the university is?' Russell made no sign either way. 'Well, it's by the river. The Colts use their pitches.'

Satisfied that he had what he wanted, Russell turned away quickly. The bar manager cum youth team coach was just opening his mouth to speak again when the door banged open. There was nothing silent about the way the boy left the clubhouse.

The man continued to prepare the room for its Sunday lunchtime session. His barmaid had arrived, the shutters were up and the cash was in the till when something occurred to him.

'Jones. He's one of the Jones boys.'

The barmaid, a young blonde woman with vast jangling earrings, turned to face him, her ears ringing like church bells. 'Who's that, Jack?'

'Some kid who was hanging round here earlier. Jones . . . Russell Jones . . . That's it. Russell Jones.'

'What did he want?'

The bar manager scratched his nose thoughtfully. 'What do the Jones boys always want? Something for nothing. Trouble.' The barmaid looked at him nervously. The man ignored her. 'Aye,' he repeated. 'Trouble.'

# **Three**

—— ⚽ ——

Everybody was thankful that, by Wednesday, the weather had warmed up a few degrees. It was still quite cool, but the continuous, raw northerly winds had been replaced by blustery south-western air, which stirred the last few fallen leaves of autumn to swirl around in noisy, angry packs. There were a few showers on and off, but on the whole conditions had improved greatly.

Double history was a thankless way to end the day, particularly when you had Mr Stewart droning on in his vacant way about pre-Norman Britain. Many of the class reckoned Mr Stewart was probably old enough to have seen William the Conqueror personally.

Chris Stephens, who normally thought history was OK, wasn't paying much attention today. Their usual teacher, Mrs Graham, managed to make history seem relevant and alive. It took someone like Stewart to make Nicky's old moan come true – that history was all about old dead people.

Chris looked across at Nicky now. As he expected, Nicky wasn't listening either, but had a small paperback propped against the inside of his textbook. Chris saw that it was the instruction manual for some piece of computer software called Fantasy Football League.

Chris half-stifled a laugh. It was that which attracted Mr Stewart's attention.

'You have something to say, ah –' Stewart didn't know any of their names, since he normally only taught the older students. Unable to complete his sentence, he pointed a crooked finger in Chris's direction.

'No . . . sir!' said Chris, stretching back and running his hand through a mop of corn-yellow hair. Out of the corner of his eye, he saw that Nicky's attention had been duly attracted, and he sat forward as Stewart approached.

'So, perhaps you'd like to tell us just why the Saxons chose Harold to be their king, instead of keeping their promise to William?'

'Well, William was French, wasn't he?' Chris asked, knowing that in times like these it was best to deflect attention with questions rather than try to make up a convincing answer.

'He spoke French, yes,' said Stewart, smirking. 'He was actually Norman, of course, which wasn't the same thing at the time.'

Chris nodded, attempting to convince Stewart by his expression that he was glad that they'd cleared that up. 'Well, there you go,' said Chris. 'We're always arguing with the French.'

Stewart looked closely at Chris, clearly not so sure now if he wasn't being taunted somehow. 'Go on . . .' he said.

Chris's mind raced as he tried to think his way out of trouble. 'Well, it's like the Euro-sceptics, isn't it? They don't want us to have closer ties with Europe, do they? Well, maybe the Saxons felt the same way back then. Or maybe they just didn't like the French.'

'Who does?' snorted Nicky. At once, Stewart went for the new target (Chris's twisted logic was obviously proving too hard to pin down).

'You don't like the French?' he asked. Chris stole a glance over his shoulder, breathing a sigh of relief that he was out of the firing line as Stewart advanced on Nicky.

'Me? Not especially. I mean, I don't care one way or the other,' Nicky babbled. 'But we've always hated the French, right? The British have been fighting them for ages. Waterloo, Agincourt . . .' His voice stumbled for a second. 'All them other battles. And these days it's just the same, isn't it? Their farmers blocking our lorries, and the EU trying to make us all speak French and measure everything in metres and litres. Just like Chris says.'

Chris remained rigidly still, facing the front. He wasn't impressed at the way Nicky was handing the baton back to him so swiftly. Off to his right, Chris could see Jazz quickly scribbling him a note. Fortunately, Mr Stewart was still fixed on Nicky.

16

'So, like most Britons, you say, you don't like the French?'

'No, like I say, it's not that I personally don't like them, although I have to say my family doesn't drink French wine, and we don't eat French bread.'

'Ah!' said Stewart, who was obviously trying to reach some point of his own. Arguing with Nicky was like driving a car that's being towed. You can do as much steering as you like, and you'll wobble about in different directions, but the end result is that you follow where he leads. 'So, your family boycotts French goods, yes? Is this because of the nuclear testing in the Pacific?'

'No,' said Nicky innocently. 'It's because they're awful. Italian stuff is much better.'

Mr Stewart reeled away from his close encounter with the alien mind of Nicky Fiorentini and rubbed his temple with his bony fingers. He caught sight of Chris, clearly remembering that he still had a potential victim to expose.

'So, coming back to you,' he said. 'You'd put Saxon resistance to having William as king down to anti-French sentiment?'

'Well,' said Chris, shrugging and gesturing with his hands. 'It's a bit more complicated than that, isn't it? We only have the word of the Normans that William was promised the crown, while Harold was Earl of Wessex, and therefore the most powerful man in England. It makes sense for the other members of the Saxon nobility to promote one of their own rather than –'

'Yes, very good,' interrupted Stewart, returning to the front of the class. Chris screwed up the note Jazz had scribbled and slipped it into his pocket. He winked at his friend in thanks.

Everyone survived the last ten minutes until the end of the day without further mishap. The buzzer sounded, and Stewart dismissed the class, beating even the quickest of the students through the door. Chris packed his school bag with his folder and books. He was in no such rush.

'That was close, eh?' said Nicky, slapping him on the back.

'I'll say. Thanks for getting involved.'

'I couldn't help myself,' Nicky explained. 'Honestly, when is old Vegetable Stewart going to retire? He makes less sense every time we see him.'

They headed for the door together, pretty well the last to

17

leave. Jazz and Mac were also hanging back, and the four of them congregated in the hall outside, fighting the tide of people heading for the exits.

They battled towards their lockers. Chris put the history books inside and pulled out his sports bag and a homework assignment. He had a busy night ahead of him. Practice in 40 minutes, followed by an hour's French homework and then a dash up to Oldcester United's ground to watch a home match.

The others had also completed swapping over the gear in their bags, so they went back into the hallway and out through the glass doors into the playground. Some fifth-years were organising a game of football under the covered way that joined two of the school's ugly brick buildings. The tennis ball they were using bounced in front of Nicky, who volleyed it into one of the 'goals' marked out by the supporting pillars. He simulated a breathy, crowd cheer. One of the fifth-formers jeered.

A car horn sounded just ahead, and they looked up. Nicky's Uncle Fabian was parked on the driveway, in breach of about 80 school regulations. It was the same every Wednesday; Nicky had to get right across town to take part in practice with Gainsbury, an average team who had been transformed since his arrival.

Although all four of them played for their school team – in fact, they were easily the best four players in Spirebrook's junior side – circumstances had led to Nicky choosing a different team to play with in the Oldcester District Youth League. No-one talked about it much any more, but Chris and Nicky had had a big bust-up the year before. There were other reasons why Chris had ended up playing with the Riverside Colts and Nicky for Gainsbury, but the fight had been at the root of it.

They'd put the trouble behind them, but they were still in their separate teams. Nicky gave them a wave as he ran off to his uncle's Mercedes.

'I still think it's funny, Nicky playing with Gainsbury,' said Jazz, who knew a little less about the story than some.

'Forget it,' Chris replied in a quiet, controlled voice. 'Two days a week we're in the same team; two other days we're not. It doesn't matter that much.'

'He must be playing well for them,' Jazz continued. 'Walshy told me that Gainsbury are having one of their best seasons for twenty years or more. They're unbeaten, except for the game they lost to us.'

The horn tooted again. The Merc slid past, Nicky grinning and waving at them from the window as if he was the Queen.

Chris, Mac and Jazz followed the Merc out through the school gates and into the short length of road outside. Hundreds of kids were milling around, talking and making plans to meet later, or agreeing what was good on TV that night. The three boys actually passed the Merc as they walked along the pavement, turning left into Stratham Road at the mini-roundabout, and heading for the riverside towpath.

'Are you going to watch Oldcester tonight?' asked Mac.

'Of course,' Chris replied.

'Don't you miss them being in the Premier League?' Jazz enquired.

Chris nodded his agreement. 'Of course, but there are some good teams in the Endsleigh.'

'My dad says it's all kick and rush in the First Division,' Mac commented. Chris shot him a sour look. 'Who are United playing tonight?'

'Leicester.'

They crossed the new road that wound round behind the school, eventually meeting up with a new retail park that was going up rapidly beside the river. On the other side there was a small playground and a footpath.

Chris led the way through the gate, along the footpath and on to the riverside walk. This had been an area of scruffy grass and discarded mattresses not that long ago, but the whole of this side of the river bank had been smartened up. There were quite a few people walking along it, moving at the same slow pace as the river: other kids from the comp; a couple of mothers pushing buggies, gossiping about a friend; a jogger, who looked as if the exercise was going to kill him at any moment; a priest from the nearby church, with a paper under his arm.

Chris looked across the river, seeing the bleak countryside that stretched off for a mile or so away from them. A few bare trees stood out against the pale grass and earth. Not a soul moved out there. No – he was wrong about that. There was someone, moving along a path under the trees. It was hard to see who it might be, because whoever it was wore a heavy, bulky jacket, with a hood up over his head. He – or she (although it would be a pretty rough woman, dressed like that!) was running briskly; moving urgently as if he or she was late for an appointment.

'Think you'll beat Leicester?' asked Jazz from Chris's right. He turned back to face the others.

'I think so. Leicester started the season OK, but their defence gives away more presents than Santa.'

Jazz laughed. They walked on steadily. The university appeared ahead of them as they followed the curve of the river bank: several low buildings and one high tower glazed with reddish glass.

'Have you ever been, Jazz?' asked Chris.

'No,' the other boy replied. 'I'm the only one in my family really interested. My father says football isn't much of a game anyway. He prefers cricket, or motor racing. He says only hooligans watch football.'

'Thanks a bunch,' said Chris, huffily.

'I didn't say that's what I believe,' Jazz said quickly. 'It's just my father. He doesn't really approve of me playing either. Says I should stick to my studies and not waste time playing a game I'll only give up when I'm older.'

Chris found it hard to believe anyone could give up football. He was glad his father was as mad for it as he was. He also found himself amazed to hear that Javinder's father wanted him to work any harder. Jazz was already in a higher year group than his age allowed, and even then he always came first in science and languages.

'Maybe he'd let you come with me and my dad sometime,' Chris said. 'We've got season tickets. Sometimes the guy next to us can't make it, so he gives us his ticket for a friend to use.'

'That would be great,' Jazz said excitedly. 'Of course . . . that still doesn't mean my father would agree.' He sighed. 'The trouble with my father is that –'

'Hey!' cried Mac, interrupting. 'What's that nutter doing?'

Chris looked ahead, in the direction Mac was pointing.

Between where they were now and the university campus, there was an area which had once been a storage depot for industrial chemicals (Chris had seen photographs from the 1930s, when all this side of the river was littered with factories and refineries). It was a small plot of land, and there had been no room for additional storage tanks, so these had been built on the other side of the river, on a small spur of land that jutted out into the current. A wide pipe arched up over the river at this point, connecting the two.

Only the depot and the storage tanks were long gone, so all that was left was the strange pipe 'bridge'. At each end, this was fenced off by a spiked collar, designed to stop anyone getting on to the pipe itself.

At least, that was the plan. However, the iron spikes had corroded and a few of them were broken. Chris had never really thought about it before, but that meant you could get across the river on the pipe. Why you'd want to, he couldn't guess, because there was nothing on the other side but fields.

Besides, the figure edging along the pipe was heading towards them. Chris realised it was the runner in the baggy coat. He had already got past the spikes, and was sliding along the black metal pipe on his hands and knees. It was slow work, and risky too. Several times, he saw the figure slip a little, losing his grip, but then snatching back hold of the pipe once more.

'I don't fancy that,' muttered Mac. Chris knew what he meant. It looked like a fast way to dump yourself in the river and a slow way to get across. The figure wasn't even halfway over yet.

Not once did it look as if he (or she . . . no, it really did have to be a he) would give up and turn back. Of course, that might be because turning round was even less possible than going on. Chris and the others found themselves walking more and more slowly, watching the boy dragging himself along the pipe. Most of the other people on the towpath had seen him too. The priest called out.

'Hey! Hey! What are you doing? Come down from there!'

That didn't sound like good advice to Chris, but he refrained from telling the priest that. The figure on the pipe was past halfway, and was tending to slip a lot less often now that he'd got the technique right. He hugged the pipe with his elbows and knees, and pulled himself along as if he was climbing up a rope.

The high brick wall around the depot was still standing, although these days there wasn't much of anything left inside, as far as Chris could see. The wall hid the boy from sight as he reached the last few metres. Chris and the others ran round towards the gate, hoping to catch up with the mysterious river-crosser. The gates were closed but they waited anyway, hoping to see him appear over the top. After five minutes, nothing had happened.

'Think he's still inside?' asked Jazz.

'Who knows?' replied Chris. 'He could have hopped over the wall somewhere round the corner, I guess. I can't see the point of climbing all that way along the pipe just to end up locked inside there.'

They heard footsteps approaching and turned to see the priest walking up with a uniformed copper. The policeman gave them a hard stare, then walked past to try the gate. It rattled, but there was a strong padlock in place and it didn't give way.

'Have you seen anything?' he asked Chris.

'No.'

'Mate of yours, is he?'

'No.'

The copper obviously didn't like the answers he was getting, so he made a big show of bending down to Chris's height so that their eyes were only a centimetre or two apart.

'So, why are you waiting for him?'

'Just being nosy,' said Chris.

The policeman was still unimpressed. 'I suppose you just happened to be walking past, did you?'

Yes, us and two dozen others, Chris thought impatiently to himself; most of them kids just like us, walking home from school, in our school uniforms, carrying our school bags. Only us three aren't on our way home, we're on our way to soccer practice at the university. Chris took a deep breath, and tried not to lose patience with the policeman.

'We're going to soccer practice,' he said, opening his bag. 'We go past here every Wednesday.'

22

'And if we don't go now, we'll be late!' added Mac, who was clearly being made very nervous by the policeman's questions.

'Well . . . you'd better run along then, hadn't you?' said the policeman in a low voice, still glaring into Chris's face. Chris thought about staring him out and seeing who'd flinch first, but Jazz tugged his arm and the three of them made off along the footpath.

'What are we running for?' shouted Chris as they reached the gate. 'We haven't done anything!' It annoyed him that the policeman could have made them act so irrationally. He looked around for the mysterious figure in the baggy coat. When he looked back at the policeman and the priest, he saw that they were still watching him. That annoyed him even more.

'Iain's off on some family errand this week, so I said I'd come and take the session,' explained the track-suited coach. The boys, gathered in a half-circle in front of him, listened closely. Sean Priest was the youth development officer for Oldcester United, the man in charge of signing players for United's youth teams. He took a close interest in Riverside Colts, which everyone said was a kind of 'B' team for the United youth squad.

He was an ex-United player, who had finished his career playing in Holland with Rotterdam FC. Still only in his thirties himself, Priest never talked down to young players. They looked on him as a kind of older brother, the sort you respect and admire. He never tried to sound smarter than them or better than them, but they all knew he was the boss, and that his ideas normally paid off.

He was leaning on the bonnet of his car, flicking through sheets of paper on a clipboard. They waited patiently for him to start.

'Right,' he said at last. 'I've got loads of announcements to make tonight, so hush up and pay attention. Did you all hear the full results from last week? Masham beat the Cathedral two-nil, Ambergate lost at North End, Parkside beat Glenham Eagles four-two. That means Parkside are still level with us on points, although we stay ahead on goals scored. Gainsbury won as well, so they're two points behind, then its Masham, Fairfield and City, North End and the Eagles. So far so good, and Gainsbury have to play Parkside next week, so one of them will drop points for sure. A draw would suit us very nicely.' He looked at Chris. 'Have a word with your mate Nicky, would you?'

Everyone laughed. Although only Chris, Mac and Jazz went to the same school as Nicky, just about everyone knew the story of Nicky Fiorentini and his feud with Chris, which was all in the past now and could be looked back on as an amusing story. It hadn't always been so straightforward.

After a few jokes aimed at Chris, the boys exchanged a few observations about the way the season had started. The Colts were becoming increasingly optimistic about their chances.

'OK, we're away again next Sunday, at Ambergate, on the Memorial Park fields. Ten o'clock kick-off. Iain's picked the same team as last week, so that's Mac, Tosh, Brundy, Zak, Tollie, Nixon, Stamp, Polly, Jazz, Chris and Rory. Phil Basford and Calloway are subs. Anyone likely to have any problems getting there? You all know where their ground is? Good. You others, I've fixed up a bit of a knockabout here, so turn up at ten and you can prove Iain wrong for leaving you out.'

The guys who hadn't made the team chuckled. The Colts only carried a small squad, with perhaps fourteen to eighteen available in any one week. Walsh and Sean Priest tried to make sure there was always something going on for the three or four who didn't get into the team, making sure that they felt included in the Colts' set-up.

'OK, second, Iain will have some letters next week for you all to take home, but you might as well know now what they'll be about. It's the best possible news, and I've been itching to tell you about it since I heard.

'A high school near Newark, New Jersey – that's the USA, in case you're failing geography – have written to Oldcester United offering to take part in an exchange programme. They want to send twelve players here next Easter to spend a couple of weeks playing "soccer".' He pronounced the word with an exaggerated American accent. 'In return, they'll take twelve British kids over there next summer.

'Now, there's one small problem,' he continued. Chris was

24

struggling to see anything but problems. If the American school had offered places to United, what was that to do with them? He waited for Priest to stop beating around the bush and get to the good news. 'The problem is that United's youth team are already taking part in a summer tournament, so we can't match up the dates. So, the only thing I could suggest to the Americans is that we send them you lot instead.' In perfect team formation, the Colts gasped loudly. Priest raised his hands to quiet down the chatter before it could start. 'The deal is this. I need twelve of you to agree to have one of the Americans stay at your home over Easter. During the day, all of you and the Americans will be invited to train with the youth squad at Oldcester United, and we'll probably try to fix up some kind of mini-tournament for everyone to take part in. The same twelve of you will then be able to go to the States in the summer.

'So, you've got to check all this out with your parents and get back to me. If there's more than twelve of you, we'll throw names into a hat and draw to see which twelve take part. If there's less than twelve of you, I'll be very surprised.'

Priest had eighteen loud and excited volunteers in front of him there and then. Chris knew he, for one, was going to start working on his father as soon as he got home, and he was prepared to bet that the others would do exactly the same. A chance to play in America! Unbelievable!

After letting them fire questions at him that he couldn't answer, and babble excitedly to each other for a few minutes, Priest silenced them once again. 'Come on, quiet down. That's not the end of the news tonight. It's not even the end of the good news.' Slowly, everyone toned down the chatter, and faced Priest once more. 'OK. Now, just so you keep things in perspective, I have some bad news for you.' He let this sink in. One by one, the boys all fell silent. 'Now, as you know, we would normally be coming up for the first round of the Oldcester City and District Youth Teams Cup. However, this year, we aren't going to be taking part.'

Chris was as surprised at this news as anyone. Last season, the Colts had lost in the semi-final of the same competition, which had been a bitter blow to the team. When he joined, Chris had heard all the stories, about how the Colts had been winning 3–1 with fifteen minutes to go, only to throw the lead away. That, on top of being runners-up in the League, had made the '95/'96 season very frustrating for the Colts, and everyone at the club was determined to do better this year.

'The reason is a little complicated. As you may know, Oldcester United have joined a national youth competition, and they are going to be playing regional games either side of Christmas. That means they can't take part in the first round of the Central Counties Youth Cup. So, I've arranged that the Colts will take their place.'

'YES!' cheered Zak, who was the oldest player in the Colts squad, and who knew the ins and outs of the various leagues, cups and competitions better than any of the others. Everyone turned to look at him. 'It's a much better competition than the District Cup. Some of the big clubs enter their youth teams. Two years ago, United played Aston Villa in the quarter-finals. It was brilliant.'

'Brilliant, but tough,' commented Priest. 'You'll have to be on your best form just to get through the first round.'

Chris already had some idea of just what that kind of step-up in competition meant from school. Spirebrook Comp were one of the best teams in the Oldcester Schools League, but they always faced a much greater challenge when they played in the County Schools Cup. Now he was moving up yet another grade with the Colts!

'OK,' said Priest, putting the clipboard down beside him on the car bonnet. 'Any questions?'

Everyone had plenty, but no-one managed to put them into words. There was a hot buzz of excitement among the whole team. The only one with anything to say was Kenny Nixon, who played midfield.

'Sean, has Iain remembered that I'm not going to be here from the end of the month?'

'Right, yes. You're off to Florida or something.'

'That's right. We go every year for a month, sometime before Christmas. Me dad needs the warm weather.'

'I don't blame him,' Priest replied. 'I think Iain has the situation under control. Phil, you covered for him when he missed a game earlier this season, didn't you?' Basford nodded. Chris noticed how his eyes lit up at the chance to get back into the side again. 'OK, then,' said Priest. 'If there's nothing else to worry about, let's get on with some practice.'

The huddle broke up, and the Colts scattered as Priest instructed them on what equipment he wanted where. He set Chris, Rory, Jazz and a couple of others in a ring, passing the ball round the circle with their heads and feet, then went off to organise other drills for some of the backs.

Rory Blackstone started the drill off, throwing the ball up and heading it towards Chris. The ball was on its third circuit around the group when Chris missed a simple lofted ball completely.

Jazz followed the direction he was looking in, towards the clubhouse. 'What is it?' he asked.

Chris took a moment longer to see if what he thought he'd seen was actually there. It had been just a fleeting glimpse, and by the time he'd turned and searched for a better view the dark shadow had gone. All the same, he was pretty sure he had seen someone lurking over among the parked cars.

'I thought I saw that kid, the one who climbed over the river on the pipe,' said Chris finally. Jazz was searching just as intently as he had been now, but Chris was about ready to give up. 'He was over by where that green car is parked, by the clubhouse.'

'I can't see anyone now,' said Jazz. 'Do you think we should run over and take a look?'

Chris was ready to agree, but then Rory stepped up to them, handing Chris the ball he had missed.

'Any chance of you two remembering why we're here?' he said in his soft, Irish accent. At the same moment, they heard Priest's whistle drill their ears, and his loud call to get on with things.

Chris shrugged at Jazz, and they turned their backs on the clubhouse and continued the drill.

Iain Walsh was a tough coach when it came to training, but even though Priest was less interested in stretching their fitness than working on their technique, the boys worked harder that week than they had all season. He didn't allow them much of a pause at all after each exercise before he was hurrying them on to the next.

After half an hour's work, he split them into two teams, and told them to play fifteen minutes each way all out. Everyone put all they had into the practice, and there was no time to dwell on the ball or try anything clever. Passes had to be quick and accurate, and everyone ran as hard off the ball as they did in possession, searching for space.

Just after half-time, a big, looping deflection carried the ball over Mac's outstretched hand for the first goal. Priest ran after the ball, which bounced slowly towards the rear of the clubhouse. He trapped it neatly under his trainer, and back-heeled it towards the pitch. Mac was picking himself up and forlornly rubbing dirt from the front of his shirt.

'Let me play in goal,' came a voice.

Priest turned round almost a full circle, searching for the source of the mysterious voice. He finally tracked it down; there was someone crouched in the shadow of the club-house wall, wearing some dark, ill-fitting clothes that blended into the background like camouflage. His face was a small circle of pale skin and wide, staring eyes framed by a hood.

'Sorry, mate, this is a proper club. We're training –'

'I know. Riverside Colts. Top of the League.' The voice used words quickly, clipping the ends of some as if impatient to get on to the next.

'That's right,' said Priest, a little cautiously.

'Let me play in goal.'

Priest didn't answer at first, even though there were plenty of reasons why he should just ignore the boy and get back to the lads he was supposed to be coaching.

He looked back over his shoulder. 'Carry on for a minute!' he called. 'I'll be right back.'

He made sure the game had restarted, then turned back to continue his conversation with the mysterious boy. The young man was still hunkered down in the deepest late afternoon shadows, as if he knew instinctively the exact spot where he would be least easily seen.

'What's your name?' he asked. The boy didn't answer. His eyes shifted away. 'Look, I help run this team. If you can't talk to me, it's no good asking me if you can play.' He turned away as he finished. He hadn't taken his first step before the boy called him back. 'What's your name?' he asked again.

28

'Russell Jones.'

'Where are you from, Russell?' The thought had just popped into Priest's head that the boy might be a runaway. His clothes had a hard, lived-in quality about them.

'Stonebridge.'

Priest nodded, stepping a little closer. He watched the boy flinch, and halted where he was.

'Just over the river. The Colts played there last Sunday.' The boy didn't react. Priest ran a hand through his blond hair and scratched the back of his neck. 'What school do you go to?' he asked.

The boy made a sour face. 'What's with all the questions?' he asked.

Sean gestured for him to calm down. 'League rules. Kids who play in the Youth League have to be at school.'

The boy considered this for a moment, shifting his weight slightly, as if his crouched position was beginning to give him cramp. He had his hands clasped tight in front of him like fists. 'I go to Stonebridge School,' he said.

Priest nodded, although he suspected this wasn't the truth. Stonebridge was a largish village just outside the city, and the only school Priest knew of there was a private primary school on an old farm. Even though he didn't have a very good view of the lad's face, Priest doubted that he was ten or eleven years old, and he certainly didn't look like the sort of kid whose parents sent him to a posh school.

Boys from the village either came over the river to Spire-brook, or journeyed a little further up the road to Crow-haven. If he went to Spirebrook, Chris would know him; if it was Crowhaven, Sean could ask Tony Fielder, one of the reserves. He considered giving them both a call, but thought better of it. It wouldn't take much to spook Russell Jones away.

'You play for the school team?' he asked. Russell shook his head. 'How come?'

This time the only answer was a shrug. Priest sighed. This was proving to be hard work. He was starting to wonder just why he was bothering. Behind him, he could hear the action on the practice pitch was as furious as ever.

'Let me play in goal,' the boy challenged again. And this time

29

he added: 'Your goalie doesn't want to do it. Let me.'

That comment seized back Priest's attention. How did Jones know that? Had he been here before?

'I'm sorry, Russell, I can't. The practice is almost over and I've got work to do with this mob before they go. Look . . . if you want to try out for a team, maybe you should try to get in at school first. I know most of the sports teachers . . . I bet I know yours. I could have a word, and then I'll come and see you play and get an idea of how good you are –'

'Why won't you let me play in goal for you?' the boy interrupted sharply. 'He doesn't want to play in goal –' He gestured with his head towards the pitch '– yet you make him. I want to play in goal, but you won't let me. Why?'

Priest imagined that he had just heard one of the longest speeches Mr Jones had ever made. Something inside him wanted to know more, but time was against him, and he couldn't make things work the way Russell wanted them to.

'I can't just let you play,' he said, quietly, trying to make the boy understand. 'The Colts are a special team, picked from the best boys in the school teams on this side of the city. If you can make it in your school team, then I'll consider you. Otherwise . . .' He looked back over his shoulder, Mac was in the process of making a low save, his body firmly behind the ball. 'As for Mac, he may moan a lot, but he's actually a pretty fair goalkeeper. The player who takes his place is going to have to be really good. But, I promise you, if you have the right stu–'

He had turned back to the clubhouse, but now all he was talking to was dark wall and darker shadow. He walked to the corner and looked towards the small patch of tarmac where a few cars – his among them – were parked, but there was no-one in sight. He hadn't even heard Russell get up.

He looked around for another few moments, then put the strange young man out of his mind and ran back towards the practice field.

'Close him down, Mac,' he called, quickly taking in the action. 'Stay on your feet!!! Good save.'

# Four

Russell's father placed his hands in the small of his back and stretched. Russell heard the bones creak.

'I hate winter,' the old man groaned. Russell, sitting across the fire from his father, ignored him. Five months ago he had been complaining because it was too hot to work.

They were sitting in the driveway of an old farmhouse, a near ruin that they were helping to restore so that it could be sold to a couple moving up from London. The power hadn't been connected up yet, and the chimneys were filled with rubble, so it was easier to keep warm out in the yard than it was inside.

Russell and his father both looked up as they heard the sound of a vehicle bouncing along the unpaved roadway. The engine was rumbling loudly and the gears screeched in protest as the driver let up the clutch too quickly. Russell was on his feet as his brother steered the battered pick-up through the gate, narrowly avoiding the fence posts on either side.

'Did you get them?' his father asked anxiously as soon as the driver's door opened.

'I did,' replied Russell's brother, a broad grin across his face, 'and I found a little extra as a bonus.' He stepped to the bed of the pick-up and threw back a tarpaulin. Most of the space was occupied by a pile of old bricks. Many of them were broken and they all looked dark with age and wear, but there were plenty of them, piled deep in the back of the truck.

Perched on top of the pile, and looking very strange balanced there, was an old enamel bath, complete with corroded taps and a tall pipe leading up to a shower-head.

'What's this now, Mick?' asked Russell's father, clearly delighted.

'I found it under all the other junk inside the out-house. There's some copper pipe too, see, and a few old brass hooks and other stuff.' He showed off these extra treasures.

Russell's dad smiled broadly, showing the gaps in his teeth. 'Excellent!'

'I'd reckon that it used to be some kind of store room, that place. When they chucked stuff out from the main building, they probably dumped it in there. Good for us, eh?'

'I'll say,' the older man replied, sorting through a few of the bricks. 'Do you think there's enough here to finish the job?'

Mick rubbed his grimy, unshaven chin. 'We might be a few score short, but we can mix in a few of them new bricks we had left over. If Russ dirties the new ones up a bit, and scrubs some of this soot and muck off these, no-one will know the difference.'

Mr Jones smiled even wider and clapped his eldest son on the shoulder. 'You've done well, you have, Mick. Russell, give your brothers a hand to unload. We can maybe get a few of these cleaned up before dark.'

Mick climbed up on to the bed and stretched out his hand to haul Russell up beside him. The door on the passenger side had already opened, and Russell's other brother, David, had more or less fallen out, followed by their sister, Marie.

'Help us get this thing off first, Russ,' said Mick, gesturing to the bath. 'And be careful. It's heavy. The three of us half-killed ourselves already getting it into the truck.'

Davey let down the tail-gate, and the four of them slowly dragged the bath down from its perch and off the back of the truck. They stored it close to the old farmhouse and covered it with the tarp.

'We'll tell them Gleason people that it's an antique,' Mr Jones said, still wearing a broad, satisfied smirk across his face. 'It needs a bit of a clean up and a few chips and bangs taken out of it, but I reckon we can tell them it cost a couple of hundred quid. What do you reckon?'

'Easy,' replied Mick, wearing the same grin (only with a full set of teeth). 'That and the bricks, and we've saved a few bob today all right!'

Father and son turned away from the batch and headed back to the truck, from which Russell and Davey were unloading the bricks. Looking up, Russell saw how pleased they both were with their 'find', their faces split with the same greedy smile. Ignore the fact that there was a twenty year age difference between them, which showed most clearly in the father's gap-toothed grin and his heavily lined face, and they could have been twins.

All the Joneses looked alike, for that matter. The same wavy, mid-brown hair (unwashed and cut by Mrs Jones with blunt shears), the same pale skin, dark eyes, long, scrawny bodies and big hands. The smiles just exaggerated the similarities. Davey grinned all the time, and Marie was easily embarrassed, which made her giggle, or snort like a donkey. Pa and Mick found delight in any petty little fiddle they could pull, like this one.

They were supposed to be labouring for Bruce MacKenzie, a huge builder who'd emigrated to Australia once and then come back. MacKenzie bought up old farmhouses, renovated them, and sold them to city folk at inflated prices. The Gleasons had bought this old farm without even seeing the work finished, and were paying for an extension and fitted designer interiors.

So long as the work got done and the Gleasons didn't complain, MacKenzie didn't care what stunts the Jones family got up to. 'Recycled' bricks and 'antique' bathtubs, removed that morning from the out-house behind the private school in Stonebridge, were just the latest in the line of scams they had pulled.

'Now, listen up, Russo,' said Russell's father. 'MacKenzie's brickies will be here on Monday. That means you've got –' He paused to count the days off on his fingers, whispering 'Thursday, Friday, Saturday, Sunday' as he raised four fingers '– four days to get them old bricks scrubbed clean and them new bricks muckied up. I want them all to look the same, you know?' Russell looked at the two piles. The old bricks, under the grime, were the dark red of cherries. The new ones gleamed almost pink. 'We'll be getting back to that other job, then. Marie can stay and help you. Mick will be back to pick you up for supper.' He gripped Russell tightly by the shoulders. 'Do you understand, now? No goofing off. I want a professional job doing on them bricks, so we can have them

Gleason people tell us how clever we are, OK?' Russell nodded. 'Good lad! I think your ma's getting fish and chips in for us tonight. Or maybe we'll stink the place up and have some of them kee-babs. Special treat for all Mick's clever work!'

Mick laughed and made a face when he saw Russell's flat, hard expression. 'You'd better be getting on with them bricks, Russo,' he said. 'Plenty of water and a wire brush should get all the muck off 'em. Eventually.' He laughed again, extremely pleased with himself. Russell knew that all they'd hear about at home for days now would be how clever Mick was, finding stuff in the grounds of that posh school.

Mr Jones waddled around to the passenger door, dragging Davey in front of him, and making the middle Jones boy sit in the middle. Mick jumped into the driver's seat, slammed the door closed and fired up the truck's ancient and abused engine. Forcing the shift into accepting one of the forward gears, he spun the truck round in a tight circle and sped out through the gates, missing one of the posts by less than a centimetre. Russell watched the truck bounce away along the lane.

Once it was out of sight, he sighed and turned to face the daunting task that lay in front of him. It took him a few moments to realise that Marie had disappeared. If he was really lucky, she'd be gone for all four days.

# Five

——— ⚽ ———

Sunday dawned bright and clear. Chris woke early, dressed and went down to help himself to breakfast. He read the sports pages in the paper, giving the report of Oldcester's brisk win over Portsmouth priority. By the time his father staggered down, looking far too sleepy to be in charge of a kettle, Chris had brewed some tea, and there was toast under the grill.

'What's got you out of bed so early?' he asked.

'I said I'd come and watch today, didn't I?' his father replied.

'Sure,' Chris responded, 'but you were pretty late in last night. I thought you might be too bushed.'

Mr Stephens worked as a production supervisor at a factory which made pipes and tubing. Every now and again, he would have to cover the night shift, or work late into the evening, as he had yesterday. Chris had spent most of the day at Nicky's, and gone home after tea. Nicky's Uncle Fabian had gone in with him to make sure the house hadn't been taken over by muggers, murderers or other maniacs, and then Chris had spent the evening alone watching TV.

'How are you going to get there otherwise? I'll be OK. Late start tomorrow, so I'll sleep in then. Besides, I said we'd go over to the Griffon Centre after; do a little Christmas shopping.'

That was hardly a major cause for celebration as far as Chris was concerned, but he was glad his dad would be able to see the game. He rarely got the chance.

They ate quickly and cleared away. Chris's kit was in a bag in the hall, and he was in the passenger seat of the Astra before his father had even found his keys or buttoned his coat.

'Important game, this?' he asked.

'Not especially,' Chris replied.

'I hate to think how quickly you could get out of the house for a really important game,' his father said, and then pulled the car away from the kerb.

They were due to give Jazz a lift, so they turned left on to the main road and made the short journey down the high street to where Spirebrook's main arcade of shops lay. Javinder's family lived over one of the shops. As they pulled up, Jazz was already at the door.

'Another one can't wait to get out of the house.'

Jazz piled into the back seat, and they set off. Chris noticed that his team mate looked a little out of sorts, so he waited until they were stopped at the lights on the new road, then climbed into the back.

'Trouble?' he asked, keeping his voice down.

Jazz nodded. 'I mentioned coming with you to see a United game. My father said no.'

'Why?'

'It's like I told you. He says that too many hooligans go to Star Park, and he's worried that I'll get into trouble.'

'We don't ever get any trouble!' Chris exclaimed. 'There's not enough of a crowd to start an argument, never mind a riot.'

Jazz wasn't finished. 'Also, he says I have to spend more time studying, not less. He's said that if I can't keep up with my work I'll have to give up on playing for either the school or the Colts. That means getting "A"s in the exams after Christmas.'

'You're joking!'

'I wish I were. Either way, I can't come to a game with you.'

'He's not being fair!' Chris insisted. How could anyone stop their kids playing football? It just wasn't right.

His father was looking at them in the mirror. 'He's just looking out for you, Javinder,' he said. 'Would it help if I spoke to him; let him know that you'd be OK with us?'

'I'm not sure, Mr Stephens . . .'

'Well, bear it in mind. If your father is anything like me, he just wants to know what's going on. It's like Chris telling me when he's inviting someone to come with us to a game . . .'

Chris gulped. He realised at once just what his father was saying. It took Jazz quite a bit longer, until they were almost at Ambergate Memorial Park.

36

'You hadn't asked your dad, had you?'

'Not as such, no . . .'

Javinder laughed. 'It looks like I'll be going to watch United *instead* of you!'

Chris didn't think this was as funny as Jazz did.

Someone else was in an even worse temper. To their surprise, the boys found that Sean Priest had turned up for the game. When they had left him after Wednesday practice, he had told them he had plans for the weekend.

'That's right,' he said when they mentioned this to him, 'but I needed to speak to you guys. Come over here, will you?' Chris's dad hesitated, until Priest caught his eye. 'You might want to listen to this as well.'

They stepped to one side, away from the rest of the team. Sean looked very put out and they quickly fell silent, realising that this wasn't the best time to make jokes. There was a small space where a few cars were parked, Priest's among them, and that's where they were headed.

Chris's father hung back slightly. Chris and Jazz waited while Priest rubbed a speck of dirt from the fire-red bonnet of his car. Then he turned and faced them.

'When you left practice last week, did you two go straight home?' Priest asked, observing them both closely.

'Yes. Mac's dad was waiting for him, and Jazz and I walked back along the river.'

'Did you see anything unusual?'

'No, not really,' said Jazz.

Chris was thinking about the boy they had seen climbing across the river, but that had been over an hour and a half earlier. He said nothing.

'You didn't see anyone hanging around the car park?'

'No.'

Sean sighed sharply, obviously disappointed that they couldn't help.

'What is it?' asked Chris.

He could see that Priest wasn't sure what he should tell them, but he then obviously made up his mind to confide in them.

'My car was broken into. Someone did the side window. They took the stereo, some kit I'd left on the back seat, and a

37

few other items I was supposed to be looking after.'

'During the practice?' asked Chris.

'That's right. Once you lot had all gone, I locked up the clubhouse and got ready to go home. When I reached the car, I saw there was some glass on the floor, and that's when I realised someone had smashed the window. I've called the police but they don't hold out a lot of hope. The university management didn't sound hopeful either.' He rubbed his scalp and sighed again. Chris knew there was more on his mind. He started to worry that maybe Priest thought *they* had something to do with it, and that was why he'd asked Chris's father to go with them while they talked. 'During the game, you know when I stayed off the pitch for a moment or two, did you see me talking to someone?'

'Not really,' replied Jazz. 'I could see you were talking to someone but I couldn't really see who it was. It was pretty dark in the shadows there.'

Chris hadn't even noticed that much; he had been concentrating hard on the game. He flicked a glance across to his father, who was listening to everything with a hard look on his face.

'One last thing,' Priest asked, clutching at a final straw. 'Do either of you two know a boy called Jones?'

'There's a Jones in the sixth form at Spirebrook,' said Jazz.

'And there's a Tony Jones plays for Manton and Hardway . . .'

Priest was shaking his head. 'His name is Russell Jones, and he's about your age.'

The two lads looked at each other. The name didn't mean anything to either of them.

'You think he nicked your stuff?'

'I don't know,' Priest said thoughtfully. 'It's possible. I think I know where he lives, so I might try and have a word with a few people, see what I can find out.' He dug into the pocket of his brown leather jacket and pulled out his car keys. He offered a quick smile to Chris's father, then turned and unlocked the door. 'Well, you'd better be going – they'll kick off without you. I'll probably see you at practice in a couple of weeks.' He climbed into his car. Chris noticed the window had been repaired already, but that there was an ugly hole in the dashboard. 'The insurance can pay for that . . . but some of the other stuff I had in the back . . .' He looked genuinely upset about whatever it was that had been taken. Chris knew instinctively that it had to be something he couldn't replace. 'Enjoy the game,' he said quickly, switching on the engine and putting it into reverse. Jazz and Chris watched as he pulled away.

'You've never said about there being any problems with stuff getting nicked from the university before,' Chris's father observed.

'There never has been, that I know of,' Chris replied.

'I wonder what got taken?' wondered Jazz.

'Something important, I guess . . .' mused Chris.

They trotted back to where the rest of the team was almost ready to go on to the field.

'Hurry up, you two!' yelled Walsh. 'It's bad enough when a team finishes with only nine players on the field . . . I'd rather not start with nine.'

They changed rapidly. Memorial Park didn't have changing rooms or a clubhouse, so they wore their kit under their street clothes. Stamp remarked that they looked like Superman changing without a telephone booth, and someone else made the joke that only Chris could change into his secret identity and look even more like Clark Kent.

Moments later, they were out on the field, and the game kicked off. Much though he was sorry for Sean Priest's problem, Chris had forgotten about them after his first touch of the ball. Nicking stuff was for morons; he'd rather play football.

Ambergate were a difficult team to play against. They packed five men in midfield and used a flat back four who worked well as a unit. Riverside found it hard to get a grip in midfield, and when they played the ball forward quickly, Chris and Rory kept getting caught offside.

With only one man up, Ambergate didn't seem to pose much of a threat themselves, but it left the Colts with four defenders marking one forward, and Tollie and Tosh weren't as adept at coming forward as they could be. Consequently, half the time Riverside seemed to be outnumbered wherever the ball fell, and the rest of the time their defence was finding itself easily able to snuff out whatever attacks came their way.

A few passers-by in the park stopped and watched spells of the game, but even they quickly realised they weren't likely to see a goal, so they went on with their jogging, walking the dog or whatever, leaving just a hard core of spectators cheering on the two teams.

Increasingly frustrated, Chris dropped deeper and deeper, looking for the ball. Nixon had taken a whack on the leg early, and Jazz looked increasingly unhappy with the physical nature of the game in midfield. The Colts were being outfought, and the strain was starting to show.

Ambergate broke from midfield. As the attack started, Chris noticed that Mac was talking to a lad in a yellow and black goalkeeper's jersey, but he raced off his line and stopped the shot with his feet. As Ambergate lined up to take the corner, Chris noticed Mac and the boy exchange another quick conversation, and Mac gave him a thumbs-up as he took up his position.

The corner went over flat and low towards the near post. Mac measured it closely as one of Ambergate's attackers took a step or two to meet it, flicking it back at the near post. Two other forwards were poised to meet the cross, but Mac plucked it from the air before it could reach them.

He held the ball, then kicked it upfield once everyone had moved off, and that more or less brought the first half to a conclusion. The Colts limped off towards where Iain Walsh was ready with drinks, bananas and tough advice. While he started on Tollie and Jazz for not working together, Chris sat down beside Mac.

'Who's your mate?' he asked. The boy was making his way slowly round the touchline on the far side.

Mac looked up and grinned. 'I'm not sure really. He was watching the game, then he came up and spoke to me. He'd noticed how their central attacker always shoots with his left foot, even though he looks two-footed when he runs with the ball. And he worked out that near post corner dodge.'

'He just told you this stuff?'

'Sure,' said Mac. Chris and Rory (who was sitting quietly to one side, listening to everything) exchanged a silent look. Mac

40

noticed. 'I don't know why!' he exclaimed, stung by their doubts. 'Maybe he's seen them play before. Maybe he's got some kind of grudge against them. I don't know.'

Chris turned and looked across the field. The yellow-shirted figure had completed his slow journey to the other goalmouth. He was stretching and jumping under the cross-bar, then sprinting and diving to the ground. He seemed to be practising against invisible opponents, racing off the goal-line to rob ghostly forwards of the ball.

'I don't know . . . he looks a little familiar,' Chris said quietly. 'What shirt is that he's wearing?'

'I thought I recognised it too,' agreed Rory, in a rare contribution.

Jazz approached, hot-faced after his roasting from Iain Walsh. Then all had to pay attention as Walsh talked to the whole team about what they had to do in the second half. He illustrated his annoyance by repeatedly smacking his fist into his other hand.

When he had finished, the boys remained quiet, finishing off their drinks. Chris tapped Jazz on the shoulder.

'Do you recognise that kid over there?' he said, pointing out the yellow-shirted kid.

Jazz shielded his eyes, and looked over to the goal. 'I'm not sure . . .' he said, 'but isn't that shirt the same one Stone-bridge's keeper wore last week?'

Chris banged his palm against his head. Of course, that was it.

'That's not their keeper though, is it?'

Everyone agreed that it wasn't, watching the boy carefully.

'It could just be the same kind of shirt!' said Mac, clearly amazed that they could be so negative. 'It doesn't have to be Stonebridge's! I bet there are hundreds of yellow and black keeper's jerseys like that!'

'With the same sponsor?' asked Rory.

'Just be careful, that's all,' said Chris, warily.

Mac turned away.

The second half started and the match picked up a little extra tempo, although chances remained as rare as dinosaur eggs. Jazz almost slipped Chris through, and Rory had one clear header that the Ambergate keeper just tipped over.

There was just as much traffic the other way though – perhaps more. Ambergate's midfield was keeping their forward well supplied with chances. Twice, the tall, narrow-faced attacker was provided with a run on goal; on each occasion, he shot with his left foot, and Mac reacted perfectly to make the save. Behind the goal, the kid in the yellow and black clapped his hands.

Chris knew his concentration was being affected but he couldn't help it. With about twenty minutes to go, the boy left Mac and went round to the touchline, where he exchanged a few words with Iain Walsh. Chris was still half-watching this when a pass from Jazz caught him by surprise.

'Wake up, Chris!' called Walsh angrily. Chris tried to chase after the player who had robbed him, but the ball was quickly passed upfield. Tollie was left stranded as the opposing full back flew past him, and the cross went over with Riverside badly stretched. Mac leapt as high as he could, but he only managed to tip the ball out to the edge of the box, where another Ambergate player was waiting. Just as he lined up his shot, Stamp slid in with a diving tackle that was way off target. He was lucky. All he got was a booking, and all he gave away was a free kick.

Chris trotted back to join the defensive wall. As he did, he saw the mysterious stranger sprint round behind the goal, helping Mac to line up his defenders with some quick, whispered words of advice. It was a dangerous position, and the lean central striker was lined up to take the free kick, watching Riverside's preparations with a wry smile on his face.

At last, everyone was ready. Chris looked back. Mac was struggling to get a clear view of the ball, edging slowly to his right to cover any attempt by the Ambergate striker to curl the ball round or over that end of the wall. Zak was standing on the left-hand post to provide a little extra cover.

The ref blew his whistle. The striker ran in, and Chris noticed him stutter slightly as he changed his footing. Instead of hitting it with his left foot, he switched his weight the other way and drilled it over the wall with his right. Zak barely moved, and Mac was stranded too far the other way to reach it. The ball fell between them and hit the back of the net.

The whole Riverside team groaned in disbelief, then turned

to take up their positions while Mac fetched the ball from the back of the net. They knew how tough it would be to come back against their well-organised opponents. Worse, they knew Iain Walsh would flay them alive if this one slipped away.

They gave it their best shot, but Ambergate continued to close down every avenue they looked to exploit. Rory hit a hopeful shot from 25 metres out, but that was as close as the Colts got to saving the game. Ambergate celebrated loudly as the final whistle blew.

The Colts flopped on to the ground by the touchline. Walsh handed out some more drinks, looking disappointed, but saying little. Mac looked gutted, his head in his hands.

Chris looked around for his waspish advisor, but the boy had disappeared. His father approached and gave him a consoling pat on the shoulder. 'You get days like this,' he said. Chris raised the most sincere smile he could manage.

'We'll talk about this at practice in the week,' Walsh said, clearly not trusting himself to offer any other comment. The other players started to drift off in ones and twos. Mac's father arrived, and Mac gathered his kit into his bag. Walsh clearly saw how much he was taking the defeat personally, and put aside his anger for a moment to go and speak with him.

'This isn't down to you, Mac. The whole team let this one slip away.'

Mac looked up. He didn't appear to be convinced. 'I couldn't reach it. Chris and I have been practising those kind of free kicks all year, and I'm getting better at judging them, but there are too many I just can't reach . . . either that, or I don't see them until the last second.'

'Their boy just pulled a trick on you, that's all. Switching to his right foot like that. You can't be expected to save everything. The free kick shouldn't have been given away in the first place . . . and it wouldn't have been if we hadn't lost possession . . .' Walsh skewered Chris with a glaring look.

Mac didn't look convinced. Tollie was arguing fitfully with one of the other players, so Walsh went off to grab them so they could help him gather up the team's shirts. They piled them into the open boot of his car, then went off before he could find them any more jobs.

Chris wasn't ready to leave matters like that. 'He's right, you know,' he said to Mac. 'You were just caught wrong-footed off that free kick. We can do a bit more practice —'

'No! What does it take to get through to you?' Mac threw his gloves into his kit bag and pulled on his jacket. 'I don't want to learn how to be a better goalkeeper. It's like you've all said all along — I'm too short to ever be any good. Fine, that doesn't worry me. But I'm not going to waste my time training hard to be second best at something I don't even want to do!'

Chris and the others kept silent. It appeared that Iain Walsh's decision had been the sensible one. After waiting to see if any of them had anything they wanted to say in reply, Mac picked up his boots and went off to his father's car without another word.

Zak, who had been watching all this take place, wandered over to take his place in the discussion. 'It's got nothing to do with how big he is,' he said (which sounded odd, coming from someone built like a telegraph pole). 'He was out of position for that free kick. He was standing much too far over to the right.'

'Why don't you tell him it was just his judgement that was at fault,' Chris remarked sourly. 'That'll make him feel a whole lot better.'

'But that wasn't his fault either,' Zak continued, ignoring Chris's barbed attempt at sarcasm. 'I heard that kid tell him that he watched Ambergate play Stonebridge earlier in the season —'

'What kid?' asked Jazz.

'The kid in the yellow goalkeeper's shirt!' snapped Zak. 'He said he watched Ambergate earlier this season, and that the centre forward always shot with his left foot. He more or less told Mac to move further over.'

A small warning light went on in Chris's mind. 'He did hit everything with his left,' he remarked, 'but that was the first time we saw him strike a dead ball. He had a bit more time to compose himself, to get balanced . . .' Jazz and Zak watched Chris thinking about what they'd seen. Chris's brow furrowed in dark concentration. 'Suppose he knew that. Suppose that kid knew that their centre forward could hit a dead ball off his right peg. He tells Mac to watch his left, and all through the match their player hits it with his left. So, when he tells Mac that he'll hit the free kick with his left, Mac listens, and gets pulled out of position.'

'You think he did it on purpose?' asked Zak disbelievingly.

'Maybe,' said Chris. The more he thought about it, the more it made a kind of strange sense. Or maybe not.

'Why would he do that? What does he get out of it?'

Chris remembered that they had been asking themselves the same thing when they had believed the kid was helping Mac. Even though things had been turned upside down in his mind, he still didn't have an answer.

'He was talking to Iain Walsh as well,' remarked Jazz.

'That's right!' cried Chris, and he jumped to his feet to go over to the Colts coach. Although he didn't really have much idea of what kind of sinister plan he was looking at, something was bothering him about the boy in the yellow and black shirt, and he wanted it sorted. His father was talking to one of the other dads, so he still had a little time to investigate.

Walsh was still looking very unhappy with life when Chris went over to him, but it was clear he was thinking about more than a lost football match. He was searching through his bag and his coat, going over the same places over and over again.

'Lost something?' asked Chris.

'You haven't seen my keys, have you?' replied Walsh, without looking up. Chris hadn't seen them, but he looked around on the ground and told a few other people to do the same, trying to be helpful. After five minutes of this, they were all prepared to admit they weren't going to find them.

'Sean must have taken them by accident,' Walsh decided.

'Is your car locked?' asked Chris's father, who had joined in the search.

Walsh nodded. 'Yes. I locked the doors before the game, and I shut the boot after I put all the shirts and other gear in. That locks automatically.'

Chris's father considered this. 'It should be all right then. We'll give you a lift if you like, and try and find Sean.'

'Actually, you could just drop me back at the university,' Walsh said. 'I'm supposed to meet Sean later anyhow, and I can always go home and get the spare set.' He looked back at his car. 'It should be all right there for an hour, shouldn't it?'

'I would have thought so,' said Chris's father.

Jazz had the bright idea of telling the park keeper what had happened, so that he could keep an eye on the car while they went off to get the spare keys.

They left Memorial Park, having thanked the home team for the game. Walsh had already put most of the team's kit in the boot of his car, so he didn't have much stuff left to carry. They all piled into the Astra; Chris's father and Walsh in the front, Chris and Jazz in the back. Mr Stephens started the car and they reversed along the street a little before finding a space where they could turn round for the trip back towards Spirebrook.

Chris leaned forward as far as the seatbelt would let him. 'You know that kid that was hanging round?' he asked.

Walsh turned in his seat. 'What about him?' he asked.

'What was he asking about?'

Walsh was still fixed on the nuisance of losing his car keys, and he obviously couldn't see what Chris was driving at. 'He's looking for a football club he can join. He says he spoke to Sean, who said that he wanted to see him play sometime.' That small warning light inside Chris's mind started to glow even brighter. 'I told him that wasn't very likely; that we didn't take on players like that, but that if Sean said we should look at him, I'd be happy to.'

Chris thought this over. He remembered what Sean had said about speaking to a boy after practice. Sean's car had been vandalised, and his radio and other stuff taken. Now another mysterious boy had appeared, and Walsh's car keys were missing.

All at once, there were bells and klaxons and other alarms going off alongside the light. Chris felt as if he had just opened his eyes on a bright day. Everything was as clear to him as it could be.

'Dad! Turn round! Go back to the park!'

'What?' his father replied, clearly taken by surprise.

'Please! I – I –' He knew he couldn't say what was on his mind; couldn't put it all together in words. 'I've left something behind.'

Chris's father sighed, and he started to scold Chris about being careless with his stuff as he found a side road he could turn round in. Within five minutes, they were back at the park.

Chris's intuition was right. The moment they reached the park, they all realised what was missing.

'My car!' yelled Walsh.

# Six

The park keeper was very apologetic, but all he'd seen was the car pulling out through the gates just a few minutes after they had spoken with him. He had assumed Walsh had found his keys after all. He'd been just that bit too far away to see the driver, but he didn't think there'd been time for anyone else to have broken in and hot-wired it.

They called the police, who said they'd speak to Walsh, but that if the keys were gone, there weren't going to be many clues at the park. Hopefully, they'd see the car before the thief could get too far in it.

Walsh asked them if he could meet the officers at the university in that case. They agreed.

There was a little bit more traffic around on the return journey, but just over fifteen minutes later they were back at the university sports clubhouse. There was no sign of Sean's car, and he wasn't in the clubhouse.

Walsh went back to the Astra after he'd checked this out. 'Sean's gone off to Stonebridge for some reason,' he said. 'Perhaps he's looking at someone.'

'They didn't have anybody special that we saw,' said Chris.

'Well, thanks for the lift. I'm going to hang round and wait for the police.' He went round to the boot to fetch his bag.

Jazz tapped Chris on the shoulder. 'Looks like he isn't going to have long to wait,' said Jazz. Chris followed the direction he was pointing and saw the bad-tempered policeman they had met before, after the incident with the boy climbing across the river. The copper wasn't heading towards Walsh, but must have been on routine patrol. Chris watched him heading towards the university's main entrance.

'Isn't that the copper we saw before?' Jazz asked.

Chris's father turned in his seat. 'What's this about you and the police?' he asked, looking very concerned. Chris stifled a groan of despair. Jazz obviously didn't even realise what he'd done.

'It wasn't us,' he explained. 'There was this boy, climbing across the old pipe over the river. That policeman thought he was with us, but we don't even know who he is!'

Jazz bolted upright in his seat. 'But look – isn't that him?'

Chris turned again and looked in the new direction Jazz was indicating. This time he was facing the main gates. Across the main road, a slender figure in yellow and black was watching the traffic, waiting to cross. He was breathing hard.

'Bloo–' Chris started, and then he realised where he was and who could hear him. 'Blimey!' he said instead. 'He must have run all the way!'

They watched as the boy jogged over the road and on to the campus. He had seen Walsh immediately and was heading right for him when he suddenly spotted the policeman. Chris watched him carefully. Just as he suspected, the boy dodged off the path as soon as he saw the copper, and circled towards Walsh past some low shrubbery and the football pitch.

'What's he doing here?' asked Jazz.

'I don't know, but I think we ought to find out.'

Chris opened the door. His father spun round in his seat, looking very put out.

'Where are you going?' he shouted.

'I have to find out who that boy is.' Chris waited to see if Jazz would follow, but his friend remained seated in the back of the Astra.

'I have to get home,' he started. 'My father –'

'Dad will take you,' offered Chris.

'What am I, a taxi service?' Chris's father cried in exasperation.

'I'll be home in half an hour,' Chris called, turning away to run over to where Walsh was watching one of the university's teams get a stuffing on the main pitch.

The boy reached Walsh first, and they had started speaking before Chris arrived. The first thing he heard was Walsh telling the boy that they didn't normally take boys who weren't recommended to them by a school teacher, but that

49

he would speak to Sean Priest and see if it was all right to make an exception. The lad was breathing hard, as if he had been running very fast.

'Hi Chris,' Walsh said in a puzzled voice as Chris came over. 'Why are you still here?' The Astra was on its way through the gates. 'Have you been left behind?'

'I just wanted a word,' said Chris.

'Can't it wait? I was just having a chat with this lad here . . . errr . . . what's your name, son?'

'Banks,' said the boy, still puffing. 'Graham Banks.'

'Well, no wonder you want to be a goalkeeper with a name like that.' The boy looked at him blankly. 'Like Gordon Banks. He was England's goalkeeper years back, one of the best we ever had. He was in the team that won the World Cup in 1966.' The boy still looked completely confused. 'No matter. This is Chris Stephens; he plays up front for us.'

'I know,' said the boy. He avoided looking Chris in the eye.

'Graham wants to play for us. I was just explaining that we normally only take lads who have been recommended to us by their schools, or who we have seen play.' Chris nodded, as if this was all much more straightforward than he suspected. 'There's a League rule that says that kids who play in the Oldcester Youth League have to be at school in the area.'

'That's right,' said Chris, forcefully. 'What school do you go to?'

'Crowhaven.'

'You're a long way from home. Isn't there a team nearer home you could play for?'

'No.'

Chris watched him closely. Mr Banks was a lad of few words, and his face carried no great expression whatever he said. He had more or less recovered his wind and was standing a little straighter. The wind tugged at his unkempt hair.

'And you don't play for your school?' Walsh was asking.

'I don't get on with the teacher,' Banks replied.

Walsh nodded his head as if he came across the problem quite often. 'That doesn't matter. You don't have to play for the school team, just go there. And you're a goalkeeper, you say?' The boy nodded and pushed his unruly hair back from his face. Walsh smiled broadly at Chris and gave him a sly wink. 'There's a turn-up for the books, eh, Chris?' The Colts' search for a goalkeeper who could relieve Mac of his duties had been a frustratingly long one.

Chris wasn't so easily impressed. 'He'll have to be pretty good to take Mac's place,' he said dourly.

'Mac doesn't want to play in goal. I do.'

'How do you know that?'

The boy's eyes narrowed. 'Mac told me this afternoon. I've heard him tell the rest of you before. He wants to play outfield. Not me. I want to play in goal.'

'You had quite a chat with Mac this morning, didn't you?'

By now, the hostility brewing between Chris and the new boy was becoming obvious. Walsh started to try and intervene, but Banks was already answering.

'Sure. What of it?'

'You gave him some advice about where to stand? How to position himself? You told him about how their striker always hit the ball with his left foot?' Chris's voice was rising in pitch.

'I noticed it early in the game,' Banks explained. 'He's better balanced on his right foot. I saw him earlier in the season too. It was the same then. He scored three goals, all with his left foot.'

'Mac listened to your advice,' Chris continued, ignoring the response, 'and it cost us the game.'

'Steady on . . .' said Walsh. The two boys were standing very close together now, face to face. Chris was just a shade shorter than the pale-faced young man in yellow and black.

The boy was hesitating now. 'If he was bigger, he would have reached the ball . . .'

'Maybe. But he isn't and you made sure he was out of position to cover the shot. What's your game, Banks? What are you after?'

The boy's eyes flashed with rage, but he was already starting to back down. Chris was so sure he was right, he carried the argument in front of him, sweeping all resistance aside.

'I want to play football,' the boy said. 'I want to play in goal.'

'Not on this team, mate. Not on this team.'

The boy remained still for just a moment longer, still face to face with Chris. But whereas Chris was up on his toes, hands clenched, poised for action, Banks had let his hands fall limply to the side. He backed off a step, turned, and ran off.

Chris watched him go, feeling a warm glow of satisfaction that was only slightly tainted by the fact that he wasn't as 100 per cent sure of his facts as he wanted to be.

'Would you like to explain to me what that was all about?' asked Walsh, who looked truly amazed by Chris's behaviour.

'There's something suss about Graham Banks,' he said, and he tried to think it through before continuing. The trouble was, whatever it was about Banks that was niggling at him refused to become obvious. 'I've seen him before, I know I have.'

'And?'

'And I think he's not who he pretends to be.'

Walsh laughed. 'What are you talking about?' he said. 'He's just a kid who's mad keen to play football. I know quite a few like that.'

Chris ignored the comparison Walsh was trying to make. 'That business this morning, with him giving Mac advice. There's something dodgy about it. At first I thought he was probably from Ambergate, but now I'm just wondering if he did it to make Mac look bad.'

'That's ridiculous! Mac had a pretty good game, except for that one mistake. And, as you've been saying all season, Mac does have a problem with free kicks in front of goal.'

There was no denying it. Chris and Mac had worked together in practice, trying to find ways to allow Mac a better sight of the ball at free kicks, or more time to react. Usually, this meant trying to cover one side of the goal with the wall and defenders on the line, while he watched the other.

'And then there's the business of your car,' Chris said. As soon as he said it, Chris knew how weak it sounded. Walsh threw up his hands in horror before Chris even completed the sentence.

'Now he's a car thief?' Walsh turned away for a moment, then faced Chris once again, looking extremely impatient. 'For goodness sake, Chris, he left the park before the game was over! Didn't you see how winded he was just now? He *ran* back here from Memorial Park. If nothing else, that means he's pretty awesome in the fitness department. I expect that's why Sean wanted us to have a look at him.'

'That's another thing,' said Chris. 'We didn't see this kid Sean spoke to the other night, but his name was Jones, not Banks. And right after Sean spoke to him, his car was broken into. Doesn't that strike you as odd?'

Walsh took a moment to consider. 'You don't even know it's the same boy! And you can't be sure that there's any connection with what happened to the cars.'

Chris started to offer the opinion that it was a pretty big coincidence, but Walsh cut him off.

'That doesn't change the facts. Banks didn't have time to steal my car. And if he had, do you honestly think he would have come back here?'

'Maybe . . .' said Chris lamely.

'Well, if he did steal it, then he's leaving it wherever he parked it,' mocked Walsh. 'Look, he's not even heading back the same way . . . he's going out through the river gate.'

Chris looked over towards the river, and saw the yellow and black shirt against the dark shadows of the river front. For a moment, Chris thought about chasing him, but he was starting to feel foolish enough already.

'So,' he said, after a while. 'Are you going to give him a trial?'

Walsh laughed. He didn't sound amused. 'I don't suppose we'll ever see him again after your exhibition just now. But if he does show the determination to come back, then sure, we'd be silly not to check him out.'

Chris nodded to show that he agreed with the Colts' manager. Maybe he'd been too hasty. Maybe not. But Chris knew one thing for sure — he was going to check out everything he could about Graham Banks, no matter what it took.

# Seven

At school during the following week, Chris found very few of his mates interested in his theories about the mysterious figure of Graham Banks. He couldn't even speak of it in front of Mac, who seemed to think that Banks represented some kind of saviour who would release him from the imprisonment of standing between the sticks. Javinder wasn't much in evidence either, since he was trying to put in more study time to keep his father quiet. No-one else in the school team knew about what had happened at Memorial Park, or was even remotely interested.

Except for Nicky. As soon as he heard the basics of the story, Nicky was intrigued to hear more.

'So, you reckon he did steal the car?' he asked Chris on Tuesday, while they were eating lunch.

'No,' sighed Chris, 'not really.' Over the last two days he had had plenty of time to realise that this was one part of the plot that didn't make sense. It would take a lot of guts to talk to someone, steal their car, and then run halfway across town to continue the conversation as if nothing had happened. Banks didn't seem the type.

Nicky scratched his chin and finished munching through one of his mother's sandwiches, which was large enough to feed most of their year group but which Nicky was slowly devouring as if he hadn't eaten for days. It was a wonder he didn't weigh 90 stone, never mind nine.

'So, what's his game, then?' Nicky pondered.

Chris shrugged. He'd thought about little else for 48 hours and it had got him nowhere. He didn't hold out a lot of hope that Nicky Fiorentini would provide many answers. 'Maybe there's nothing more to it than some kid who wants to play in goal for the Colts . . .'

Nicky wrinkled his face in disgust. Chris might have spent the weekend thinking about things, wondering just how much was real and how much was imagination, but the mystery was all new to Nicky, and spending time thinking about it was far better than preparing for double geography.

'Let's review the facts,' he said with determination. He opened a notebook and drew his pen with a flourish, imagining that he looked like the bloke in *Taggart*. He wrote the words 'CAR THIEF' in large letters at the top of the page, which seemed to Chris very clear evidence that Nicky had made up his mind already. He sighed. There was no way to deflect Nicky when he was in this kind of mood. 'First off, there are these two kids who want to play in goal for the Colts. Thingy Jones –'

'Russell,' advised Chris.

'Right. Russell Jones.' Nicky wrote the name on the first line.

'We don't know for sure that the kid who spoke to Sean was called Russell Jones though,' said Chris. Nicky looked up impatiently. He clearly wasn't prepared for his investigation to stall so quickly. 'Sean just asked Jazz and me if we knew anybody called Russell Jones. He didn't even say that he knew for sure that this was who nicked the stuff from his car. In fact, he didn't say much at all.' Nicky looked so cross at this point that Chris decided to throw him a crumb of comfort. 'But Iain Walsh said that Banks had spoken to Sean before, and my guess is that he's the kid he was speaking to at the university that Wednesday, before his car was broken into.'

Nicky scribbled out the name 'RUSSELL JONES' and wrote 'BANKS' underneath, with a large space beside it to the left. After a few seconds, Chris realised what he was waiting for.

'Graham,' he supplied. Nicky wrote it down as 'GRAEME'. 'I think it's G-R-A-H-A-M,' said Chris, but then realised that he didn't know for sure one way or the other. Nicky looked up, waiting for the next clue. 'All right,' he said. 'And you reckon that this Graeme Banks and Russell Jones are the same person?'

'I can't imagine that two kids would just appear out of the blue wanting to play in goal for the Colts . . .'

'Actually,' said Nicky, obviously happy to be given such a clear opening, 'I find it hard to believe even one goalkeeper would want to play for your lot.'

Chris recognised the gibe for what it was and thumped Nicky on the arm. They wrestled for a moment, but Nicky was still too interested in detective work to be shaken off the scent so easily. He recovered his pen, and wrote '= RUSSELL JONES' beside 'GRAEME BANKS'.

'The trouble is,' Chris insisted, 'we just don't know that for sure. Even if Sean did speak to Banks, this Russell Jones might be someone completely different.'

'Nah!' Nicky groaned, shaking his head. The neatness of the theory appealed to him too much. 'Remember, you said the kid who Sean spoke to kept in the shadows, almost like he was hiding. And this Banks kid? You said he was pretty strange too.'

It didn't sound much like evidence to Chris, but Nicky was happy, so he kept quiet and waited for Nicky to move the investigation on to the next subject. Fiorentini was writing again. He wrote the word 'CARS' on a line on its own, then he added 'WALSH'S' on the next line, directly under 'GRAEME BANKS', and 'SEAN'S' beside it, under 'RUSSELL JONES'. Finally, he added a third new line, with the words 'STOLEN' and 'BROKEN INTO' in the two columns.

'That's what ties it all together,' he said. 'That's what makes it certain that Jones and Banks are the same person. Or maybe in the same gang.' He stopped to think about this idea, which sounded pretty good, and made the whole thing much more gritty and exciting somehow. 'Connected, anyway,' he concluded. He stuck the end of the pen between his teeth and chewed on it as he considered what they had so far. 'OK,' he said after a while. 'What do we know about him?'

'Who?'

'Jones/Banks,' muttered Nicky threateningly, jabbing at the words on his notepad.

'We don't know anything about Jones,' Chris said, looking down at the accumulated evidence. He noticed Nicky glowering at the way he refused to accept that the two were definitely one person. 'All Sean said was that he thought he knew where he lived, and that he was the same age as us.' He looked up. 'Roughly.'

'Aha!' crowed Nicky, who hadn't heard this bit before. 'And how old did you think Banks looked?'

Chris accepted the inevitable. 'Yeah. The same . . .'

Nicky wrote the words 'SAME AGE!' above where he had written 'GRAEME BANKS = RUSSELL JONES', and drew a ring around them.

'Great,' he said, with a little worried look at his watch. Double geography was looming ever closer. 'OK. What did you find out about Banks?'

'Just that he goes to Crowhaven Comp,' said Chris. Nicky didn't write this down straight away but looked up as if Chris had left out something important. Chris realised what it was. 'Just over the river, about six miles away. It's not a big town, so I don't suppose the school is that big.'

Nicky's geography was notoriously poor. He could just about place Britain's major cities on a map, provided they had a Premier League team, but that was it. Chris always joked that Nicky and he used to walk to school together because otherwise Nicky would never find it.

'OK, that's the next stage,' said Nicky. 'We go over there, and ask if anyone knows a Russell Jones or a Graeme Banks.'

'When?' asked Chris, who wasn't sure that Nicky meant it.

'Tonight, after practice. We'll go home, get our bikes, and ride over there.'

'You're joking! It's six or eight miles!' There were plenty of other reasons too, he felt sure, but the school bell interrupted his train of thought.

'All right . . . we'll get the bus,' insisted Nicky once the shrill bell had given up. He closed his pad and put it back into his school bag. 'Phone your dad and tell him you're coming over to my place.'

Chris tried to think of a way in which he could persuade Nicky that this wasn't such a smart idea, but he couldn't. Besides, if he was honest, he was as curious about the mysterious boy in yellow and black as Nicky was; perhaps more so. And it would be really cool if they could find out who had stolen the stuff from Sean Priest's car, or maybe even get it back.

'OK,' he said at last. Apart from anything else, he knew that if he didn't go, Nicky would head out there without him.

Nicky had a knack for getting himself into trouble. Of course, Chris knew that Nicky had a knack for getting *him* into trouble too, but that was something he'd have to worry about later.

Compared with Russell Jones, Chris had very little to worry about. The target of Nicky's new investigative obsession was, at that moment, somewhat closer than eight miles away. In fact, Russell was just over the river, squatting on the edge of a small copse of trees, shivering with cold under his long, baggy coat. From just after first light, he had been hiding out in the scrubby growth on the other side of the lane from the house. He'd spent all Monday doing much the same.

He had a perfect view of the partially restored house from where he was hiding. He could see the pile of bricks he had made, stacked in a neat cube, shrinking now that MacKenzie's brickies were using them for the extension. In the distance, standing in a bed of weeds, he could see the bathtub under its tarpaulin cover, the shower-head standing up above the grey blanket like a submarine periscope. He and Mick had moved it from the side of the house on Sunday. Russell wasn't sure why.

Of course, he wasn't sure of very much, just at that moment.

For most of each of the last two days, he had just watched MacKenzie's men working and waited for them to go. He'd taken one or two walks around the fields, but he was too tired to go far and – besides – he was terrified he'd be seen.

To pass the rest of the time Russell thought about football, and about what it would take to convince one of the two men he had spoken to that he should be given a chance to play in goal. And he thought about how that dream – which had never seemed to have much chance of success anyway – seemed to be fading now anyway.

Russell still didn't understand how things had got so bad for him so quickly. He thought about that, too. Over the last two days, he'd had plenty of time to think.

After leaving the university on Sunday, he had rushed back to Stonebridge, crossing the river by the same precarious route he had followed before, and then headed across the

58

fields and alongside the by-pass to reach Stonebridge FC's ground.

Sneaking into the clubhouse, which was by then full of the usual lunchtime crowd (which meant about fifteen customers, if you counted the dogs), he had slipped the yellow and black keeper's jersey into the laundry bag, where the rest of the Stonebridge youth team's shirts had been tossed. He hoped everyone would assume that it had been in there all along, and that no-one would ever guess that it had been removed before dawn that morning so that Russell could turn up at Ambergate and make a good impression.

He knew taking the shirt was wrong, but he couldn't expect Riverside to give him a chance if he didn't have any kit. The Stonebridge goalkeeper could always find a spare or wear one of the Under-17s shirts. Russell had grinned, imagining him moaning.

Russell had always intended to take the shirt back straight away. He knew that Stonebridge FC was such a shambles that a missing piece of kit wouldn't be reported right away, and no-one would be that surprised when it turned up again later.

However, he had almost been caught as he sneaked back out through the main doors. Jack Whistler, who ran the youth team and the bar in the same haphazard manner, had been talking to another man on the front step, and Russell almost collided with both of them as he made his escape. What was worse, Russell recognised the other man at once. It was Sean Priest.

Ducking back through the doors, Russell had squatted on the floor in the dark, dirty hallway, listening through the gap in the twin doors as the two men continued their conversation. After a while, he had realised they were talking about him.

'Oh aye, the Jones family are trouble all right,' Whistler had said. 'The old man is barred from the club here, and his eldest son, Mick, is a nasty bit of work as well.'

'What about Russell?' Priest had asked. Russell's heart had leapt at the sound of his name.

'I don't know that much about him,' Whistler had said. 'He's kind of the odd one out in the family.' He tapped the side of his head and explained. 'He's got a lot more upstairs than the rest of them. But if he's got Jones blood in him, he'll turn out to be another wrong 'un. None of that lot will ever turn out any different. He's been hanging around here – says he's watching the football. I didn't recognise him at first. He wears this old baggy coat and a sweatshirt with a hood on it – half the time you can't even see his face. Of course, now I realise that he was checking the place out, looking for a chance to nick stuff from the club.'

'What makes you say that?'

'A few odds and ends have gone missing. Nothing much, not until this morning. Cans of drink, bits of food, that sort of thing. Then today, I arrive and find someone has broken in through the lav window, forced their way into the office, smashed into the cupboard and stolen the cash tin. And guess who I haven't seen all day? Russell Jones.'

Russell had thought about trying to prove Whistler wrong and himself innocent by making an immediate appearance, but he hadn't liked the way the conversation was going, so he kept quiet and still.

'Think he took it?'

'You tell me,' Whistler had replied. 'First Sunday I haven't seen him hanging round since the season started, and this happens. And a goalkeeper's shirt has gone missing. Like I said, he's football mad.'

'Did you call the police?' Priest had asked.

'Yeah. They came and took some fingerprints and stuff, but I don't think they found much.' There was a short pause. Russell had found himself thinking about fingerprints. He had looked back at the dressing room door; imagined the old cupboard, and the window sill in the loo, and the backs of the chairs in the bar – there were hundreds of places where the police could find his prints.

And then he had thought of the shirt at the bottom of the laundry.

'What's your interest in him?' Whistler had continued.

Priest had taken in a deep breath. 'Much the same, in the end. He came to see me, said he wanted to play for the Colts. I told him how that was going to be difficult. Next thing I know, he's disappeared and my car has been broken into.'

'Tough,' Whistler had sympathised. 'Lose much?'

'The radio, a couple of quid. Worst of all though, I had some stuff in the back . . . certificates for some of the lads who took part in the United trials last season, and some personal stuff, from my playing days. A few medals, my Under-21 England cap, that sort of thing. I was loaning them to United for their trophy room.'

'Now that is rough. You can't replace stuff like that.'

'No,' Priest had replied, and his voice sounded sharp and bitter. 'It's my own fault, though. I should have locked them in the boot.'

'Aye, well, odds are the Jones boy is your man,' Whistler had concluded. There hadn't been a reply. Russell had sensed that the conversation was just about finished.

He had felt like rushing out there and then to deny everything, but he didn't expect anyone would believe him. Certainly not Whistler, who never had a good word to say about anyone. As for the other man, what chance did Russell have of convincing him? Then he had started thinking about fingerprints and the shirt in the laundry . . . The fear of being caught had made him desperate. He had gone back and dragged the shirt from the pile of dirty kit, stuffing it inside his coat. Checking to make sure the coast was clear, he had gone back into the hall, ready to make his escape.

He had listened at the main doors. There was no talking outside and he could hear the sound of a car pulling away. He had reached out to open the door, his fingers actually stretching for the handle, when a shadow had fallen on the other side of the frosted glass, and the door had started to open.

There was no time to turn back. Whistler had walked through the door and found Russell in front of him, frozen like a rabbit in a car's lights. Whistler had been almost as surprised as him, but then he had seen the sleeve of the goalkeeper's jersey poking out from under Russell's coat.

'You little –' he had started to curse, reaching out for Russell's arm. At that same moment, the inner doors, the ones that led through to the bar, had opened, and Madeleine, the barmaid with the massive earrings, had come out into the hall.

'Phone, Mr Whistler . . .' she had said, and then she'd caught sight of the ferocious expression on his face, and she had jumped back, her earrings pealing like there was a church wedding going on in her head. In that moment, while Whistler was distracted, Russell had sprung forward, dodging past him, evading his grasping hands, and had crashed through the open doorway and into the cold air outside.

He had raced across to his secret entrance through the fence, with Whistler in pursuit. He had dived through the hole and swung left along the embankment, heading towards some abandoned farm buildings. Whistler had given up the chase shortly after, when Russell had ducked through some hedgerow on to a bridleway that followed the old railway line.

He hadn't stopped running then, though. Russell hadn't stopped running until he had reached the house MacKenzie was building for Mr and Mrs Gleason. He had spent the afternoon hiding inside, crying in frustration and fear at the way his plans were falling to pieces around him.

Later on, things had managed to get worse.

Mick had arrived at the house while it was just still light, racing through the gate in the pick-up. Russell had stayed hidden. He didn't want to be found by anyone, not even his brother. Mick, though, had seemed to guess at once where he was.

'Russo! Come out! It's me, Mick!'

Russell had descended the stairs from the bare bedrooms on the first floor to find Mick in what was to be the kitchen. His elder brother was leaning on the half-finished worktops scratching at his chin and wearing a repulsive, wide grin, which had disappeared the moment Russell had started to smile nervously in return.

'I don't know why you're smiling, Russo,' he had said. 'You're in big trouble, mate.'

'I haven't done anything!' Russell had protested automatically.

His brother had allowed the cruel grin to creep back across his unshaven face. 'Now, that's almost true,' Mick had replied. 'You didn't finish them bricks like Dad asked, and you haven't kept an eye on Marie like you were asked to. No, instead you've been out thievin'!'

62

'That's not true! I haven't been stealing; I wouldn't!' His voice had become very loud as he tried to make Mick believe his denial.

'Don't deny it!' Mick had yelled back. 'We've had the police turn up at home, frightening the old lady and getting Dad into a right old state. They say you've nicked stuff from some football club, and maybe even nicked a car! What are you going to say about that, eh?'

'Nothing – honest!' Russell had felt his face flushing bright red even as he spoke.

'You always were a poor liar, Russo. You should never try to pull the wool over my eyes.' Russell had known it was the truth. Ever since he was little, Mick had always been able to catch him out, no matter what little secret he had been trying to hide. He had considered telling him the truth now, about the football and taking the goalkeeper's jersey and all, but he knew it would sound feeble after he had already been caught lying.

Mick had grinned like a shark once again. He had reached out and put his arm on his brother's shoulders. 'Never mind,' he'd said. 'I won't rat on you. Even though you haven't shared any of the stuff you took, you're me brother, and I won't turn you in.' He had cast a quick eye round the house. 'You'd better stay here until the heat dies down.'

Russell had nodded his head in agreement. Mick had lifted up a bag and put it on the counter at Russell's side. 'There's some food and some clothes. Sleep in the house during the night, but be gone before MacKenzie's boys get here in the morning. I'd stay away from home and from anywhere where people might see you.'

Miserable and wretched, Russell had agreed to do everything as his brother had instructed. Mick had offered him some words of encouragement but Russell hadn't really heard them.

'Right, I'm off then. Oh, wait . . . there's a little job you can be helping me with first.' Mick had led Russell outside. 'I want this old bath shifting out of sight,' he had said. 'It'd be just like MacKenzie to pinch it from us. Come on, we'll put it at the end of the garden.'

They had heaved the old bath from the side of the house

and hidden it among tall grass and tangled thorns where it couldn't be seen from the house. The work had left Russell exhausted. He had gone back inside with Mick and climbed back up the stairs, carrying his bag with him.

'Remember! Keep out of sight!' Mick had warned. Several minutes later, while he ate some sandwiches and crisps he had found in the bag, Russell had heard Mick set off in the van. He had then settled down to spend the rest of the day and the long night alone in the Gleason's unfinished home.

Russell remained in the bushes, watching as MacKenzie's builders finished work for the day, packed up the gear and drove away. Once he was sure they had gone, he straightened up and made his way back to the house.

The last two days had passed slowly. He was cold, stiff and hungry. Mick had promised someone would bring him some more food, but he hadn't seen any of his family since Sunday. He was starting to think they might have abandoned him. He was also just starting to wonder whether it might not be a better idea to get caught . . .

He went back into the house and waited for a couple of hours. Darkness fell and there was still no sign of Mick or anyone else. Finally, he picked himself off the floorboards, went downstairs, and then stepped out into the yard. He wasn't sure what he was doing, or where he was going, but he wasn't going to spend another night alone in that house.

He dragged his coat more closely around him, and was halfway to the gate when he jolted to a stop. Voices! He heard someone laugh, and then someone said, 'Look, there's a gate.' There was someone in the lane!

Russell froze, not knowing what to do. Hunger was making him slow-witted. He knew he couldn't hope to reach the door of the house before whoever it was came past the gate. Rooted to the spot, Russell fought the panic that was rising up in his guts and waited to see what trick fate would play on him next.

# Eight

Not unusually, Chris and Nicky were arguing.

'I just don't see why you have to gob off to everyone!' Chris exclaimed, looking up into the clear night sky as if he was talking to the stars.

'I don't!' Nicky protested, his hands spread wide in a gesture designed to make him look innocent. 'They were the ones causing the trouble.'

'Really? How do you work that out?'

'All that business about us being nosy-parkers, trouble-makers and what-not. What was their problem?'

'It was the way you asked the questions!' Chris complained. 'Barging in like that and demanding to know if anyone knew someone called Russell Jones or Graeme Banks, like you were Inspector Morse or something.'

'It worked, didn't it?' Nicky replied. 'They told us!'

That was true, Chris admitted to himself, but hardly the point. Just as planned (by Nicky), right after football practice they had left school and caught a bus out to Crowhaven. They'd reached the comp at about 5.30pm, and – of course – it was deserted. Naturally, Nicky's plan hadn't allowed for the fact that kids at Crowhaven go home at 3.30pm just like everyone else.

Wandering back into the middle of the small town, they'd found some kids queuing outside a chippy. The boys had decided a bag of chips fitted both their appetites and their budget, so they had joined the queue. At this point Nicky had started questioning them about the mysterious Russell Jones/Graeme Banks.

Graeme Banks was easy enough to track down. That was the name of the PE teacher at Crowhaven Comp.

65

Then they had asked about Russell Jones.

'How did you put it?' Chris asked now, trying to remember Nicky's exact words. 'I think it started "Do any of you lot know a thieving little toe-rag called Russell Jones?"'

'What of it?' snapped Nicky. 'They didn't exactly turn out to be his best mates, did they? In fact, we weren't in any bother until you said we were friends of his.'

'I had to say something. You'd got them mad with you, calling them country bumpkins, or sheep, or whatever it was.'

'That was later,' Nicky insisted. 'They were already looking for trouble by then!'

The argument about who had said what when would easily last them until they got back to civilisation. What they could both agree on was that the kids at the chip shop had become very agitated about being questioned about this Jones character, and that the two of them had been chased down the road by a bunch of sixth-formers. Nicky had lost all their money when he chucked it at the quickest of those pursuing them. They had been herded away from the main road and out into the country by a mob of about 40 Crowhaven students. Word had spread quickly about Chris and Nicky, and their questions . . .

Eventually, they had lost the chasers but found themselves somewhere outside the town, a good way from the main road, but at least on the right side of Crowhaven to find their way back to the city. Chris had a compass in his kit bag, and they were using it (along with the stars – Chris was pretty sure he had found the Pole Star off to their left) to find their way back along footpaths and bridleways. Well, Chris was using it. Nicky wouldn't have been able to tell you whether they were north, south, east, west, up or down from Oldcester to begin with.

'Well,' said Nicky, for whom the day was never complete unless someone had threatened to pound him into jelly, 'we found out what we needed to know.'

'What's that?'

'Russell Jones and Graeme Banks are the same person. Well . . . not really. One of them's a teacher. But the kid who *called* himself Graeme Banks doesn't exist. He's Russell Jones.' Chris continued watching the night sky above the dark trees. There was a thick coating of leaves on the ground under their

66

feet. 'And I don't think he goes to Crowhaven School,' said Nicky, a few metres later. 'Probably been bunking off for years.' He allowed that fact to sink in for a few moments before he added, 'I think that proves he's our thief.'

'Just because he plays truant doesn't make him a car thief,' Chris replied, with a pointed look at his friend.

Nicky snorted. As far as he was concerned, bunking off geography every now and again was just proof that he wasn't a glutton for punishment. Nicking off school altogether was clearly proof of a cunning criminal mind.

Chris felt pretty uncomfortable about Jones himself, but the incident outside the chippy had put a little doubt in his mind. Anyone who had that many enemies sounded more like a sad act than a criminal hardcase.

Besides, Chris had a natural soft spot for the underdog. It came from supporting Oldcester United all those years. He wandered on, gazing up at the skies and thinking about football . . .

'You're lost, aren't you?' Nicky complained, bringing him back to reality with a bump.

Chris was about to tell him that he knew for sure where they were, while Nicky could get lost in his own back garden, when he saw the lane ahead.

'Look, a road. And there's a house just up the way. Maybe they'd let us use the phone.'

Nicky laughed abruptly. 'You'd better let me call Uncle Fabian. I don't think your father is going to be very pleased with you.'

Chris's face showed that he believed the same thing, and that made Nicky laugh again.

'There's a gate . . .' said Chris, directing Nicky towards the opening.

Moments later, they came face to face with a young boy in the driveway. They almost bumped into him. It was so dark and the boy had on such a dark, shapeless, baggy coat that they wouldn't have known he was there if it hadn't been for the way his pale, wide-eyed face was lit by the moon.

There was a moment when everyone was quite still, quite silent. Nicky had his hand up in a kind of wave, and his mouth was opening to speak.

He got as far as 'He —' before the boy exploded into movement. Nicky was left standing there as the boy turned on his heel as if he was spring-loaded, and took off back past the house into the blackness of the garden. Then Chris rocketed off after him. They were both ten metres away and vanishing fast as Nicky said '—llo.'

Off in the distance, he heard Chris yell, 'It's Jones!' Nicky finally set off in pursuit.

It was so dark it was easier to track their quarry by sound rather than try and catch sight of him. The garden behind the house was thickly overgrown, and all three of them blundered through the vegetation. Chris yelled at Nicky, and Nicky yelled back. Their voices sounded at once both distant and very loud, with a kind of spooky echo.

Chris stopped, breathing hard. His breath made a small mist in front of his face, and he waved it aside, trying to see what had happened to Jones. It didn't seem possible, but their prey — who had only been a few feet ahead when they started — had vanished in the gloom. He could hear Nicky thrashing about behind him, but Jones had gone silent.

'Damn!' whispered Chris. He dropped lower, hoping that Jones would lose him too, and started to creep forward in the direction he thought he'd seen Jones last. Coming further out from the shadow of the house, where the moonlight cast a chill light on the waist-high grass, Chris found he could make out a little more detail. He stalked a little further forward and turned in a long, low circle.

Even though his eyes were accustomed to the darkness after their long walk, everything still appeared to be a shape-less tangle of grey-green in the tangled garden. But just ahead, there was a solid-looking shape cowering in some deep weeds. It hadn't moved for a while. All around it, plants were being stirred by a slight breeze, but this thing kept quite still.

What's more, it seemed to be holding a stick.

Nicky caught up and Chris pointed out the shape to him. Nicky narrowed his dark eyes. He grinned, gave the thumbs up to Chris, and started to circle round to his left. Chris stayed where he was. He thought he heard a soft, metallic tapping.

After what seemed an extraordinarily long time, in which he twice heard Nicky stumble over something and land on the ground, cursing, Chris started to think that maybe the shape wasn't their target. Before he could advise his friend, however, Nicky had launched himself at it like a guided missile, uttering a blood-curdling yell.

The scream was cut short by a dull 'BONG', as if Nicky had found some ancient, distant doorbell and pressed it. The dull, echoing chime lasted for several seconds, punctuated by Nicky's loud cursing.

'It's a flamin' bathtub!' he yelled loudly. Chris struggled over to him, kicking his way through clinging nettles and tall weeds. Nicky was sitting on the ground, rubbing his head. In his fist, he was gripping the corner of what looked like a large blanket or a heavy sheet.

He had pulled it from what was, in truth, a bathtub. The moonlight reflected off the white enamel and the corroded metal of the taps and fittings. The stick turned out to be a pipe with a shower-head on it. Nicky had bent this over 90 degrees when he tackled it.

'What kind of person puts a bathtub at the bottom of the garden?' growled Nicky. Chris bent over to pick him up, then stopped. His eye had been caught by some objects inside the tub, some of which were catching the light.

'Look at this!' he told his friend.

The shiny objects turned out to be medals, spilled from an envelope. There was also some kind of hat, and another envelope with eight or nine pieces of paper in it. Chris searched a little more thoroughly, and found what felt like some framed photographs and a half-sized ball.

'Jackpot,' he breathed, as he realised what he'd found. It took Nicky another few moments.

'Told you!' he laughed, helping Chris to pick it all up. They put what they could into their pockets and prepared to struggle back with the rest. 'It had to be Jones all along! I knew it!' Nicky said, and he continued to congratulate himself as they went back towards the front of the house. Chris knew from bitter experience that Nicky would be able to keep on reminding him how clever he was until they found their way back home. He prayed it wasn't that far.

Russell watched them go from the hiding place he had found in the trees. He had used his familiarity with the ground to lose the blond-haired kid, and had settled back to watch them attack the bathtub. When their stupidity turned to triumph, he had been as amazed as anyone.

The two boys went off along the lane with their prizes, their voices carrying on the air for several long minutes. Only when he was sure they were gone did Russell extricate himself from the branches of the bush above him and brush the leaves from his coat.

He wasn't sure how they'd found him, but he was sure that the light-haired kid was the striker who played for the Colts. Stephens, or whatever his name was. They had to have come looking for him. But when they'd found whatever it was that was hidden in the bathtub, they'd been even happier.

He still had no idea what was going on, or just why everyone was after him, but Russell knew that this was about a lot more than just a goalkeeper's jersey. Or maybe not. Maybe the shirt — which he carried folded up under his coat — was still the key to everything he wanted. He smiled for the first time in days, and turned away from the house.

He was still hungry. It was time he was going home.

# Nine

The following morning it rained so hard Chris felt sure that the Colts' Wednesday practice would be abandoned. Rain lashed against the classroom windows and damp gusts of wind swirled up the last leaves of autumn and dashed them against the building.

By afternoon, however, the worst of the weather was over, and there was even a little weak sunshine to lift the gloom. Looking out over the playing fields, Chris could see that the ground was too wet to play on, but he made up his mind to go to the university practice pitches anyway. Even if the football was cancelled, Chris had an added reason to be there that afternoon.

When the final bell rang, he tried to round up the others. Jazz was a little reluctant, thinking it might be better if he went home and got stuck into some homework rather than waste an hour going to a practice that wasn't even going to happen. In the end, though, his curiosity got the better of him.

'Why are you so keen?' he asked Chris. 'We'll never play in conditions like this – Walsh will just send us home.'

Chris had a big, stupid 'I know something you don't' grin across his face. Moments later, Nicky appeared, wearing an identical smile.

'You don't even play for the Colts!' Jazz snapped at Nicky.

Fiorentini wouldn't give away the secret. 'Maybe not, but – like you say – practice will be cancelled tonight anyway.'

This non-answer only served to intrigue Jazz even more. He packed his books away and waited to see just what they were up to.

'Where's Mac gone?' asked Chris, looking round.

'He ducked out really quickly when the bell went,' said Jazz.

71

'Maybe he needed the loo or something . . .' They set off to look for him, but he had as good as disappeared. One of the girls in their class said he had been met by his father and that they had already driven off.

'He's been acting really strangely, too,' Jazz observed warily. 'It must be catching.'

'I didn't want him to miss this,' said Chris, a little put out.

Splashing through puddles, they ran from the school grounds and along the river bank. Chris and Nicky seemed to be really struggling with their bags, as if they were carrying more than just books and their training gear.

'What's the hurry?' Jazz protested. 'We'll be much too early.'

But they didn't slow down, and they were soon close to the walled-off area at the end of the pipe. All three of them looked across the river, clearly thinking the same thing.

'No sign of the mystery boy today,' said Jazz. Chris and Nicky were grinning at each other again.

'I don't think we'll be seeing him again,' said Nicky, smirking.

As it turned out, they weren't too early, they hadn't seen the last of Russell Jones, and the silly grins Chris and Nicky had been wearing all day were about to become a thing of the past . . .

⚽

'I don't believe it!' gasped Chris.

'He's got some nerve!' Nicky snarled.

Jazz looked at them both, and at the small group on the all-weather pitch tucked in the shelter of the university science block. 'What? What!?' he asked urgently.

They all looked over at the small group working at one end of the pitch. Iain Walsh was off to one side, with another man who Chris recognised as Mr MacIntyre, Mac's father. Mac was there too, hitting shots at goal from passes Walsh supplied. Walsh was running back and forth, collecting the balls as they came off the surrounding wall, keeping up a constant stream of lobbed crosses, encouraging Mac to hit them all first time.

That just left the kid in goal, wearing a yellow and black shirt, who was managing to keep out most of Mac's volleys. The three of them were standing at the fence, close by the gate, watching the action. Every now and again, Jazz looked at his two companions. There was hatred on their faces. Neither of them said anything and neither did he. Instead, they just watched as the drill continued.

Russell had fast reflexes and a natural, cat-like agility. At such close range, there was no way he could keep out everything Mac fired at him, but he was doing pretty well. They could hear Walsh offering advice or praise after each strike: 'Good . . . again . . . try to gather those into your stomach . . . again . . . good . . . that's better . . . no, stand up until he's hit the ball . . .' and so on.

Finally, Chris couldn't take any more. Hefting his bag to his shoulder, he slammed open the gate and walked swiftly across the all-weather pitch.

The drill ended as soon as Walsh saw them. 'Chris – hi! I'm glad you're here. I've got some news for everyone –'

'Funny that,' said Chris bitterly. 'I've got some news of my own.' Walsh shot him a warning look, as if to remind Chris just who was in charge of the Colts. His foot was resting on one of the balls, but his casual stance changed the moment he caught the acid tone in Chris's voice. 'What's Jones doing here?' Chris demanded. He looked past Walsh towards where the goalkeeper was standing. 'That is your name, isn't it, "Banks"? Your real name?'

'He's explained all that to me –' Walsh began.

'That's not the only thing he needs to explain.' Chris dropped his bag to the floor.

'Button it for a moment, Chris,' said Walsh, pointing at his lips for emphasis. 'You said your piece last Sunday. It's my turn now.'

Chris opened his mouth to continue venting his anger, but Walsh repeated the gesture even more forcefully, his eyes flashing a warning he couldn't ignore. Chris lapsed into a sullen silence.

Behind where Chris stood defiantly in front of him, Nick and Jazz walked on to the pitch. Walsh waved them over. 'Jazz . . .' he said warmly, '. . . and Nicky, right?' Jazz smiled back nervously. Nicky's features matched Chris's black expression. 'With all this rain we've had today, I didn't expect to see so many of you here.'

73

'Clearly,' remarked Chris. Walsh moved round to face him more directly, putting himself squarely between Chris and Russell Jones, who remained some distance off, leaning on the five-a-side goal's crossbar. Jones looked pale and nervous.

'Pack it in,' Walsh instructed. 'Listen to what I have to say before you fly off the handle again.' There was a brief pause while Walsh made sure Chris understood. The seven of them formed a small circle, with the Colts manager at the centre. The lights from the science block cast a yellow glow over the proceedings – they hadn't bothered with the floodlights, even though the low, grey cloud made everything appear closed in and dark. 'OK. First off, I've got some news about Sunday. Mr MacIntyre has agreed to buy the team some new kit, to replace the stuff that was in the boot of my car when it got pinched.' Chris shifted, slightly taken aback by this news. In the face of everything else, he hadn't expected the confrontation to start off with news about some new shirts – although it also occurred to him that it was a very generous thing for Mac's dad to do. Walsh misunderstood Chris's reaction. 'Didn't it occur to you that we might have a problem in that department? All the kit was in my car when it was stolen, remember?'

Chris gritted his teeth. 'Oh yes. I remember.' He was staring at Jones as he said it.

'There's no money for new kit, so I didn't know what we were going to do for Sunday's game. Anyway, Mr MacIntyre's company have agreed to sponsor the Colts and buy us new kit. I'm picking it up later tonight.' He looked round the circle. Jazz appeared to be hesitantly pleased with the news, but he was the only one to even attempt to meet Walsh's smile. 'A bit of gratitude wouldn't go amiss . . .' Walsh continued. Chris turned his head and caught Mr MacIntyre's eye. His face and posture softened somewhat as he did so. Mac's dad was a really decent bloke and Chris had always got on fine with him. It was hard to say thanks to him and still stay mad with Jones, but Chris did the best he could. 'There's more good news,' Walsh continued. 'Some of the stuff taken from Sean Priest's car has turned up.'

That news really did take Chris aback. 'How come?'

'Jones found it,' replied Walsh, and he stepped back slightly

74

so that Chris and Russell could make eye contact. Chris stared at Jones, who stared right back. Chris couldn't believe that Jones would have the bare-faced cheek to tell that lie right in front of him.

'He can't have!' spluttered Nicky in the background.

'Why not?' asked Walsh. Nicky obviously decided against replying for now. 'It's quite simple really,' said Walsh. 'When he was here before, Russell thought he saw who it was who was hanging round Sean's car. When he heard what had happened, he went to see them and got the stuff back. Well, some of it anyway. The radio, some silver medals, a watch . . .' Walsh looked over his shoulder at Jones, then back at Chris. 'He's not prepared to say who it was. Maybe the police will think differently, but I think Sean might say that if the rest of the stuff came back, then he'd be happy to forget about it.' He paused for a moment, and Chris could see that the manager was testing his reactions, as if – for some reason – he wanted to be sure Chris understood exactly what it was that he was saying. 'Apparently,' Walsh continued, 'there's even a chance my car might turn up.'

Chris opened his mouth to speak, and Walsh waited while he struggled to find the right words. They were a long time coming. His voice seemed to be stuck in his throat. 'So . . . great. What's that got to do with tonight?'

Walsh was relaxing, clearly convinced that the sting had gone out of the situation. He took a step towards Chris and lowered his voice. 'In the circumstances, it would be a bit ungracious to tell the lad we wouldn't look at him, wouldn't it?'

Chris bit his lip. There were so many ways he could begin to tell Walsh what he and Nicky had discovered about Jones, and so many objections he could raise, he didn't know where to begin.

Walsh took another long look round the circle. 'Look,' he said. 'It's no secret that Mac wants a chance to play outfield, and Jones is busting to play in goal. Ignore the business with the stolen stuff, ignore the missing kit and all that, and you still come back to the fact that it makes sense to take a look and see if it could all work out. So, I'm taking a look at what Jones can do between the sticks.' Once again, he turned a leisurely circle, facing them all one by one. 'That's all I'm promising anyone. Jones gets a chance to show what he can do in goal, Mac gets the same chance to make a grab for one of the midfield places. That's all. Next Sunday, Mac will still be in goal. Even if Jones makes the grade, he still has to wait until we get him signed up properly. Does everyone understand?'

Mac's father nodded. 'That's all we've ever wanted, Iain. Just give Mac a chance.'

Mac was grinning broadly, though he hesitated when he saw how Chris still appeared to be uncertain.

Jones nodded, his face etched with nervous anticipation. He was so pale he looked almost ill.

Jazz shrugged and said, 'Sure.'

Walsh completed the circle until he was face to face with Chris.

'Chris?'

Chris didn't reply. He still couldn't make the pieces of the puzzle fit as neatly as they had last night, when he and Nicky had returned from their long trek across the country bearing the prizes they had recovered from the bathtub. Certificates for some of the players who had taken part in the last set of trials at Oldcester United; photographs and mementos from Sean Priest's playing career; an England Under-21 cap with Priest's name on it; a half-sized match ball with the signatures of AC Milan's Championship-winning side of the early nineties on it – Gullit, van Basten and all those other illustrious names.

The same prizes that were now in the sports bags he and Nicky had carried in triumph all day.

Chris felt confidence slipping away from his grasp like water spilling through his fingers. He was on the verge of accepting everything Walsh said, when a more certain, combative voice piped up from behind.

'Hang on, you can't do that!'

Walsh almost flinched from the rage and conviction in Nicky's voice. 'What do you mean?'

'You can't just give him a place in the team, just like that!'

'You haven't been listening, Nicky. What I said was –'

'Oh, I heard what you said all right,' Nicky blazed on. 'Mac gets to try this, Jones gets to try that. But the fact is, Mac's dad has offered to buy you some new shirts, so you're prepared to do anything to keep him happy. I bet you'll make absolutely sure that everything comes out just like they want, even if that means having someone on your team who might, just might, have nicked your kit in the first place.'

Walsh was moving close to matching Nicky for anger. 'You don't know what you're talking about, son.'

'Yes I do! We've been checking up on Russell flamin' Jones, and I'm telling you – there's no way you can let him play for the Colts!'

'It may have escaped your memory, Nicky,' Walsh snapped in response, 'but you don't get a vote! You play for Gainsbury Town, not the Colts. So mind your own business!'

'Yeah, well, it is my business!' Nicky said, knocked slightly sideways but still keeping his balance. 'League rules, right? You can't play in the Youth Teams League unless you're at school full-time. So ask Jones when was the last time he set foot inside a school. Go on, ask him!'

Everyone had turned to face Jones. Small, dark disks had appeared under his eyes. His eyes were wide; small dark irises in a broad expanse of white.

'Is that true?' asked Mr MacIntyre.

Slowly, and after a considerable delay, Russell nodded.

Everyone fell silent, even Nicky, although Chris could feel his friend was almost ready to burst with all the other facts he had stored inside.

'Why don't you go to school, Russell?' Mac's father continued in a gentle, coaxing voice.

'The kids at Crowhaven don't like me, don't like my family. I used to get into fights all the time. And it's true what I said before – the PE teacher was never going to let me play football for the school. He didn't like me.'

'Thank you!' crowed Nicky, like a lawyer who has just scored some brilliant point in a courtroom.

Everyone ignored him – they were all focused on Russell Jones.

'How long have you been skipping school?'

'A year . . . maybe a bit longer . . .' Jones replied quietly.

'That's a lot of time to have missed,' Mr MacIntyre said. He was watching Jones very closely. 'Think you could catch up?' Jones shrugged. Mr MacIntyre hadn't finished yet. 'Want to give it a try?'

Jones shrugged again, but then looked up. 'Yes,' he said.

During this part of the conversation, Mac had stepped closer to Jones. Now they were only a short distance apart and Mac was offering the other boy a friendly smile. 'I'll help you catch up,' he said. Jones smiled back and nodded.

The tension had gone out of the situation like air from a balloon. Chris felt drained. He watched as Mac and Jones grinned at each other. It appeared that MacIntyre had accepted Crowhaven's outcast.

'So, we can get that sorted,' said Mac's father. 'I suppose there'll be a little delay while the League makes sure that he's prepared to go back to school properly, but we can sort that out later. So long as he's prepared to give it a go, nothing's changed in the meantime, has it?'

Everything was falling into place. Chris wondered if he should just accept the situation. Perhaps he was wrong about Jones after all. Perhaps –

Whenever Chris felt doubt about anything, there was one thing he could rely on. It took more than a little sympathy to get Nicky to walk away from a good scrap.

'Hang on, hang on!' Nicky started.

'Leave it, Nicky,' said Chris quickly.

'Eh? But –'

'Leave it.' Chris turned back to face Walsh. 'OK. Maybe he could be eligible for the team. Maybe it does all make sense. But can he play? Is he good enough?'

Walsh placed his hands on his hips. 'That's what we're here to find out, isn't it?' he said.

'Fine,' said Chris. 'Then let's try this. We'll go two on three. Me and Nicky on attack, Jazz and Mac defend, Jones in goal. Let's see if he can stop us scoring.'

Walsh seemed a little suspicious of the plan at first, but he obviously recognised that Chris would need to be convinced if Jones was ever going to get a fair crack of the whip.

'Good idea. We'll play for ten minutes. Let's go, gentlemen . . .'

Chris walked briskly to the side of the pitch, dropping his bag against the fence. Nicky approached him, looking puzzled. Chris was already changing into his training kit.

'What are you doing, Chris? We don't have to play against

Jones. We've got all the stuff in our bags that proves —'

'That proves nothing. Don't you see? Jones has got them all believing he's innocent. If we tell them about what happened last night, do you think they'll believe us? You have to admit it was pretty lucky us stumbling over him like that. So, if they believe him, that means we'd have to be lying. And that would mean they'd think *we* took the stuff!'

'What?'

Chris didn't want to repeat it. It sounded absurd, but he had picked up this feeling that Walsh had a small doubt in the back of his mind about the way Chris had been behaving. The last thing he wanted to do was fan that spark by suddenly producing stolen goods from his bag, along with some fantastic tale about how they'd found it.

'No. We do it my way. Jones may think he's clever, but he's actually made it simple for us. All we have to do is show him up and he's finished. Do you get it? We've got to put on a show and make him look more like a cart-horse than a goalkeeper.'

Nicky grinned. It was just the sort of plan he'd have thought of himself. 'Yeah . . . I get it,' he replied.

They slapped palms; Chris on Nicky, then Nicky on Chris. By the time they had checked the lacings on their trainers and straightened their kit, they were fired up and ready to go.

'You've got no chance, Jones,' hissed Nicky.

Chris beckoned Nicky closer and they exchanged a few words on tactics.

Walsh blew his whistle.

'Let's do it,' said Chris.

Russell Jones stretched his limbs and tried to get the fog out of his brain. He could see Chris and Nicky running out on to the halfway line, looking fast and sharp. He knew how good Chris was from having watched him in action against Stonebridge, and he thought he knew where his strengths and weaknesses lay. But he'd never seen Nicky, and he had certainly never seen Chris and Nicky together.

Jazz and Mac tried to give him an idea of what he was in for.

'Nicky will go wide to the right,' said Jazz. 'I'd better try and take him. If he can, he'll try and beat me and draw you to block him; then he'll set up Chris for a tap-in.'

Russell tried to take it all in. He felt tired, slow-witted and nervous. It was as if everything depended on the next ten minutes; all his plans and dreams. They couldn't come true, could they?

'Or he'll hit an early cross for Chris to run on to,' Mac was adding. He'd seen plenty of those in practice for Spirebrook's school team. It was as if Nicky knew instinctively where Chris would be, and Chris knew where Nicky would deliver the ball. They were a deadly team. How could he make Russell understand with just a few words?

'OK,' called Walsh. 'Ten minutes. Defenders, stay in your own half. When you get the ball, clear it upfield into the other half, and the attackers can start again.'

'*If* they get the ball,' sniped Nicky.

'They'll get the ball,' added Chris. 'They'll be picking it out of the net every two minutes.'

Walsh shot him a warning glance and threw the ball out to him in the other half of the field. Russell watched as Chris knocked it sideways to Nicky with his first touch. That was what he expected; Nicky would create, Chris would strike. He remembered watching Chris against Stonebridge. Equally strong on either foot, and lethal in the air, Chris was a predator, a hunter. He had an explosive change of speed, even if he wasn't the fastest thing on two legs running flat out. Give him a few inches of space and his control and shooting power made him deadly. Mac was in for a torrid time.

And that, Russell knew, meant that he would have to be on his best form to stand a chance of keeping Chris out. He shook his head and slapped his face, trying to clear some of the cobwebs from his brain. He was hungry and exhausted. On top of the cold, damp day he had spent in the fields near the house, this had left him slow and stiff. Finally, he hadn't slept last night. He had had an urgent task to fulfil, and he needed the cover of night to get it done . . .

He found himself wondering – what would be tougher? This challenge against Chris and Nicky or his escapades in the darkness? He remembered vividly –

A harsh shout from Jazz brought him back to the present. Nicky had slipped outside him and was receiving the ball back off the surrounding wall, and heading towards the goal area. Chris had slid away from Mac's marking and was clear at the back post. Russell stepped forward quickly, standing tall, trying to make himself a big target Nicky couldn't get past. As best he could, he tried to cover both the shot and the cross . . .

At a speed he could barely even see, Nicky checked back inside, drawing Mac towards him and changing all the angles. With barely any back-lift, he then flicked the ball into the semi-circle. The ball was perfectly weighted and placed just in front of Chris. He swept it into the empty goal with Russell unable to do anything more than fall back on his rump.

The ball was spinning on the floor by one of the posts. How long had that been? Russell wondered. Ten seconds?

He picked the ball out of the goal and punted it upfield. Chris and Nicky were already on their way back, having high-fived in celebration. Chris chased the ball down, turned, and stroked the pass across to his partner.

'Stay with your man, markers,' yelled Walsh. Russell straightened his shirt and set himself to watch as Nicky came in again. His adrenalin was pumping now, making him a little more alert. Even so, his limbs still felt heavy and his brain was functioning very slowly.

Jazz was more of a creative midfielder than a ball-winner. In a less intense atmosphere, everyone would have been prepared to admit that he was almost as capable of doing to Nicky what the winger was doing to him. Right now, though, even though he didn't have anything at stake, his blood was up, and it was clear that he wasn't prepared to be made to look a fool while Chris and Nicky proved their point.

Nicky was snaking towards him, the ball seemingly tied to the end of his boot by invisible string, taunting him with small feints to right and left. Jazz backed off, trying to keep Nicky cramped for room, and trying to stay balanced while he looked for an opportunity to tackle.

There! Nicky had let the ball run just a little further ahead. At once, Jazz threw out his foot to steal it away. To his horror, it wasn't there. Nicky had touched it again, flicking it over the tackle, pushing it past Jazz's increasingly overstretched leg. As

Jazz hit the tarmac floor, Nicky was already gone.

Russell heard Mac curse, but this time he stayed with his man, keeping close to Chris, and goal-side. That meant Russell could deal with Nicky more confidently. He stepped off his line again, narrowing the angle and trying to cut down on Nicky's options. This time, Nicky went wider, almost to the goal-line. Russell stood up, moved to his left, and then watched as Nicky drew back his right foot.

Crack! A flat, hard shot, low to his left. Russell fell sharply and threw out his left leg. He got some of his shin on the ball, and watched it spin off to the left, hitting the back wall. He lost sight of it as he hit the deck hard. By the time he had scrambled back to his feet, the ball was already in the centre of the goalmouth, and Chris and Mac were both lunging for it.

Mac half-blocked the shot, but it still crept slowly towards the net. Russell tried to throw himself at it, but too late. It crept in and he only got his hands on the ball as it settled in the net.

'Damn!' yelled Mac.

Walsh clapped his hands and urged the defenders to pick themselves up. 'Good first stop, keeper, but you were too slow getting up. Come on, concentrate.'

Chris followed Nicky back over the halfway line.

'Two down, thirty to go,' said Nicky, grinning. Then he added, 'He's got quick reactions, I'll say that for him.'

Chris was surprised at Nicky's compliment. 'Yeah . . .' he replied.

'That would have been a corner on a full pitch,' Nicky continued. 'He's pretty good at closing off the angles.'

The ball was on its way upfield. Chris backed off, letting Nicky collect it. 'You're not changing your mind?' he called.

'No way!' Nicky replied, frowning. 'It just means he's a decent keeper, that's all. The other stuff is still the same.'

Chris nodded. Nicky took the ball under control, flicking it up on to his thigh and chest. Jazz had closed up to the halfway line, watching as Nicky went through his leisurely antics. Nicky smiled and Jazz slowed to a stop, hands on hips as he waited for Nicky to stop fooling around.

Allowing the ball to drop close to the ground, Nicky

volleyed the pass across field to Chris and took off like a bullet from a gun. Jazz turned, realising he'd been suckered, but it was too late. Chris hit the return first time, past Jazz and towards the corner, then he changed up a gear too and set off towards the goal. Jazz was beaten and Mac was committed to going into the corner after Nicky. He was in the clear.

The cross came over, struck with Nicky's usual accuracy and low flight. It angled across the goal towards the far post, right into Chris's path, even though Nicky hadn't looked up. Chris dipped his head towards the ball's path, preparing to steer it into the corner. This was a classic Chris and Nicky combination; the kind of goal they had scored a hundred times.

Only . . . this wasn't a goal. To his amazement, as Chris ducked to meet the ball, he found Jones there too. The keeper reached out and tipped the ball away an instant before they crashed into each other.

It was a pretty heavy hit, but Chris managed to control his fall and landed feet first, with his hands outstretched. Jones wasn't quite so lucky, rolling over Chris's back and falling backwards on to the hard surface.

Walsh raced over, obviously fearing that he might have smacked his head on the tarmac, but Jones was no more than a little stunned and winded. Even so, Walsh announced that he'd seen enough.

'It's only been a couple of minutes!' cried Mac.

'We scored twice though,' replied Nicky tartly.

'I've seen enough anyway,' said Walsh. 'You're all going at this like it was a heavyweight boxing match, not football. I'm not prepared to see anyone get hurt over this.' The boys stood in a small circle around Walsh and the fallen Jones. The coach pulled him to his feet. 'Besides, I've seen all I need to see for now. You're not bad, Jones. You're strong and you're brave, which you'll need to be. You've got good reactions but you don't move quickly enough when the ball's played across the goal. Also, you just haven't played enough. Your positioning is faulty, except when it's just one on one; you against a single attacker.'

'So . . . what does that mean?' asked Jones.

'It means you're not a better keeper than Mac, not yet. Maybe you could be, I don't know. But you need a lot of training and you need some match practice. I can't promise you that here.'

Everyone took a moment to think this through.

'So, if I can get into another team, you'll look at me again?'

'Yes. Meantime, I want you to come along to practice so we can work on your fitness and keep an eye on you. Actually, you may even get a game or two – in midfield. We're going to be a bit light there in a couple of weeks when Kenny Nixon goes off . . .'

'Wait a minute –' Chris started to protest.

Walsh ignored him. 'But first we'll have to get you registered, and we have to get you enrolled at a school.'

'Perhaps I can help there,' offered Mr MacIntyre.

'And you could play in goal for the school team!' said Mac. 'Flea would be OK with that idea, I bet –'

'No, I mean it, wait!' said Chris, his voice rising. Even then, the others ignored him, but this time it was because Nicky's voice was raging louder still.

'You're going to give this . . . this . . . fraud a place in the team, just like that?' Everyone there – with the exception of Jones – knew that last year Nicky hadn't been offered a place with the Colts, and that this had brought him and Chris to blows. It was clear he wasn't going to be happy with the idea of Jones just walking into the side – not even as temporary cover in midfield.

'Like I said, Nicky, you don't get a vote in this team. In fact, nobody does. I decide who plays. Understand?'

'I understand,' Nicky snapped in reply. 'But you're not in charge of Spirebrook's school team. What if Flea won't go along with your little plan?'

'That'll be up to him. Frankly, though, I can't see what his problem would be. If Jones enrols at Spirebrook and he's good enough to make the team, Mr Lea will decide if he plays . . . just as I decide who pulls on a Colts jersey. Do you get it now, Nicky?'

Chris had listened to all this, seemingly calm but boiling inside. When he spoke, his voice had the raw sharpness of ice crystals in the wind. 'You keep saying you'll decide who plays,' he told Walsh. 'But that's not quite true. You can't make someone play who doesn't want to.'

'But Jones does want to play, don't you?'

Chris didn't bother to look to see what Jones would reply. His eyes were fixed on Walsh. 'I'm not talking about Jones. I'm talking about me.' Walsh turned back. 'If Jones plays for the Colts,' Chris continued, 'I don't.'

There, it was out. Chris was suddenly aware just how cold the evening was becoming. Worse, the rain was starting up again. He shivered, and told himself it was the weather that was causing it.

'You don't mean that, Chris.'

'Yes I do.'

There was a long pause while everyone faced up to the enormity of what was being said. The rain splattered on the red tarmac surface of the all-weather pitch and drummed on the windows of the science block. There was a distant rumble of thunder. It had become very dark all round.

'You're right, I can't make anyone play,' said Walsh at last. 'I also can't let any one player dictate how the team is run. If you won't play with Jones, Chris, then you won't play.'

Chris had known that was how it would turn out. He nodded, once. 'We agree on something, then,' he said. A moment later, he turned away, walked across the pitch to the fence, picked up his bag and headed for the gate. Nicky followed him. No-one said a word; not when the gate slammed shut behind them, nor for a long while afterwards.

# Ten

Oldcester had a League game at home to Southend that Saturday. Chris and Nicky went through their familiar routine. Nicky arrived at the Stephens house early, carrying a huge bag of food his mother had packed for them. Actually, it often seemed as if she had packed food for both teams, ref, linesmen, coaches, substitutes and a good proportion of the crowd as well.

Then they caught the bus into the city centre. Oldcester was a small city; an old industrial town that had boomed once in the Victorian era, and then again in more modern times. It had swallowed up outlying villages and towns like Spirebrook, but there were large spaces of open countryside away from the main routes in and out of the city, dividing the suburbs. Some maps of Oldcester made it look almost like a star, with broad arms along the main roads, but deep indentations where there were no houses or factories.

The city centre itself was compact. There were two main shopping streets, and a broad market square beside the City Hall, beyond which it was a short distance to the river. Three old bridges and one relatively new one crossed the river here. Right beside one of these bridges lay Star Park, the home of Oldcester United. It was a 28,400 capacity, all-seater stadium, rebuilt completely in ten years from the early 1980s, with bars and restaurants in the Easter Road Stand, and executive boxes all round.

Seats JJ121 to JJ123 were in the Easter Road Stand, above the halfway line. Chris, his father and Nicky were in place by 2pm.

'Brilliant,' said Chris's father, rubbing his hands. 'This is the sort of day you play good football on; cold, but not really cold;

no wind; a little sunshine to brighten things up; a damp pitch, but not too wet, and no rain on the day.'

'During the European Championships you said football could just as easily be a summer game as a winter one,' said Chris, who never missed a chance to point out his father's inconsistencies.

'Did I? Well, I was talking nonsense. Besides, it's different on the telly . . .' Chris and Nicky giggled. Nicky was already delving into his bag to find something to tide him over; Chris opened his programme. 'Should be a good game this afternoon,' his father continued, unfastening the top button of his coat. 'Beat this lot and we could be six points clear at the top.' United had been relegated from the Premiership last season. This year they were almost unstoppable, and they were leaving the rest of the division behind. 'If the Colts are lucky, this weather will hold for tomorrow, and you can get back to winning ways too,' he continued. Chris tried hard to concentrate on his programme. He saw Nicky look across out of the corner of his eye. Then his father leaned forward, blocking the view. 'Oh no, silly me,' he said sarcastically. 'You don't play for the Colts any more, do you? I know you told me, but I keep forgetting. It's probably because I don't know why.'

'Leave it, Dad,' moaned Chris.

His father leaned back in the bright red seat and ran his hand through his thinning blond hair. 'Fair enough. I know I'm just the taxi driver anyway. Tell me, do you still want me to give Jazz a lift tomorrow, or have I resigned as well?'

'Dad!'

Mr Stephens left it at that. His tactics over the last few days had been to keep bringing up the subject in short bursts, trying to draw Chris out. It was close to working. Chris was hopeless at keeping secrets.

'Anyone want anything to eat?' asked Nicky, trying to help Chris by changing the subject.

'No thanks, Nicky,' Chris's father replied. Then a moment later he added, 'Have you got a game tomorrow?'

'Yes,' said Nicky, sounding embarrassed. 'Kenbridge Park at home.'

'Let's hope the weather stays like this for your sake, then.' That was the end of the latest skirmish, and Chris could relax.

'When are you going to take that bag to the office?' his father asked, nodding at Chris's bulging kit bag. He'd lugged it all the way there, having to carry everything because Nicky was overloaded with supplies.

'In a minute.'

Chris found himself fidgeting with the handles. He wanted to leave it as near to the kick-off as possible to go down to the office under the stand and hand over the stuff he and Nicky had found. Sean Priest's office was right behind the main office where the ticket enquiries were handled, and Chris had decided he couldn't face him.

The speaker system was playing the new Echobelly single. Chris and Nicky suspected that the DJ had a soft spot for indie music; he played some really unusual stuff. It suited them fine, but some of the older supporters had written to complain – there was a letter in this week's programme. He settled in his seat to listen. Almost immediately, the music was faded down and the announcer's voice echoed round the ground.

'Would Chris Stephens and Nicky Fiorentini come to the front office under the Easter Road Stand? That's Chris Stephens and Nicky Fiorentini . . .'

Chris looked up, his mouth wide open. Looking across, he saw that Nicky was equally dumbfounded. Only his father didn't seem surprised.

'Go on, off you go. I'll stay here and look after the supplies.' Chris started to smell a rat. His father, a notoriously bad actor, was trying to look innocent. 'You might as well take the other bag with you,' Mr Stephens added.

Chris took hold of the handles and tugged it out from under the seat. He and Nicky made their way along the row to the end, and then descended the steps to the rear of the stand.

'What's all this about?' asked Nicky.

'Search me,' muttered Chris.

There was a line of people in front of the office window that looked like it might not clear before kick-off. The boys stood in the open space behind the stand, wondering what they were supposed to do next. Just along from the window, a steward was waving at them from a door marked 'Private'.

They made their way over, the bag slung between them.

'The tannoy told us to go to the front office,' Chris told him, looking back at the queue.

'You could end up waiting all day for them,' the steward said. 'Come through here . . .'

The doors led into a short passage. Ahead of them, a flight of stairs climbed up into the interior of the stand. The walls were lined with large, framed photographs of special moments from Oldcester's history, such as Peter O'Grady's match-winning header in an FA Cup Final from the 1950s.

Other photos went back to the club's foundation in 1902, and divisional winning teams from the 1930s, when Oldcester had climbed up to the Second Division. There were recent pictures too, such as when Paul Maguire got his hat-trick in the Autoglass Final of 1993.

Chris and Nicky had seen these pictures before, less than half a year earlier when they had visited Star Park after their trial. Even so, they were always worth looking at again. Chris pointed out that the only person who didn't have his hands raised to celebrate Maguire's goal was Maguire himself – he'd had his back to goal when he turned to shoot, and he had spun a full circle and missed the ball hitting the back of the net.

The steward waited for a moment while they lingered in the hallway, then started to climb the stairs, beckoning that they should follow. Chris started to point out that they were supposed to be reporting to the office, but then mutely followed the man.

At the top of the stairs there was a crossroads with a set of double doors in front of them that the boys knew led to United's trophy room and museum. Off to the left there was an executive dining room, where the club's directors wined and dined before the game. The boys heard laughter and the clink of glasses from behind the closed doors.

The steward, still ahead of them, opened the doors into the trophy room. Unusually, the lights were off. Hesitantly, Chris and Nicky stepped towards the doorway, realising that something unusual was about to happen, but not knowing quite what.

The lights came on suddenly, flickering once or twice, but

then bathing the room in its customary bright neon light. It was crowded with people, but they stood back from the doors, a crescent of smiling faces welcoming Chris and Nicky in. Right at the centre of the semi-circle stood Sean Priest, wearing a sharp grey suit (with a hideous purple Tazmanian Devil tie) and a wide grin of pride and pleasure.

Chris and Nicky almost froze in the doorway, but instead they allowed themselves to be drawn in. A flashgun fired from off on the side somewhere. From beside Priest, United's chairman, a giant of a man with a bushy black beard, was stepping forward with his hand outstretched.

'At last, our other guests of honour have arrived. Which one is which? Chris? Nicky?' He'd guessed the wrong way round, but no-one corrected him, least of all those whose names they were. Chris had just spotted his father at the edge of the throng – and Nicky's parents, Uncle Fabian and other assorted relatives were blocking off one end of the room like a crowd of protesters at the gates of a strike-bound factory.

'Come in, come in,' urged the chairman (who went by the unlikely name of Dennis Likely). 'Bring the lads a drink, somebody. If we don't help them get over the shock, we'll need the St John Ambulance.'

People were laughing and applauding, and flashguns were popping all over. Chris and Nicky found themselves at the centre of a slow-moving scrum, being steered towards an empty cabinet at one end of the room. Dennis Likely was like a mountain over their heads.

'Right,' he said, in a loud, booming voice, 'now you'll all have to bear with me as I repeat myself for the benefit of our new arrivals. You were all invited here to join with us in paying tribute to Sean Priest, who as a player and now youth team manager has a record of over twelve years' service with the club. We've all forgiven him now for going off to Rotterdam for a couple of years in the middle.' People laughed at what was an 'in' joke among United circles and Likely held up his hands to quiet them. 'No, it's true. Even though they got a bargain at £2.2 million, we got the better bargain when he retired and came back to Star Park to transform the youth team set-up, making it one of the most successful young player development schemes in the country.'

There was a short outbreak of applause. A liveried waiter appeared with tall glasses of Coke for Chris and Nicky. Mr Likely waited for them to be served, and then continued.

'Part of what we are here to acknowledge today is that achievement. Thanks to Sean, we have laid the foundations for a new type of youth policy. Along with representatives of some of the bigger clubs, Sean has been speaking to the FA and the government about introducing the kind of School of Excellence for young players that they have on the Continent. What we want is to take the most promising players and bring them into a special kind of school, sponsored and run by Oldcester United. The young players at this school will be given the best kind of coaching to improve their fitness and playing skills. Everything will be looked after – their diet, their physical well-being and their education. In addition to training, the boys will complete a full programme of school education by top-quality teachers.'

More applause. Much of this announcement was going over Chris and Nicky's heads (literally, given that Mr Likely was about two metres tall). However, they were getting the gist of it, and were as caught up in the excitement of it all as everyone else.

'It isn't going to happen overnight – there are still some legal wrangles to be sorted out – but it is going to happen. Oldcester United will have a proper school, built on the old Magpie Car showrooms site on the other side of Easter Road. We'll attract the brightest and best young players from all over, and we'll turn them into a team that will make Oldcester into one of the greatest clubs in the Premiership.

'I don't want to keep on about this, because today is about Sean and honouring his achievements. But the school is all down to Sean's hard work. I just wanted you all to know that.'

The throng of people were clapping once again. Chris put the bag down and joined in.

'So . . . what today is really about is how we can say thank you to Sean for all he has done for the club. He made over four hundred first team appearances for United, and never gave less than his best. He helped us win promotion to the top flight back in '87, and won a few other trophies besides.

91

So, in honour of his achievements, we decided to do two things. First off, we'll be having a testimonial game in January. Two select elevens will be playing here on 9 January; Sean's Friends against Sean's Foes. As you can guess, this means he gets to pick both teams himself, which is some kind of record I'm sure . . .'

The audience laughed. Nicky tugged at Chris's sleeve, and they exchanged a look that made it clear they still had no idea what they were doing there.

'The other thing we have arranged,' Mr Likely continued, 'is a special exhibit here in the trophy room. As I said, Sean has won a few things in his time, and he's collected all kinds of knick-knacks on his travels. Very kindly – or because his wife, Trudi, has decided she doesn't want them cluttering up the house, I'm not sure which – Sean is loaning some of these things to the United club museum. This cabinet behind me will be a record of Sean's career. Sean has said we can keep the stuff for as long as we like, but I did warn him I might want the space for the Endsleigh League trophy at the end of the season . . .'

This time everyone cheered. Though mystified, Chris and Nicky were enjoying themselves enormously.

'Now, the sharp-eyed among you might have noticed that the cabinet is empty. That's because some light-fingered thief broke into Sean's car when he was bringing the items for display to the club. It looked for a while as if all we would have to show would be an empty case.

'But that's why we have these extra guests of honour here today,' he continued, and he dropped his huge hands on to Chris and Nicky's shoulders, which made them both stagger. 'These lads here . . . Chris Stephens and Nicky Fiorentoni, two young United fans who are also, I might add, being watched very carefully by the club, managed to find the stolen items.'

Chris had felt the penny drop just before that last part, and he was beaming with pride and flushing bright red with embarrassment as the announcement came towards its conclusion. Even though Mr Likely had managed to get the names the wrong way round (tapping Chris's shoulder when he said Nicky's name and vice versa) *and* had pronounced Nicky's name incorrectly, he couldn't have felt more honoured and elated if he'd scored the winning goal in the Cup Final. It was a bit odd that no-one was clapping or anything though . . .

'So, all we have to wait for now is for the lads to actually give us the stuff back!'

Chris found himself back in the real world with a start, realising what everyone was waiting for. With Nicky's help, he hefted the bag and handed it to the chairman. Flashguns snapped, people applauded, and there was a deafening cheer from the Fiorentini clan.

A waiter produced champagne while Mr Likely delved into the bag and started taking out some of the items they had recovered from the bathtub. The boys were even allowed a tiny sip of the stuff themselves. Then there were more photographs and questions – they were even interviewed for the local TV news. People were still telling them what a great job they'd done when someone announced the match would kick off in five minutes.

In all the excitement, Chris had nearly forgotten that there was also the small matter of a game United had to win . . .

The celebrations were even more joyous after the game, which was a cracker. Southend hadn't gone to Oldcester hoping to eke out an away draw; they had gone looking to catch Oldcester off-guard, and scored early. An equaliser just after half-time set up a frantic last 40-odd minutes, until United's Dutch ace, van Brost, hit a screamer from 25 metres to get the three points.

Having already had the privilege of watching the game from the director's box, the boys were then treated to a huge meal in the dining room, sitting at the top table with Chris's father, Nicky's parents, Sean Priest and his wife, and Mr Likely. There were still more photographs.

There was so much food, it was a sure bet Mrs Fiorentini had done the catering.

Chris had recovered his wits by the time he forced dessert down and the adults were drinking coffee.

'How did anyone know about us finding the stuff?' asked Nicky. There was only one answer: Chris turned to his father.

'I admit it – I phoned the club on Thursday and talked to

Sean. You said you were going to give the stuff to Iain Walsh after practice on Wednesday, but then when you came back from that and you still had the bag full of stuff –'

'How did you know?' asked Chris.

'I looked, of course. I know I'm not supposed to pry into your things, but I'm a father – we do this sort of stuff by instinct.'

'So you and Sean set all this up?'

'No, that was all Mr Likely's idea.' The chairman turned at the mention of his name, and beamed at the boys.

'But you knew this was going to happen?'

'Of course.'

'And you managed to keep this a secret?'

'That's another thing we fathers are very good at. We can only lie with a straight face about the really important things.'

Chris grinned at the admission, and leaned back in the chair to make room for the vast quantity of food he had eaten. Sean Priest looked over and stood up, then made his way over to their end of the table.

'Come on,' he said. 'There are some people I want you to meet.'

Chris stood up, dropped his napkin on his seat, and waited for Nicky to get up too. They walked along behind the table, following Priest down some steps to the main part of the dining room.

'Over here,' he said, directing them towards one of the centre tables.

This had been a day of plentiful surprises already, but it seemed it wasn't over yet. Eight very familiar faces were seated around the table, and they all looked up as Sean approached.

'Lads,' he told them, 'I've brought over some really famous people for you to meet. You might want to get their autographs. This is Chris Stephens, and this is Nicky Fiorentini. Or Fiorentoni, as our chairman prefers to call him.' Nicky giggled nervously. 'Boys, these are some of the has-beens who will be playing in my testimonial. I'll give free tickets to the game if you can name all eight.'

It was an easy challenge. Chris could have rattled off the names in his sleep.

'Stuart Pearce, Dennis Wise, Des Walker, Lee Chapman,

Gary Mabbutt, Robert Rosario, Mike Hooper and Peter Schmeichel.'

'Too easy,' said the big Manchester goalkeeper, grinning. 'Hello, Chris; hello, Nicky. Good to see you again. Why aren't you wearing those shirts I gave you?'

Chris and Nicky had met the blond Dane when they had visited Old Trafford the year before. He had given them a present of two signed United jerseys. Chris's was on the wall of his bedroom.

'Quite handy England having a game mid-week, eh?' said Priest. 'It meant I could invite a few of the lads up to check on their form. I'm going to have all the best ones on my Friends team, and put all the duds with the Foes.'

'Just be careful who you put where,' said Stuart Pearce, with only the slightest trace of a grin on his face.

Sean held up his hands. 'No offence, Pearcey, but you have to play for the Foes. After some of the tackles you've hit me with over the years, it wouldn't feel right having you on my team . . .'

Everyone laughed. Schmeichel borrowed a couple of chairs from a neighbouring table, and they all made room for the boys to sit down.

'Sean says you boys play a bit yourselves,' said Dennis Wise, leaning his chin on his hands. 'Signed up for Oldcester yet, have you?'

'Hands off,' said Priest. 'I saw them first.'

'And if you don't want them, they'll come to United,' said Schmeichel, putting his arms round the boys. 'The real United, that is.'

The others all jeered. They were soon laughing when he told them the story of when Chris and Nicky had visited Old Trafford, and found him and Ryan Giggs warming up before a game. 'This one tried to beat me from forty yards,' he said, jabbing Nicky in the back with his forefinger.

'Are you two going to get signed up for this new school, then?' Lee Chapman asked.

'Nah, they wouldn't want to do that,' said Wise before Chris could answer. 'Proper lessons and teachers and stuff? Instead of playing football twenty-four hours a day? That's not your scene, is it, lads?'

'Actually, I think it would be brilliant,' said Chris quietly.

Wise winked at him. 'I was only kidding. I think it's brilliant too. I hope you make it.'

'If you can, anyone can . . .' joked Gary Mabbutt, and he started the first in a line of stories about Wise's time at Wimbledon. Priest gestured for Chris and Nicky to follow him after the third or fourth, just as Wise was starting to fight back, reminding them just who had won an FA Cup medal, and which of them had ended up on the losing side . . .

'Now they've started, they'll keep that up for hours,' Priest told the boys.

'Have you played with all of them?' asked Nicky, trying to work out who would be on what team in the testimonial.

'None of them, actually,' said Priest. 'But you get to know some of the opposition players better than others after a few years in the same division. I had to mark Lee twice a year, for example, when he was with Leeds and then West Ham. Whenever we were waiting for a corner, or there was some stoppage or other, he'd tell me jokes. Good 'uns too, as I remember. The first time, I was laughing so much he got a hat-trick. I got wise to him after that, but he's always been a tough forward to keep from scoring.'

'He's not as good as someone like Rush, though,' said Nicky, 'or Andy Cole, Les Ferdinand or Collymore –'

Priest held up his hand before the list could get any longer. 'Maybe not, but it's not always as easy as saying this player is better than another. For example, did you know that Rush has only ever scored one goal against Oldcester? A game I wasn't playing in, by the way. Now, a lot of it's just luck, but I always felt I understood how Rush played, whereas there are other strikers I always felt much less comfortable with. Robert Fleck used to give me nightmares when he was at Norwich.'

'So, who else is on the Friends side?' asked Chris.

'Most of them are players I was with here at Oldcester or at Rotterdam. A few of them are people like Lee or Gary; guys I really respect and get on with. The lists aren't finalised yet. Tell you what though, you'll have to come along to the warm-up before the game. It's bound to be a great laugh.'

Chris could think of nothing better.

While they had been talking, they had wandered through

to the trophy room once more. The empty cabinet stood at the far end of the room.

'It'll be great when it's got everything in,' said Priest, smiling. 'I still can't believe it's happening. Especially after all the stuff got stolen.' He turned to face Chris and Nicky. The smile had disappeared. 'Do you want to tell me what happened? What's been going on?'

The quick change of mood caught Chris off-guard. He remembered how he'd felt on the practice pitch, when it had seemed that whatever he said would sound hollow and untrue after Jones had taken the other stuff back.

Nicky, who was more gifted at being evasive, stalled for time.'What do you mean?' he asked.

'What do I mean?' repeated Priest. 'Well, it's hard to know where to start. All the gear I was bringing to the exhibit gets stolen; then Iain Walsh gives me a call and says that this Russell Jones kid has recovered half of it, but that he won't say who took it. Then your dad rings me up, Chris, and he says you two have found the rest of it while you were out on some "walk in the country". Finally, Iain says you've packed in the team.' He took a moment to let that lot sink in. 'It sounds to me like you've got a lot to explain.'

'You don't think we nicked it, do you?' asked Chris desperately. There was a horrible sinking feeling in his guts that told him he and Nicky were about to be accused of everything they knew Jones was really guilty of.

To his intense relief, Priest's face lost the stern expression it had worn while he was detailing the events of the last week. 'No!' he insisted. 'I know you wouldn't do anything so stupid and destructive, not even for a joke. Besides, there was no way you could have broken into my car, and from what I hear it's the same with Iain's. That isn't what this is all about. I just don't understand how you and Jones both ended up with my stuff, or what happened to Iain's car — and most of all I don't understand why you're walking out on the Colts, Chris.'

Chris couldn't even begin to explain it himself.

After all, what could he say that would make sense to anyone else? It was no big secret that he had disliked Jones from that first meeting, and he had no idea what had caused that, other than irritation with losing the match at Memorial Park, and Jones's part in Mac's mistake. Then there was the business with Sean's car and Iain's car . . . and there had to be some connection there between Jones and the thefts. Even if he had taken some of the stuff back, it didn't mean he'd stolen it in the first place. Even if *that* wasn't true, he had to be involved in it somehow to have been there when Chris and Nicky had discovered the stash in the bathtub, and to have 'found' the more valuable items . . .

There was no doubt in Chris's mind that Jones was involved. But he wasn't as sure as he wanted to be that Jones actually was the thief, and there was no way he could make a solid case to anyone else. It was his instincts that were telling him something was wrong.

How was he supposed to explain them to Priest?

'Errr . . . um . . .' was as far as he got. When he realised that he wasn't even going to be able to stall as efficiently as Nicky, he closed his mouth and settled for silence.

Priest waited patiently for a while, but it was clear that Chris wasn't going to say anything. He didn't even bother looking at Nicky; he could be even more stubborn than Chris. Besides, although Nicky was closely involved, he wasn't Priest's problem.

He tried one more tack. 'Look, I honestly don't care about the stuff, Chris. Don't get me wrong, I would have been gutted if it had been lost for good, and I'm as pleased as punch to have it back. But they're just possessions, just things. None of it's real. I'm not interested in catching anybody out or getting anybody in trouble with the police. So, if you're protecting someone, don't worry about it.'

'I'm not,' said Chris quietly.

'OK, fine. I'll tell you something else. I used to think that playing was the most important thing in the world, but it doesn't even begin to compare to the pleasure I get out of coaching, and running the youth teams. If we make this School of Excellence happen, it'll mean more to me than anything I ever achieved in my playing career.

'You're good enough to make it, Chris. You too, Nicky. You were borderline last year. Next spring, I expect you both to walk into the youth team here, provided you keep practis-ing and playing the way you have been. And then there's the Central Counties Cup and the exchange visit with the Americans. I just don't understand how you can throw all that away.'

Chris could only find one way to explain it. 'It's a personal thing.'

Priest didn't react one way or the other to that. 'Between you and this Jones boy?' Chris nodded. 'Chris, this isn't playground football. You can't always pick who plays on your team and who doesn't.'

'I know. I just can't play with Jones.'

Priest had been leaning back against the door during this whole conversation. He always tried to put some distance between himself and the players when he spoke to them, so that he didn't have to look down at them. That was one of the best things about him as a youth coach; he never made the boys feel that they were worth any less than him.

A loud peal of laughter rose from the dining room, and Priest straightened as he looked through the part-opened door.

'We'd better get back. Your parents will think I've sold you to Inter Milan and run off with the money.'

Nicky nearly made a loud protest. Before they had come to England, the Fiorentinis had been AC Milan fanatics. Uncle Fabian still said they were the greatest team in the world, even though he went to see United play whenever he could. However, even Nicky found it hard to make a joke at a time like this.

'Have you signed for anyone else?' Priest asked. Chris shook his head. 'Don't. Leave it a week. There may be a way of sorting this out that none of us have thought of yet. Just be patient, Chris, and look on the bright side. Things can't get any worse.'

# Eleven

But they did.

Mac's father was an architect who did a lot of work for the county council. He didn't get to design a lot of fancy buildings (there wasn't a lot of call for opera houses or museums, and the river almost disappeared under the weight of its bridges), but an architect of any kind counted as being pretty posh in Spirebrook. There were plenty of the other parents who saw him as being pretty smart, and that was before he appeared on *Mastermind* (fourteen points on the life and works of Isambard Kingdom Brunel, twelve points on general knowledge; he'd come second in his heat by two points).

In addition to being smart, Mr MacIntyre also had pretty good connections through his work for the council. Thanks to him, the light railway that was being built out to the university was likely to be extended to Spirebrook via the old railway bridge over the river, which he'd discovered was as solid as a rock at a time when the people developing the site were hoping to get it pulled down.

So, when Mr MacIntyre said he'd see to it that Russell Jones was enrolled at Spirebrook Comprehensive, he didn't waste time. Jones had been in to see the head, Mrs 'Andy' Cole, on the Friday after the ill-fated confrontation on the all-weather pitch, and on the Monday Chris arrived to see him stepping from the MacIntyres' car in a brand new uniform, with a brand new bag and a smart new haircut.

'I don't believe this!' howled Nicky.

And it managed to get worse. The head of year, Mr Campbell-Waterman, put Jones in the same class as Chris, Jazz and Nicky.

'Next thing you know, he'll be living at your house,'

Nicky muttered to Chris.

'Didn't you know?' asked Jazz, who clearly hadn't cottoned on to just how much Chris and Nicky were offended by Jones's presence. 'He's living at Mac's house.'

They were feeling a little better by the end of the day, by which time they had established that Jones was going to find catching up on the year he had missed extremely tough. He was completely at sea in French, and hopeless at science.

'He's only just able to read and write,' said Nicky fiendishly.

On Tuesday, it was geography, and Nicky wasn't so cheerful. It turned out that Jones was quite good at geography, particularly by comparison with Nicky (but then, who wasn't?). Chris had harboured a secret hope that Jones wouldn't appear for a second day after the way the first had gone, but Jones had arrived in his bright new uniform and had taken his place on the opposite side of the classroom from Chris and Nicky. He was sticking at it, even when he appeared to be really struggling.

Nicky was already close to wanting to knock his brains out.

The tension increased as the day wore on. Chris and Nicky had noticed Jones arrive with a full kit bag as well as his books. There was no doubt in anyone's mind that they were all going to meet up on the soccer field again that afternoon.

Nicky wasn't that patient. During lunchtime, he sat with a deep scowl on his face, picking at the six-course meal his mother had packed for him in what the whole class called his 'lunch crate'.

Jones was playing football with some of the older boys on the playground. Mac was playing too, and he *never* got involved with that crowd.

Nicky was already growling before Jazz arrived, so it was hardly his fault, but it was his presence that finally sparked Nicky into action.

'Decided to come and sit with us, have you?' he sneered. 'I thought we weren't good enough for you any more.'

Javinder looked completely bemused. 'Have I done something to upset you?' he asked, casting a quick glance at Chris at the same time.

'How can you just buddy up with Jones? How about a little bit of loyalty?'

Jazz's eyes opened wide; he clearly wasn't in the same frame of mind as Nicky at all.

'Are you talking about geography? Mrs Robinson paired us off, Nicky. I didn't ask to work with Jones –'

'Not just that,' Nicky continued, worrying away at it like a dog ripping at an old blanket. 'What about last week? What about the way you took Jones's side against us?'

'In the football? It wasn't my idea that we teamed up like that! I –'

'You know what I mean. Afterwards. How come you didn't say you'd quit as well? Walsh might have been able to cope with losing one player, but what if he'd lost two, eh?'

'Hey! It's easy for you to act tough about it! You didn't have to quit the team or anything!'

'That's not the point –'

Chris leaned over and stopped Nicky from leaping to his feet. 'You're right. That's not the point. It's not Jazz's fault, so let's not lose sight of what the problem really is, OK?'

To Chris's surprise, Nicky settled back in his seat. He tore off a hunk of ciabatta bread between his white teeth and sat munching it, glowering out across at Jones, who was running through the opposition defence with the ball at his feet.

'I'm not going to take sides over this, Chris,' Jazz continued. 'If I quit the team, my father will make it very difficult for me to join another one.'

'It's OK, Jazz,' Chris replied in a low voice, staring out at the frantic, wheeling game in the playground. 'I know how it is.'

'That's not all though, Chris,' Jazz continued. 'I think you're wrong. You're a mate, so I won't take sides against you, but I think you've got Jones wrong.'

Chris turned to face Jazz, and felt Nicky lean across to stare into his dark, wide eyes as well.

'What?!'

'I think you're wrong, Nicky.'

'I don't believe it! Look, Javinder, he nicked the stuff, OK? How else do you account for him just finding it like that?'

'He says he guessed who might have taken it, and went and got it back.'

'Well, he's lying!' roared Nicky, loud enough for people in other schools to hear, never mind everyone at Spirebrook.

'He lied about his name, didn't he? He lies about everything! He took the stuff himself, and brought it back when he realised we were on to him!'

'He explained about the name thing. He knew Iain or Mr Priest would check up on him at school. If they'd asked for Russell Jones, all they would have heard would have been bad news –'

'I wonder why!'

'They didn't like him, Nicky. He's different. I know how he feels.'

Nicky backed off slightly at that point. It wasn't hard to remember that there were kids at the school who had given Jazz a hard time when he first started. There were always morons prepared to have a go at him for being a 'Paki', even though he was born and bred in Spirebrook, and knew as much about Pakistan as he did about the moon.

'That's not the same thing!' Nicky muttered. He was still leaning over Chris, his finger waving in front of his friend's face as he developed his argument with Jazz. 'Look, we know he's involved in the robbery thing. Don't forget, we saw him that night, when we found the stuff at that deserted house. Jones was there!'

'Maybe he was looking for it, like he said.'

'Then why did he run off?'

'Why would he run away from you, Nicky?' mocked Jazz. 'I don't know. Give me a micro-second to think about it.'

Nicky slumped back in his seat, still scowling. He clearly wasn't very happy with the idea that anyone could be neutral in this dispute.

'So, you're telling me,' he grumbled, 'that you think it was just coincidence that Jones was searching for where this mysterious "mate" of his hid the stuff, at the same time as we stumbled across him. Yeah, that sounds very likely.'

'It's not that strange,' Jazz said, clearly trying to make a reasoned argument in the face of Nicky's outright hostility. 'You were looking for Russell because of the stolen gear, and he was looking for the gear. You just ended up in the same part of the world, that's all.'

Nicky made a kind of snorting sound, which signified that he considered that about as likely as Mac's chances of becoming the tallest kid in the school. Chris had noted the subtle way Javinder had started using Jones's first name . . .

The bell that finished off the lunch break sounded soon after. Judging by the cheers, the team that Russell Jones was playing for had won. That did little to improve Nicky's temper, and when Griff – who had been the captain of their school team last year but had now moved up – approached, things went rapidly downhill.

'Good player, your new mate,' he said.

It was an innocent enough remark, but Griff's face was stuck in what looked like a permanent smirk, so anything he ever said appeared to be sarcastic or teasing. Nicky leapt to his feet, which brought him halfway to matching Griff's height.

'He's not our mate!' he yelled.

Griff pushed him down, his eyes glittering. In the last few weeks, he had started wearing his lightish hair very short, and he had an earring in his right lobe. Always a little rough, Griff now looked pretty menacing.

'What's your problem, Fiorentini?' he snarled. They had always had this slightly tense relationship, and things were much worse now that Griff was in the senior team.

'We've got enough losers at this school, without adopting another one,' Nicky retorted, trying to find a way he could get up without Griff pushing him back down again.

'You should know,' snapped Griff, and he shot a glance at Chris and Jazz, who were keeping very still. 'You're supposed to keep mad dogs in a muzzle,' he told them and he and his mates stepped away and went through one of the nearby doors.

When Nicky looked up again, all he could see was Russell Jones, standing alone in the middle of the playground. He'd seen it all. Nicky was almost ready to go completely hyper.

'You can fool as many of these other suckers as you like!' he roared at Jones. 'But not us! We *know* you're a crook. And one way and another, we're going to prove it!'

Jones walked away, finding a more distant door through which to enter the building. Chris and Jazz waited with Nicky while he calmed down (or at least until he didn't look as if he might pick a fight with one of the teachers). As they finally got up to make their way to their next class, Nicky pulled Chris back so that Jazz went on a few paces ahead. He was out of earshot when Nicky hissed into Chris's ear.

'That's what we have to do; prove it. We have to *prove* Jones is a thief.'

'How?'

'We follow him. Everywhere he goes. Sooner or later, he'll meet up with this "mate" of his, or he'll go nicking again. That's when we get him. That's when we get even.'

Chris agreed. Even though he didn't feel nearly as hot under the collar as Nicky, the Jones situation was starting to get out of control. It had to get sorted. Chris wanted to get his life back to how it had been before – that meant they had to get Jones out of the way.

'Does this mean tramping round a lot more fields?' he asked.

Nicky grinned, recovering his sense of humour now that they had a course of action. By the time they reached Mr Muir's English class, their plans were set. Starting with tonight's school football practice, they were going to use every hour they could spare to keep tabs on Russell Jones. Nicky, of course, had to excuse himself from Wednesday nights and Sundays because of his commitments with Gainsbury Town, but that wasn't a problem. Chris had suddenly acquired a lot of free time on those two days. Remembering that only made him more determined.

'Fine,' he said. 'Let's do it.'

# Twelve

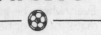

Mr Lea – Frank Lea, which is why everyone, even half the school staff, called him 'Flea' – was nearly two metres tall, and almost the same across. He had played as a rugby union prop forward in his younger days (back in Victorian times, according to some of the gags), and still turned out as a Number 8 for a veterans' side. He was huge. New first-years sent to find 'Flea' with a 'message' would almost faint at their first glimpse of this huge mountain.

Spirebrook didn't play rugby, but Flea liked to challenge the hardcases in the school by getting them to try and tackle him while he ran back and forth across the soccer pitch, from touchline to touchline, over and over again. Chris remembered seeing him carry Griff and Fuller – another of the wild men in the year above his – on his back for twenty metres while they tried to haul him down. Then, as if he had just noticed they were there, he shrugged his shoulders and they both slammed to the ground.

There was a playground rumour that the only kid who had ever managed to knock him down now played loose head for England. There was another rumour that the kid involved had actually been hospitalised for a year, and now grew flowers at a nursery behind Spirebrook's Methodist chapel.

But for all his ferocious size, Flea could be a very gentle, docile man when he wasn't wearing his rugby shirt. His style as a soccer coach was to coax the boys into good habits, not scream and bellow at them like some of the other managers they had seen.

That didn't mean that you could cross him, though. Flea was in charge of the school team, every bit as much as Iain Walsh ran the Colts or Sean Priest controlled Oldcester's youth teams.

This year — much to Chris's surprise — Flea had made him team captain. Sadly, the school team hadn't looked quite so sharp this year after having made the County Schools Cup Final the year before; too many players had moved up a level, and the new crop weren't quite as good. Results had been patchy, but Flea wasn't too disappointed. It had been a quiet year, with no major dramas or crises to be sorted out.

All this was very clearly in Chris's mind as he watched Flea put Russell Jones through his paces in goal. The PE teacher was feeding passes to Chris's strike partner, Phil Lucas. Phil looked a little like Linford Christie, only with wider eyes; he was big and strong, and hit the ball very hard off his right foot. Jones was stretching first one way and then the other as Lucas tested him on the ground and in the air.

Chris had to admit that Jones had pretty good reactions and that his judgement was pretty good in these one-on-one situations. He could tell that Flea was impressed.

Nicky jogged over from where he and some of the others had been dribbling in and out along a line of cones. Chris was using some new shooting walls Flea had obtained — four tall boards, about half the width of a five-a-side goal. He stood in the middle and shot against each board, one after the other, turning in a circle as he met each rebound with a fresh volley.

The ninth shot clipped the top of the wall and the ball sailed off. Mike Hurst chased off after it. Chris stepped out and let one of the senior team players take his place.

'What do you think?' asked Nicky.

'I don't know,' Chris replied.

'What are we going to do if Flea wants to pick him?'

Chris thought for a moment. 'I don't know,' he said again.

Nicky obviously decided he was never going to get the answers he wanted from Chris, so he went off to take his next run along the cones line. Chris saw him shoot off-balance at the end of the run, missing the goal by miles, to the jeers of some of the others. It appeared Nicky was as distracted as he was.

Flea came over, looking quite satisfied. 'What do you think, Chris?'

'About what?'

Flea's smile disappeared. 'About Jones! Pretty good keeper, don't you think?'

'He's a fair shot-stopper,' Chris conceded, 'but I'm worried just how much he can know about the rest of the game. He hasn't played much, you know.'

'That's true. Maybe we should try him out in a game though? See what happens?'

Chris tried to find another objection quickly, but he couldn't. His one consolation was that Mrs Cole wasn't going to let Jones just walk on to the school team. She had very strict rules about that sort of thing.

'Maybe . . .' he replied.

Flea started smiling again. 'How about Thursday?' he asked. Chris was stunned. Flea was producing some paper and a pen from his shirt pocket. He scribbled a diagram on it, showing where he wanted to play different people, using their initials. 'Here's what I have in mind; we put Mac in midfield, playing just in front of the back four –' He paused while he added Doughnut Packham, Neil Shelby and Mike Hurst in a line '– then we put "Munster" in the centre of midfield with Stapleford, Jazz wide left, Nicky on the right, and you and Phil up front.' He completed the line-up by adding the initials RJ under the defenders, completing the diagram with a little goal under those two letters. Flea considered what he had sketched out for a moment, turning his head to look at it sideways. He appeared very cheerful about what he saw. 'That's actually not a bad line-up, all told. We're still not as strong in defence as we were last year, but I think Mac will win a lot of ball for us playing through the middle like that, and Jones should help us keep a few more clean sheets, don't you think?'

'You think Jones should play Thursday?'

'Sure!' said Flea, beaming. 'Why not? It's only Hemmingford, so it's not a big game – and besides, we're not going to do anything in the League this year. If we give Jones a run, we'll see how things look before the Cup starts . . .'

Clearly no-one had said anything to Flea about the situation with him and Jones. Chris felt as if the newcomer was taking over his life, bit by bit. Soon he'd have to wait for Jones to go first before he could have a bath . . .

'What about Mrs Cole?'

'Oh, she won't object, if I put it to her right,' said Flea. That appeared to be that. Flea continued to hover over Chris, waiting. 'You OK with the plan then?'

'Sure,' said Chris, faking enthusiasm.

Flea put the diagram in his hand and propelled him off towards the others. 'You can break the good news to the team, then,' he said, turning away to deal with the seniors.

'Why don't you just shoot me and have done with it?' Chris asked as he walked across the playing fields with the diagram in his hands. He gripped the paper with the very tips of his fingers and thumb as if it might burn him.

He decided he'd better get to Nicky first. He was over with Doughnut, 'Munster' Adams and Phil Lucas. Chris caught his eye.

'What is it?' asked Nicky once he had jogged over.

Chris showed him the piece of paper, looking up quickly. Flea was looking in his direction, but seemed to turn away quickly to yell something at Griff.

'Jones is in the team for Thursday,' said Chris hurriedly, pointing at the initials. Nicky snatched the sheet from him.

'WHAT?!!!'

Nicky's voice echoed across the field. Some of the others looked up and started to meander their way over. Nicky's voice had sounded so amazed, they probably thought Chris was telling him some outrageous bit of gossip, so naturally they wanted to get over as quickly but casually as they could.

Chris used the brief time they had left to confirm what he had just said. 'He plays Thursday.'

'How come? Did you tell Flea we didn't want him?'

'Yes,' said Chris, tiredly lying rather than trying to explain the situation to Nicky.

'Did you tell Flea we wouldn't play if Jones did?'

Chris wasn't prepared to spin the lie out that far. 'That wouldn't make sense, now would it? If I keep that up, I may never play football again. Besides, we're going to follow Jones, right?'

'Right . . .'

'So,' said Chris, rushing to explain things to Nicky before the others arrived, 'it doesn't make sense to quit the team and then show up so we can follow him. He'd be bound to smell a rat.'

Nicky narrowed his eyes and nodded, clearly impressed at just how devious Chris could be. 'Good point,' he said. Chris was pretty pleased with it himself.

The others were close enough now that they had to leave it there. Chris took the team list back and waited for the last of them to gather round.

'OK,' he began. 'Thursday's game here after school against Hemmingford. Here's the team that Flea has selected.'

He made sure he emphasised just who had chosen the team, and shot Jones a sharp look before he started to read the first name.

It almost caught in his throat.

After the practice, Nicky pulled Chris to one side.

'Are you ready?' he hissed.

Chris nodded. Jones had just put the last of his kit away, and was heading for the door with Mac. Nicky held Chris back for a moment, and then they stole out into the gathering darkness in pursuit.

It took less than a minute for the first flaw in their plan to be exposed. Mac's father was outside the school gates. Their quarry was going to be driven home.

'How come he's getting a lift every day?' said Nicky.

'Never mind that!' urged Chris. 'Come on!'

Nicky was still complaining as they broke into a run. 'He only lives a few roads from me . . . he's never given me a lift before.'

'Come on!'

It made better sense to turn back from the main gates, cross the school grounds and use the new back gate to go out on to the lane, which now wandered through the retail park. However, it took them a confused moment or two to realise that as they watched Mac's father steer his car away from them. They passed Griff and a few of the others going the other way, and then overtook Doughnut just as he was opening the back gate.

It was a frustrating run, chasing after a car which had been out of sight within seconds, and Chris was starting to feel foolish by the time they reached the traffic lights on the main road. Opposite them, Church Hill climbed up steeply. Already pretty tired after practice and their run so far, Chris groaned inwardly at the sight.

Then they saw the MacIntyres' Audi pull up at the lights. It must have caught every other light along the main road to have only got that far.

'Quick, duck out of sight!' Nicky's voice rasped, and they swerved violently into the entrance to the supermarket, very nearly managing to get run over by a Volvo which was negotiating its way in.

They watched as the lights changed, and the Audi turned left and climbed the hill ahead of them. They then had to wait for the pedestrian lights to change in their favour. By the time they were across the road, the Audi's brake lights had vanished from view over the distant brow of the hill.

Wearily, they slogged up after it, going past Nicky's turning and reaching the top of the hill where a blackened old church stood on one side opposite a modern primary school. Off to the right, a wide avenue dipped down briefly and then climbed back up again to reach the summit of Church Hill. This was Sailing Ship View, a cul-de-sac of large modern houses built along a track that had been created when an old sailing ship had been taken up the river just before the First World War, accompanied by river barges and hundreds of small craft.

Sailing Ship View was what counted for posh in Spirebrook.

Chris and Nicky hesitated. They could see Mac's house from where they were.

'What do you think?' asked Chris.

'We need to get closer,' Nicky said. 'We can't see the other end of the road from here. He might be able to slip out there along a footpath or something.' It didn't sound likely, but Chris didn't want to argue.

He set off, trying to stick to the shadows. He'd gone about five metres before he realised Nicky wasn't following him.

'What is it?'

'This is stupid,' said Nicky. 'There's no point us both being here. And we've got homework too . . .' Chris knew what was coming. 'I tell you what, you take the first shift, and I'll be back in an hour to relieve you. Or an hour and half, tops.'

He disappeared before Chris could argue, leaving him alone

in the street, equally torn between wanting to uncover Jones's deceit and needing to throttle Nicky Fiorentini.

Muttering some pretty vile comments to himself, Chris stalked along the street, keeping a close eye on the MacIntyre house. The Audi was in the drive and Chris could hear the engine ticking as it cooled. Lights were going on both downstairs and up. Just as Chris was walking along on the other side of the road, he saw Mr MacIntyre step to the window to draw the curtains, and he had to make a quick sprint to the cover of a tree.

For much of the next hour, that piece of excitement was about all that Chris could remember. More and more, this was starting to look like a stupid idea. And a cold one too.

There really wasn't anywhere much to hide. At its end, the cul-de-sac had a turning circle for cars, ringed with houses. The old lane to the end of the hill continued as a footpath between two of the dwellings. Chris hid there.

He had a good view back along the road even if he couldn't see much of the MacIntyre house, except for a hedge and a cherry tree marking the boundaries of the front garden, and the upper floor.

Chris wrapped himself in his school jacket as best he could, watching and waiting. By his reckoning, at least three hours went by before he saw someone skulking along the road from the crossroads.

'About time too,' said Chris. He was about to whistle at Nicky when the figure passed under one of the two street lights in Sailing Ship View, and Chris saw that it wasn't Nicky — not even close. This was someone much older — nineteen or twenty maybe — with designer stubble, close-cropped hair (probably brown — it was hard to tell under the street light) and a curious half-smile across his mouth. He was wearing all black — denims, a leather blouson and a baseball cap, and moved with a stealthy, cat-like grace even though he had his hands in his pockets.

Chris found himself moving into the shadows instinctively.

The young man took a quick look around, then crossed the road, halting at the end of the MacIntyres' driveway. Chris almost lost him in the shadow of the cherry tree, but he could just make out the blunt, hard features of his face.

He watched the house, and Chris watched him. Neither of them moved for several long minutes. Finally, the stubble-jawed face smiled privately again, and the man backed away from the drive, turned and ran off.

Chris released the breath he had been holding. He didn't know why, but he didn't like the look of the stranger. There was something quite chilling about the way he moved, making no sound even in the stillness of the quiet November evening.

In fact, Chris knew he was afraid of the guy – he could feel a small icy hole in his guts, which wasn't just the cold or the empty feeling in his belly. This was someone you ought to cross the street to avoid.

Which was precisely why Chris decided he had to follow him. If there was a connection between the man and Russell Jones (and surely there had to be!), Chris knew it would lead him to the answers he needed. Screwing up his courage, he stepped out of the fenced-off passageway and set off in pursuit, trying to stay as close as he could to the hedges and trees of the smart gardens along the way.

The man turned left at the crossroads, back on to Church Hill. Just before he went out of sight, he looked back along Sailing Ship View. Chris froze in horror, sure he would be seen. Then he realised that he was between the two street lights, and that the only reason he could see the guy so clearly was because he was being back-lit by the distant lights of a car approaching the crossroads from the opposite direction.

Almost shivering, Chris waited a moment and then jogged very tentatively towards the crossroads, down the incline and then up the little slope at the end. He slowed as he reached the corner, and stretched his neck to look round, making sure the man had moved on.

He couldn't see him, and he was more frightened than ever, convinced that the man would just leap out from the garden on his left. He looked again. Someone was walking up the hill, he noticed, but there was no sign of –

There! The man had crossed the road and was trotting past the chapel. Chris let out a long sigh of relief. He could feel his heart pounding. Trying to follow this guy was going to be more of a strain than he'd thought.

He stepped around the corner. There were few cars

parked along the steep slope of Church Hill, but Chris hoped he'd be able to keep at least one of them between himself and his quarry at all times. Those and a few trees, and he'd maybe have enough cover to prevent the guy from seeing him.

'Hey, Chris!' came a shout.

Once again, Chris froze on the spot. The brown-haired man was looking across the street, watching as Nicky came labouring up the hill. He turned his head a little more and caught sight of Chris on the corner. Their eyes met. Chris felt that same, sickening chill in his stomach as the man's mouth creased in that awful, confident smile, and then he turned away and continued to descend the hill once more.

Nicky finally reached the corner, blowing a little hard. He took one look at Chris and burst out laughing.

'What's the matter, did I frighten you? You look as if you've seen a ghost!'

'You idiot – what was the idea of shouting at me like that?'

Nicky seemed quite offended. 'What's your problem? We're nowhere near Mac's house, are we? Speaking of which, aren't you supposed to be watching? How are you going to see any-thing from round here?' Chris was almost ready to scream in frustration. 'Sorry I was so long – Mum made me wash up. It's only quarter to seven, though. Not too late ... uh-oh. What's all this about?'

Nicky was looking past his friend's shoulder. Chris finally looked away from the rapidly disappearing figure of the unshaven man, and turned to see what Nicky was gawking at.

The car whose headlights Chris had seen approaching the crossroads was pulling up against the kerb beside them. It was a pristine N-reg white Vauxhall with lurid red and orange stripes along the side, an array of lights on the roof and the word 'POLICE' in red lettering on every surface, just to make sure people got the message.

'Great,' muttered Chris. 'How much worse can things get?'

As always, whenever Chris thought that, his guardian angel, who took a lot of time off and had a great sense of humour, decided that there could always be a cloud inside every silver lining.

# Thirteen

Chris didn't have a lot of experience of being questioned by the police, so it struck him as richly ironic that the driver of the police car should be the same officer who had encountered him on the river bank with Jazz and Mac, the day they had seen that idiot climb over the river.

The idiot who had turned out to be Russell Jones. Wasn't it funny how everything always came back to Jones? (No! thought Chris, it wasn't funny at all.)

What's more, the copper had a photographic memory when it came to faces. His first words were 'Don't I know you?', and he managed to recall the entire episode within a minute or two, including the fact that there had been a theft from a car in the university grounds later that very same day.

'I believe that's where you said you were going when I saw you,' he said, his eyes lighting up as he put two and two together and came up with something like twelve.

One of Mac's neighbours had put in a call when they saw someone hiding in the shadows outside the drive. The officer knew it wasn't Chris — the caller had specifically said it was someone tall and with very short hair. Chris's blond mop and Nicky's well-groomed sweep of black hair hardly fitted the description. Even so, the copper was pretty sure he could smell a conspiracy, or a gang maybe. He clearly didn't believe Chris for a moment when he said he had been thinking of visiting a mate's house but had changed his mind and had met up with Nicky instead.

Nicky, of course, had an alibi when it came to establishing where he had been at the time of the call. In fact, he had about ten alibis, because the Fiorentini clan had eaten tea in their usual large numbers. While Mrs Fiorentini supplied the constable with cups of tea and cake, Uncle Fabian explained that Nicky was his nephew, that he had been at home from about 5.30 until 6.30, and that Chris was his best friend and team mate, and would never get into any trouble.

Any slim hope that the policeman would accept that as conclusive proof of their innocence disappeared when he insisted that he would drive Chris home. The words '. . . to make sure you keep out of trouble' weren't actually spoken, but they might as well have been. The copper clearly wanted to see where Chris lived.

He didn't add to the problem by actually taking Chris to the front door, but it didn't make a lot of difference. His dad was outside talking to the guy who collected the football pools money, and saw Chris stepping out of the police car. Given that it was also 7.45 (they usually had dinner at 6.30), Chris knew he was in more trouble than he could deal with.

⚽

The punishment wasn't too bad — extra chores, a week's grounding and a heavy parental silence that was a lot worse than being shouted at. However, Chris knew he would be under close scrutiny at home.

Chris met Nicky at the usual place the following morning. Fiorentini, of course, was perfectly OK; quite jolly, in fact. His family had forgotten about the incident as soon as the policeman left, and he'd watched cable TV with his cousins until nine, finished his homework and gone to bed to sleep the just sleep of the untroubled and innocent.

Chris, on the other hand, had slept poorly, had finished his homework that morning, and felt as if his whole life was becoming a grim nightmare. He wondered how old you had to be to join the French Foreign Legion (and did they demand that you could speak French?).

He gave Nicky the gist of the story as they walked to school. Chris's father had made it very clear that he was to be home immediately after school that night.

('Right after practice!' was actually what he'd said first, and then he'd added, 'Oh, no! Silly me! You don't go to football practice on Wednesdays any more, do you! I keep forgetting. I wonder if I'd remember if I just knew why!' There was more in the same vein.)

'What about Jones?' cried Nicky.

'What about him?' sighed Chris, too tired and too miserable even for that.

'We're keeping tabs on him, remember?'

'So, you watch him!'

'How can I? I've got practice tonight!'

The two of them shouted at each other at increasing volume as they covered the next few metres.

'Look . . .' said Chris, too fed up to argue with Nicky (and that was *really* fed up), 'forget Jones. This isn't going to work.'

Faced with Chris being reasonable, Nicky backed away from the argument as well. 'I guess you're right. It's not as if we saw anything anyway.'

Chris embarked quickly on reminding Nicky that *he'd* seen about two hours of TV in his own home, and that only *Chris* had actually been in a position to see anything to do with Russell flaming Jones. That row carried them to the turning that led to Spirebrook Comprehensive, at which point Chris told Nicky about the mysterious unshaven man.

'Wow! Really? Now that is a development!' Nicky considered the information for a minute. 'Who do you think he was?' Chris had no idea, but Nicky was able to offer several. 'An accomplice, do you think? Maybe he helped Jones nick the stuff, and Jones cheated him out of his share when he brought it all back. Or is he some underworld enforcer, come to get Jones for snitching? Or maybe he's a member of a gang who Jones owes money to . . .' Nicky had some experience of the latter situation, and knew how easy it was to fall in with the wrong crowd. That didn't mean he had any sympathy for their enemy, however. 'Wait, I've got it!' Nicky cried out a second later. 'Think about it! Jones has conned his way into Mac's house. What if he's casing the place, getting ready to let his partner in so they can rob Mac's family?!' Chris considered this for a moment, and it didn't sound too stupid. The man might have been waiting for a signal from Jones, saying that he'd left a door open or something. That meant . . . 'We have to keep an eye on Mac's house, in case he comes back!' said Nicky excitedly, finishing Chris's thought off for him.

'I can't!' said Chris in despair.

'I could be back by half-five or six at the latest,' Nicky urged him.

'No! Besides, Jones will be at the Colts practice, won't he, not at the house.'

'Maybe that's the plan,' mused Nicky quietly, scratching the top of his head. 'The place will be empty –'

'Well, I can't watch the house *and* Jones, can I?' asked Chris, and he realised as he said it that he had more or less just agreed to do one or the other.

'OK. It's easy,' said Nicky, and he used his fingers to count off the points of his master plan. 'First off, you go to the practice. Then if Jones is there, you can check the house. I'll meet you there. If he doesn't go, then we'll know we're right about him and his mate turning over Mac's place.'

'What then?'

'Call your mate, the policeman . . .' suggested Nicky.

Nicky vanished almost immediately after the last lesson, probably to make sure that Chris couldn't try and wriggle out of 'their' commitment to keep up the observation on Jones. In fact, even though he couldn't explain it to Nicky, Chris had more or less decided that all he would do was make sure Jones went off towards the university grounds with Jazz and Mac, and then head home. He really didn't need a fight with his father . . .

Hanging back as the rest of the class gathered their gear at the end of the day, Chris watched Jones out of the corner of his eye. A few of the other kids were getting used to him now, and he was laughing and joking with Christine Blake (the biggest airhead in the class) and her mate Rachel. Chris waited impatiently. Finally, hoisting his bag on to his shoulder, Jones left the room and headed for the lockers.

The others were there waiting for him. Jazz saw Chris watching them, so he had to pretend to be waiting for a word with Mr Campbell-Waterman, the head of year. Fortunately, as soon as he saw him, Soupy Campbell told Chris he didn't have time to talk to him now, so Chris was able to leave the hallway and find somewhere else from where he could keep an eye on things.

Eventually, he found a spot over by the dinner hall, which gave him a straight if somewhat distant view of the main gates and the playing fields. He loitered in the doorway and waited for the trio to appear.

After about three or four minutes, he started to wonder if they were coming. The crowd of kids milling around the gate was already starting to thin out, and there was no sign of them. Chris stuck his head out from the doorway and looked towards the gate. Nothing. Then he scanned across the playground and the playing fields. There were a few kids out in the lane, or on their way out to it through the new gate. Although the wire mesh fence partially obscured the view, Chris became pretty convinced that three of them were Jones, Jazz and Mac.

Fine. That told him all he needed to know. Chris lifted his back from the door he had been leaning on and took his first step down towards the path leading to the gate.

He stopped immediately, then ducked back rapidly. He was pretty sure he hadn't been seen. The man had been looking across the playground, towards the building at the other end of the covered way. Chris had barely emerged into view. He couldn't have been seen!

Cautiously, he peered around the edge of the porch. To his relief, the stubble-chinned man was still looking in the same direction as before. Chris breathed a sigh of relief. The guy looked just as sinister by day as he did by night, his face quite hard and bony. He had his hands jammed in the pocket of the leather blouson and a cigarette between his lips.

As Chris watched, the curious smile he had seen before appeared suddenly on the guy's face. Christine and her posse were about to by-pass him when he removed his hands from his pockets, flashed them the smile and said something. The girls replied, and one of them pointed off towards the field gate.

You didn't need to be a lip-reader to know what had gone on. Christine's mate had just told Bullet-head where his mate Jones had gone. The man's face froze like ice for a moment, then he allowed the smile to return, offered the girls some last piece of conversation (at which they giggled), then turned and ran back out through the gate.

119

Impulsively, Chris rushed after him. It wasn't something he dared think about.

He reached the gates just in time to see a car setting off and heading left, down the road that led through a small, modern housing estate to the footpath through the kiddies' playground and the riverside walk beyond. It was a Honda; an old car, lovingly cared for . . . Though it had changed colour and was wearing new number plates, Chris recognised the sporty roar of its engine and the small dent in the back bumper.

It was Iain Walsh's car.

Chris was sure he was right. For a moment, he was even more certain that he had to try and follow the car; then he realised – the driver was looking for Jones, and Chris knew where Jones was going.

He took off, racing as fast as he could; as fast as if he was chasing down a through ball with only the goalkeeper to beat. He imagined it like that in his head. He was past the last defender, and there was just the keeper to beat; a keeper in a yellow and black shirt.

'All I need is one bit of proof . . .' he muttered to himself as he raced along the street. 'Then you're mine, Jones . . .'

The Honda had stopped up ahead, at the junction with the new road, the same road that ran behind the school and on which he had seen Jones walking minutes before. But Chris knew that Jones and the others would have turned off as soon as they reached the point where the river curved round to meet them, and would have passed through a small alley between two houses on to the riverside footpath. The driver of the car wouldn't be able to see them from the junction.

He heard the engine rev, and knew the stubble-headed man had reached the same conclusion. Wheels spinning, he turned right on to the new road. Chris knew that the road looped round in a broad arc, finally connecting with the main road near the university gates. It was the long way round, much like going around three corners of a square. With luck, the lights at the end of the road would be red, and the car would face a long delay. Chris knew that the shortest way to reach the university playing fields was along the river. His way.

He reached the junction and paused only to make sure the

Honda was still moving away. It had almost disappeared around the curve.

Chris ran across the road, through the gate on the other side and past the playground. As he emerged from the other end of the footpath, he stopped. He could see along the riverbank from there, and it was as busy as it ever got at this time of day. Some kids from the comp; a few mums with younger kids, having picked them up from the small primary school at the back of the housing estate; students walking from the campus towards digs in Spirebrook. Chris's eyes were fixed on just three of them, walking in a compact group towards the university.

Mac had produced a tennis ball, and they were passing it between them, running back and forth along the towpath. Chris remained where he was hiding, knowing that he would be seen if he stepped out into the open. The distance between him and the others gradually widened.

Chris cursed impatiently. He wanted to stick close to Jones, knowing that soon his accomplice/fellow gang member would try to make contact. At this rate, though, he'd be left well behind. What should he do now?

Just then, Mac scooped the ball over Jazz's head, and it landed with a faint plop in the river. Chris heard them groan, and they moved to the river back to investigate the possibility of fishing it out.

That made up his mind. Chris doubled back along the footpath, and turned on to the new road, charging along the curving street as quickly as he could. His bag banged against his thigh, which slowed him a little, but at least it wasn't very heavy (not too much homework tonight, luckily!). He pulled the handles up his arm and tossed the bag over his shoulder.

As the long, gradual curve unwound, Chris spotted a turning on his left. It was a narrow road Chris didn't know that well, lined with old terraced housing and leading down past some half-demolished factory buildings at the other end. Chris remembered that it led to the old chemical depot by the river, the one with the pipe that stretched over the water to the other side. When he'd last seen them, Jones and the others hadn't reached that far. This might be a way of catching up with them without being seen.

He turned left and pounded down the street. He could hear his footsteps echoing off the walls of the old houses. Nothing else stirred much, although there were a couple of women talking at one of the doors. At the far end of the road, outside the abandoned factories, there was no sign of life at all, although there was a ratty old pick-up truck parked at the kerb, at the point where a set of bollards almost blocked the road (a couple appeared to be missing). Beyond them lay the paved riverside walk, and beyond that, the high-walled depot.

This was the one point where the riverside walk didn't actually follow the river but jinked inland for about 50 metres, before angling back towards the water on the other side of the depot. That 'detour' would have slowed the others down, assuming they had finished retrieving Mac's ball.

Even so, Chris was conscious that they could appear ahead of him at any moment, so he slowed his pace to reduce the amount of noise he was making, and angled his run so that the pick-up blocked the view from the corner. All he could hear was his heart pounding.

As he covered the last few metres, Chris reduced speed still further so that he was walking by the time he reached the truck's tail-gate. He could see the missing metal posts now; two of them, lying in the gutter behind the truck. The holes where they normally stood were visible in the roadway. A gap just a little wider than the truck that had been left.

Leaning against the dirty rear of the truck, which was covered in rust, white paint and mud in roughly equal measure, Chris found himself breathing hard from his exertions. It had been quite a run. He put his bag down on the roadway and bent over, his hands on his knees.

He heard a gate rattle but ignored it. Shortly after, he heard voices. This time he straightened up, aiming to look over the back of the truck bed through its grimy windows, so that he would see whoever appeared along the path. As he stood up, he realised something was blocking his view, and he instantly recognised what it was – the almost-shaved head of Jones's accomplice. The man was standing in front of the truck, leaning lightly on the bonnet. Chris couldn't believe he hadn't seen him there before.

He ducked back down and listened as the voices came closer. They were distorted by a strange, resonating echo off the walls of the depot and the abandoned factory buildings, but he could recognise Jazz's piping, clear voice and Mac's dirty laugh. Jazz was explaining the Spirebrook challenge to Jones, who clearly didn't believe him.

'It's true!' Jazz insisted. 'You can't play for the team unless you can kick a ball over the wires!'

'Sure, sure,' said Jones.

'We've all done it!' Jazz insisted. Chris could remember being present when Jazz had taken his turn. It made him feel quite sad now.

'I'm not falling for that, Jazz,' Jones said. The voices were becoming clearer as they came closer to the opening.

'Trust me,' said Javinder. 'I wouldn't lie to a mate.'

Chris heard Jones start to reply, but he was cut off before the first word by a hard, crisp voice which silenced everyone else immediately. Chris found himself almost not breathing.

'You ought to listen to him, Russo. Never lie to your mates. Or your family. Trust is a very important thing, you know?' There was a long pause. 'Nothing to say, Russo? Well, as it happens I need to have a word with you. It's a bit of luck us bumping into each other like this, isn't it?' Again, silence. Chris edged to the side of the truck. 'Would you be free now, for a word? Just for a minute?'

'Russell . . .' That was Mac's voice, sounding nervous, urging caution. Chris could imagine the worried frown on his face.

'It's OK,' said Jones. 'Just give me a minute.'

Chris slowly sank down on his haunches, peering under the right rear wheel arch to watch as Mac and Jazz slowly moved on ahead down the path, looking back over their shoulders. After a few moments, they disappeared behind the wall of the abandoned factory on the other side of the road. Chris hoped they didn't go too far out of sight.

The man waited until they had gone before he spoke up again. Chris shifted, turning round and creeping towards the other side of the truck.

'What do you want?' he heard Jones ask.

'Now, that's not the friendliest greeting, is it, Russo?' 'Russo' didn't bother to reply. 'Are you starting to get above yourself, now that you're living in that fine big house with that nice architect man and his family?'

'Who says I'm living there?' asked Jones lamely.

The man snorted. 'Well, I suppose it could just be that you've gone there for your holidays, Russo, but it doesn't look like it to me.' There was a lot of sarcasm in his voice as he said this, which disappeared as if by magic as he continued. 'I told you, didn't I – I've always got my eye on you.' The voice, with its strange musical inflections, sounded dark and menacing. Chris bit his lip, as nervous as if he was the one being confronted. Suddenly, the man's voice was all light and cheerful once again. 'And look at you! Nice new clothes, shiny new bag. You've even had your hair cut!'

'I'm not the only one,' Jones said softly.

The man laughed. 'Do you like it? I thought it made me look a little bit more professional.' He laughed again, ending abruptly when he realised he was the only one enjoying the joke. 'Do you remember our profession, Russo? Do you remember how we put food on the table?' Jones chose not to answer. Normal service had been resumed. 'You remember . . .' the man goaded him. Chris was completely still now, hovering close to the corner of the truck. He waited for Jones to answer, but even though Jones kept to his customary silence, Chris didn't have to wait long for the unshaven man to provide the answer. 'We steal things.'

YES! That was it; that was what Chris wanted to hear. There was no doubt any more, not in his mind at least. He had the proof at last. OK, it wasn't anything he could show to anyone else, but his own uncertainty was banished now, and he would make sure Jones was exposed if it was the last –

'No.'

Jones had replied in such a low, gentle voice, Chris almost missed it while his mind was turning cartwheels to celebrate Jones's unmasking. He forced himself to concentrate.

'What was that?' asked the man.

'No,' Jones repeated, with a little more conviction. 'Not any more.'

Chris edged forward a fraction more, hoping he might be able to peek around the edge of the truck as he had done on the other side. Nothing. He realised they must both be standing directly in front of the vehicle's bonnet.

Bullet-head was obviously allowing this information to sift into his head, because nothing was said for a while. When he next spoke, his voice sounded as brittle as glass. He was trying to be light-hearted, changing the subject as if Jones hadn't denied him. It sounded more like a threat.

'When were you thinking of coming home, Russo?'

'I don't know.'

'Ma's worried.'

'I'll come and see her . . . I'll come and explain.'

'There's more to it than that, Russo. You've got responsibilities. With that bungled job at the sports store, and then us losing all that other stuff that I lifted from that bloke's car –'

Chris's heart jumped. Things were getting really interesting now!

'That wasn't my fault. It was stupid hiding it in the bathtub. You said it yourself, MacKenzie would have helped himself to it, and all he had to do was walk down the garden . . .'

'Is that what happened, Russo?'

'No,' said Jones abruptly. 'Some lads from the school up the road found it . . .' Chris noticed how vague the answer was, concealing more than it revealed.

'And what were they doing at the house, these friends of yours?'

'I don't know,' Jones replied quickly. And then he added, 'And they're not friends of mine. They play football for the school team. One of them used to play for this other team, the one I'm going to practise with –'

'The blond lad, yes I know. I've seen him around.'

Chris felt his stomach tighten. He'd seen the guy once before today; how could Bullet-head have 'seen him around'? The thought that he might have been followed for days made Chris's blood run cold.

'Then you know he hates me . . .'

'I do . . .' the man said thoughtfully. 'Why would that be, I wonder?'

'He thinks I stole the medals and stuff,' Jones replied flatly.

There was a short pause. Chris was finding it hard to take in everything he had heard, but his brief certainty about Jones was evaporating quickly. He was replaying some of the conversation in his head when Bullet-head spoke up again.

'But you did steal it!' he said.

Chris almost jumped upright. He felt his shoulder bang against the back of the truck. He had an instant to fear that he'd given himself away, but Jones was busy denying what the man had said. Maybe his little slip wouldn't be noticed.

'I didn't!' Jones had cried.

'Oh, but you did,' the man said, and Chris found himself becoming more confused than ever. 'Oh, I'm not talking about stealing it from the car, Russo. No, I did that. Like I keep telling you, there's not a minute of the day or night when I don't have my eye on you . . .'

'You . . . you've followed me?'

'I have,' explained the man. 'I saw you break into the clubhouse at Stonebridge and steal that goalkeeper's shirt –'

'I only borrowed it!'

'Very handy, it was, seeing how you did it. I paid the place a visit meself a bit later. In and out; three hundred quid in the cash tin. Very handy. Old man Whistler told the police it was you, you know, because of the shirt . . . That's why I told you to keep away from home for a few days. Looking out for you, I was. If it wasn't for me, the coppers would have caught you for sure.'

Jones uttered a kind of strangled cry. It took Chris a moment to realise that he'd cried out 'Mick!' Somehow, being able to put a name to the face wasn't as comforting as it might have been.

'Then I followed you here that other time. That was a bit trickier. I had to leave the van when you went haring off across the fields. I don't know why you want to be a footballer, Russo – you could be a cross-country runner! Then you started crawling over that pipe, and I thought, no, that's not for me. I went back and got the truck. I didn't have much hope of finding you, if I'm honest, except that there aren't that many places to get to from where you were. And I thought, sure, and if he was going into the city or whatever, wouldn't he have just followed the main road? I figured that meant you had to be heading for the university.'

Chris pictured the geography in his mind. The house where

he and Nicky had discovered Jones was more or less directly west of where the pipe crossed the river, and the university was more or less east of the other end. Jones had just gone in a straight line rather than hike to the main road and go round . . .

'As I'm passing the university – not the first place I would have looked for you, as you can imagine – what do I see? A bunch of lads playing footie. And there's my own sweet little brother running round in his new jersey. So . . . I thought –'

'Yes, OK, I get the idea,' said Jones. Chris silently cursed him for interrupting. All this detail was just what he wanted to hear.

'No-one much around; just these lads playing football, and there's my brother skulking around in the car park. I thought you might have been doing a little work for yourself, sort of like freelance . . . Little secrets, kept from the family.' The man's voice had changed tone. The slightly melodic, charming accent was nowhere near as evident now. Chris felt the truck move – the guy must have lifted his weight from the hood. 'So, I parks the truck and comes for a look-see. I couldn't find you, but there was no-one around watching the kids, and they were all much too busy playing their game to pay me any attention. So I find meself a nice car and – BOSH –' He mimicked the sound the glass had made '– I does the window, opens the door, and what do I see? Lots of nice little silver medals and cups and stuff like that. Mementos, is that the right word? Mementos. All neatly packed in a box or two, they were. So I stashed them out of sight under some crates and boxes behind that little clubhouse, and came back for them later, when the heat had died down. You know – it seems the police think you might just be responsible for that too.'

Not just the police, thought Chris, biting his lip. He'd listened to the story closely; it all seemed so obvious once you could see the whole picture.

'Why, Mick? Why did you want to get me into trouble?'

'I'm coming to that. First, though, we have to talk about the car.'

Chris knew how this story was going to turn out before Mick started. He turned his head, looking back up the street and to both sides. Sometime soon, he was going to have to think just how he was going to slip away without being noticed.

Then his memory jolted, as if the computer inside his head had just unlocked a secret password. The car; Iain's Honda. Where was it? Had Mick actually had time to drive round to the university, park it by the sports field and then walk through the gate and along the towpath to here? It didn't seem likely. And if he had, didn't that mean he'd just driven Walsh's stolen car on to the very parking area where Walsh himself would be at any moment?

That didn't make sense . . .

'That was easy. There they all were again, watching the football, or watching you run round the pitch at half-time. It was easy to get the guy's keys from his jacket. It's not much of a car — I would have preferred it if that other guy had hung round. A nice red BMW — now that's what I call a car. Of course, it wouldn't have been worth as much with the radio being nicked . . .' Mick laughed. 'But I happened to know where I could find one!' He laughed even louder. His amusement ended abruptly. Chris imagined he wasn't happy that no-one else joined in. 'Once everyone had gone, I just drove it away. There wasn't much inside worth nicking — just a few balls, and kit and stuff.'

'What did you do with it?' asked Jones.

'Sold what I could; chucked the rest.'

'And the car?'

That was what Chris wanted to know, too.

'I was hoping I might be able to sell that too. It's got a nice new coat of paint and new number plates . . . I took it to a bloke I know this afternoon, but he only offered me £250, and I think I could get £500. What do you think, Russo? Isn't £500 a fairer price?'

There was no answer. Chris lowered his head and peered under the truck. Bent like that, he could at least see their legs; Jones in school grey, the guy in black jeans. The man had his feet crossed at the ankle; Chris saw he was wearing tan cowboy boots under his denims.

'Is that all?' Jones asked finally.

'I think so. I think so. The police are only really looking for you because of the Stonebridge thing, but they have the two cars on their files, and there are witnesses who could very easily put you at the scene both times. It wouldn't take an awful lot of thinking for them to realise that you're quite the little master criminal.'

When Jones next spoke, Chris heard his voice start to break with emotion.

'Why are you doing this, Mick? Why are you stitching me up like this?'

'Now, I said I'd explain, and I will. I just thought it was important that you understood just how much trouble you were in.' The voice took on the icy, menacing tone once more. 'You do understand, don't you, Russo? You understand that I'm the one who can make or break you now? I can protect you or I can dob you in . . . You understand that clearly, don't you?'

'Yes . . .' Jones choked.

'Then get this straight as well. I knew you were starting to drift away from us, after that robbery at the sports shop. I knew all about your little visits to the sports ground, and your little games, all by yourself. Lord, how many times did you kick a ball against that fence? All that running and jumping around; what did you think you looked like?'

The man had settled back against the front of the truck, relaxed now that he was in control.

'That woman . . .' Jones said.

'What woman?'

'The security guard . . .'

'Her? Aw, she was all right. I'm not stupid like you, Russo, I read more of the paper than the sports pages. She spent a few days in hospital and she was as right as rain. I blame her company meself. Fancy putting a woman in a job like that! Her mate, now, at least he could handle himself. I had a lot more trouble with him after you ran off, I can tell you.'

'So . . .'

'They never got a good look at us, and no-one's ever asked us any questions. You see? You got yourself into a state for nothing.'

'You could have said . . .'

'I could have, yes, but I didn't. Other things on me mind. Like how to stop me kid brother running off on us. 'Cause I

129

knew that was what you were dreaming of, Russo, while you played your little games, all alone. I knew you was planning to run off.'

'I . . .'

Chris knew Jones couldn't deny it. He'd seen how hungry Jones was to play football; that much, at least, he'd been right about all along. Equally clearly, this Mick guy was never going to let him. Jones had only ever had one choice . . .

'So, where would that leave us? Me, your ma and da? Soft-brained Davey and Marie with her head off in the clouds . . . Did you think I was going to let you run off, and leave me to look after all of them by meself?' Chris jumped as Mick banged his fist against the truck's radiator. 'No chance, Russo. No chance. I need you to help me with jobs like that sports store. There's places you can go that I can't. And it's only fair that you do your bit and help me put bread on the table. You're not running out on us, Russo. I've work for us tonight. Another one of them big stores, just up the road from here. Electrical goods. Should be worth a few bob, eh?'

'I can't!'

'You can't, or you won't?'

'I can't!'

Chris heard the man growl angrily. It took him several moments to recover enough to be able to speak once more.

'Forget it, then. I've got a back-up plan anyhow.' Looking under the truck, Chris saw Jones had backed off several feet. He didn't blame him. Chris didn't doubt in the slightest that being in Mick's bad books was something you'd avoid if you had the choice. 'Go on, off with you. Go and play football with your little pals. Don't you worry about your family; don't you worry about your own flesh and blood. I'll take care of them . . .'

Jones took a few hesitant steps off in the direction Jazz and Mac had taken. If it had been Chris, he would have been halfway to the city centre by now, but he knew the subtle threads Mick was pulling to keep Jones close. Even a lousy family was better than no family at all.

'Go on!' goaded the man. 'You've got your new family and your new friends. You don't need us any more.'

'That's not how it is . . .' choked Jones. 'I just don't want to steal any more. I want to do what's right. And I want to play football.'

'No-one's stopping you,' Mick snarled. 'Go on . . .'

Jones took a few more steps, moving across the road towards the narrow pavement on the other side. Chris could see his face now. He looked pale and sick, dark rings showing under his eyes. He kept backing off, never once looking away from his brother.

'Just one thing,' Mick called before Jones could disappear around the corner. 'I'll still be keeping my eye on you, Russo. All the time. And if I once get the notion that you might try to tell people about some of the things we've done together . . . well, I just hope you can keep running as fast as you did across them fields, 'cause I'll help the police put all those little clues together and you'll be banged up faster than you can spit.'

Jones's eyes glistened, but his jaw stayed shut tight. It looked as if everything had been said. He retreated the last few steps away from the truck and disappeared around the corner. Chris could hear him running off along the walled pathway, his footsteps joined by two others.

That was that. Chris understood it all perfectly now. He'd had Jones wrong all along. The real villain of the piece was his sinister brother. Chris knew he'd been stupid so far, but it would be easy to put that right. With what he'd heard, it should be easy to turn the tables on Mick Jones and get his brother off the hook.

He looked around for the nearest place he could hide, anticipating that Mick would soon start the truck and head off.

There was a doorway about twenty metres away. If he kept low and moved quietly, he'd make it without Jones's brick-headed brother ever knowing he'd been there.

Chris was just about to get up on to his toes and run over to the door when a hand fell on his shoulder. He was dragged upright and pulled around beside the truck, pressed flat against its flank.

'Hello there,' said Mick Jones, fixing his fingers tightly in Chris's hair. 'If you don't have any plans for the evening, would you mind helping me out?'

# **Fourteen**

'Let me go!' cried Chris. He wanted to raise his voice into a shout, but Mick Jones thrust a hand over his mouth.

'Sure, that's going to happen,' mocked the man, lowering his face to glare into Chris's eyes. 'I know you. You were following me the other night – and you play football in that team that Russell's with now.' He grinned cruelly. 'And I'm guessing you're one of those that took my stuff from the house . . .'

Chris replied, 'Your stuff?', but it came out sounding like 'Mmer mmmff?' thanks to the fist jammed in his mouth. Mick's grin broadened and his eyes glittered like glass.

'Don't even think about screaming for help. No-one much walks up this part of the pathway, so the odds aren't in your favour. Whereas you can be absolutely certain that I'll break your neck if you so much as squeal. Understand?' Chris nodded. Bullet-head copied him, nodding at the same speed, mocking Chris's frightened expression. 'I'm glad we understand each other,' he growled, pulling Chris away from the side of the truck. 'Now, just stay smart like that and maybe you'll live a little longer . . .'

The practice didn't go well. Walsh recognised that several of the team were distracted. In part he put it down to nerves about the forthcoming first-round match of the Central Counties Youth Cup. They'd drawn Kettering, who were one of the strongest youth squads not attached to a League club. The Colts' senior team might be able to hold their own,

132

especially with home advantage, but Walsh was starting to have real doubts about his junior XI.

Jones was having a nightmare time in goal. His concentration looked completely shot, and he was looking very slow and half-hearted. Walsh was starting to have second thoughts about telling him the good news — that his registration in the team had come through, and that he could start playing for them immediately. Still, Walsh thought, maybe he was just more nervous than the others. Jones seemed to have a great deal to prove.

Walsh was also having difficulty elsewhere. Mac was working hard to convince him that he could play midfield, but although he was tackling like a tiger, he actually looked smaller now that he was in the midst of all the other boys. And both Stamp and Polly were good ball-winners in midfield, so he didn't really need a third. What he needed was someone who could play like Jazz did; feeding the front players with accurate passes.

He looked across the field to where Rory Blackstone and John Niells were working together on shooting practice. Rory was his normal reliable self, but Niells wasn't a great substitute for Chris. He was a willing, honest lad — brave in the air and a fair passer of the ball — but he didn't have Chris's acceleration, two-footed shooting or ability to beat a defender one on one.

From looking like a well-balanced, better than average side, the Colts were starting to look very much as if they'd be out of their depth on Sunday.

Walsh had no idea what had gone wrong. He could see the obvious things — like Chris being missing, and Nixon too — but he couldn't understand how so much bad luck could have descended on the team at the same time.

He decided to put off the more difficult decisions he had to make by dealing with the senior team first. He called them over, read out the team list, and sent them on their way. Then he looked through the second page on his clipboard again. He could feel the younger players looking at him as he stood poised with his pen between his lips. Finally, he realised he couldn't put the decision off any longer. He rested the board on his knee and pulled off the top of his pen with his teeth.

Under the line which read 'RIVERSIDE COLTS JUNIOR XI'

he crossed through the word 'JONES' and wrote 'MACIN-TYRE'. Further down, he removed Mac's name from the list in midfield and added 'SANDERS'.

After that, under the heading substitutes, he wrote 'JONES' as the fourth name on the list of five. That left one line blank. There was little point in adding the normal reserve goalkeeper – Jones could act as cover there – so that meant a spare outfield player. But who?

Finally, after even more thought, he wrote the name 'STEPHENS'. It was wishful thinking, but perhaps he could persuade Chris to change his mind before the weekend. He was still registered as a player, after all. Walsh could always change his mind later.

He called the boys over and told them the team. He didn't mention that he had Chris down as the fifth reserve, and none of them noticed that he was a name short. He saw the look of disappointment in Mac's face as his name came up first, but that wasn't his primary concern right now.

'Listen,' he told them. 'Don't get this game out of propor-tion. Yes, it's a bigger competition than the District Cup; yes, the opposition will be good. But so are you, when you have your mind on the job. Mac, Jazz, Rory, Tollie . . . I'm talking to you guys especially. You can take Kettering. Just get it together between now and Sunday, OK? If any of you need to talk, I'll be here on Thursday, and I'll make sure I'm here early on Sunday. Meantime, stay away from all the kids with runny noses, and try to turn up looking more like a winning team on Sunday, OK?'

They drifted off in ones and twos, without the enthusiasm he expected. Walsh noticed that Mr MacIntyre had arrived to pick up Mac and Jones, and that Mac told him the news about him playing in goal with his head held low. He thought he heard Mac's father tell him not to worry, that things would turn out all right soon.

Walsh was hoping that was right.

Then he noticed another car in the same row as the MacIntyres' Audi. The Astra's door opened and John Stephens stepped out, then jogged briskly over towards Jazz and Mac. Walsh watched heads being shaken in answer to whatever question Chris's father posed.

Mr Stephens then ran over to talk to Walsh, holding the collar of his jacket closed. Walsh wondered why he wasn't wearing a coat – December was just around the corner, and the wind was chilling.

'Hi,' called Walsh as the other man approached. 'Everything all right?' He could tell by his expression that it couldn't be.

'You haven't seen Chris, have you?' asked Mr Stephens.

'Errr . . . no. Should I have?'

Mr Stephens hunched his shoulders and looked around the playing fields. 'I guess not. I just hoped he'd come here tonight.'

'I was wishing the same thing myself, not three minutes ago,' observed Walsh with a concerned smile.

John Stephens looked up. 'He was under strict instructions to come straight home from school. Chris may bend the rules sometimes, but he hardly ever breaks them. I thought he might have decided to come here and make peace, you know? Get his place back on the team?'

'You know about the problem with Russell Jones, then?' asked Walsh.

Mr Stephens shook his head. 'No. And right now, I'm not too worried about it. I'm starting to worry, Iain . . . This is the one place I was sure he'd come if he didn't come home.'

Walsh could see how concerned Mr Stephens was. 'I understand. Look, let's grab a few of the lads before they all disappear, and see what they know. Have you tried Nicky yet? The school? Maybe Sean knows something . . . I tell you what, my new car has a mobile phone. Let's start checking round.'

They walked over to Walsh's new Vectra. Along the way, Walsh explained about Chris's 'resignation' from the Colts.

'Do you think there's a connection?' asked Mr Stephens, and then, immediately, he added, 'Should I call the police?'

'Leave it a while,' said Walsh. 'Chris is a bit sore about the Jones thing, but I don't think he's run off or anything. He'll probably turn up soon. And there's a lot we can do before we have to call the police.'

# **Fifteen**

The police were out in force the following morning.

No-one at the Colts knew anything, nor any of Chris's mates at school who Mr Stephens rang that first evening. He couldn't speak to Nicky, who was off at practice early on, and then at the cinema that evening. Uncle Fabian, though, rang back later to say that he had picked Nicky up from school to take him to Gainsbury, and that he hadn't seen any sign of Chris at all. He promised to get Nicky to call if he knew anything else.

Walsh caught Sean Priest at Star Park just before he left. Sean didn't have any answers either.

From about eight o'clock onwards, John Stephens and Iain Walsh were out in their cars, touring backwards and forwards around Spirebrook. They spoke to everyone they could find, but no-one had seen anything of Chris.

Mr Stephens called the police at 9.30.

Mrs Cole called an all-school assembly on Thursday morning. Rumours were already flying round the school, prompted by John Stephens' phone calls and fuelled by the presence of two police cars in the school playground that morning. Getting everyone into the one large hall was a squeeze, but they finally managed it.

Mrs Cole was on the stage, flanked by two police officers on one side and John Stephens on the other.

Griff tapped Nicky on the back with his foot. 'What's all this about, Fiorentini?'

'I think they're looking for Chris . . .' Nicky replied softly.

All over the hall, kids were whispering and quizzing each

other about who knew what. Mrs Cole stood up and the whole room fell into a hush instantly.

'Pay attention, all of you. Now, there's no immediate cause for alarm, but a student at this school hasn't been seen since the end of school yesterday. As a precaution, the police have been called in. The student in question is Chris Stephens of Year –'

Mrs Cole was almost drowned out as the whole hall reacted in shock and dismay. As captain of the lower school's football team, Chris was known to just about everyone. Several hundred voices started discussing what might have happened; those few who didn't know Chris started pestering others to find out who they were talking about, and were quickly told to shut up.

Mrs Cole raised her voice to bring everyone's attention back to the front of the hall. 'I'm sure all of you will want to help as much as you can. The first thing to do is find everyone who might have seen Chris after school . . .'

The assembly descended into chaos. The police told everyone to try and remember everything they had seen at the end of the day. If anyone knew anything at all, they were to go to the sixth-form study room, which was being set up as an incident room.

The chaos continued as the school became the focus of the police's immediate enquiries. No-one could concentrate on anything else. Chris's class mates were taken off separately so that a young detective sergeant named Clifton could speak with them first.

They were all in a state of shock. All of them homed in on Nicky, unable to believe that he didn't know something.

'I was at football practice!' he said over and over.

The DS, with a uniformed woman constable in tow, arrived soon after. He sat on the desk at the front of the room and tried to get them to talk him through the end of the day.

'You were all together in Mr Stewart's history class, right?' asked Clifton.

They all nodded and answered 'Yes, sir,' as if they were joined by wire.

'Nothing unusual about the lesson?' Mr Stewart had been his usual electrifying self, sending them to sleep with a fascinating exposition of the importance of the Domesday Book. 'So, who saw Chris leave at the end of class?' the detective asked, looking around the room.

They looked around at each other too, all trying to remember who had left first, and who last. Finally, Christine Blake put up her hand.

'We were here almost to last,' she said, with a nod in the direction of Rachel Manchester. 'I think Chris was still here when we left.'

That was how most of them remembered it. Chris hadn't really spoken much to anyone, but hadn't rushed from the room.

'OK, then what?' asked Clifton.

'I saw him downstairs,' said Jazz. The DS walked over to his desk. 'He was waiting outside Mr Campbell-Waterman's office. I was collecting my kit for football practice. I think Mr Campbell-Waterman must have told Chris to come back later, because then he went off out of the main doors.'

The DS wrote all this down carefully. After that, he tried to find someone who had seen Chris actually leave the building. There was no-one – in fact, nobody had seen Chris at all after that, it seemed, until Christine Blake managed to get a few more of her brain cells working than usual. She remembered that she had seen Chris at the school gates, and that he'd run straight past her and her mates, and off down the road to the left.

The copper looked quite pleased at this extra information, and tried to get Christine to remember what time this was, but she couldn't achieve that.

'We were chatting at the gates for about five minutes,' she recalled.

Nicky paid just as close attention to these various clues as anyone else. He'd drawn a little diagram on his pad, showing the school buildings, the covered way and the paths leading to the gates. Asking around, he knew that Chris hadn't been loitering around near the gates, or on the paths after he left Soupy's office. Which meant that no-one had really seen what Chris had been doing during those five minutes before Christine saw him running off that way (which was bound to be nearer ten; Christine and her mates could chatter for an hour and swear it had been less than a quarter of that).

'Did anyone see Chris after that?' asked DS Clifton. No reply. 'Do any of you walk that way after school?' Again, there was no reply. Nicky looked across; Jazz and Russell Jones were looking at each other in a way that suggested that, no, they hadn't walked that *exact* way . . .

'What about you guys?' Nicky said, focusing on Jazz, who he knew he could crack easiest. 'Didn't you go that way to practise with the Colts?'

The DS thanked Nicky, and said that he'd ask the questions, if that was OK. He then more or less repeated what Nicky had asked.

'Not exactly,' said Jazz. 'We went out the back way, along the lane – I mean the new road. After a while, you end up on the river . . .'

'I know,' said DS Clifton, flicking back through his notebook. 'The Colts – is that the team Chris used to play for?' Jazz nodded, looking quite miserable. 'The one he left recently after some row?' Jazz nodded again. 'And do you happen to know much about this row?'

Jazz lowered his eyes, looking even less happy than before. 'Chris was having problems with another player on the team. He told Mr Walsh – he runs the team – that he wouldn't play if – if this other boy continued to play for them too. Mr Walsh said he wouldn't choose, so Chris quit.'

'I see,' said Clifton. Nicky waited for him to pounce on Jones. Instead, the plain-clothes officer went back to trying to work out where Chris had gone. 'Chris went off down the road towards the river at roughly the same time as you were there. Did you see him?' Jazz shook his head. 'Did you see anything unusual at all?' Clifton continued. Once again Jazz shook his head, his eyes down on the table. Nicky watched him, and he wondered if there was more to this than met the eye. He couldn't imagine that Jazz would lie about anything that might help explain what had happened to Chris. At the same time, Jazz wasn't acting like himself at all.

As the DS turned his attention away from Jazz to make sure no-one else had anything to say, Nicky spotted Jones glance towards Javinder. Although Jazz didn't look back, it was a look that said, 'Keep quiet, don't say anything . . .'

They *knew* something.

DS Clifton had finished his questions for now. He stood up, trying to reassure Chris's class mates that things were probably nowhere near as bad as they looked, and that Chris would turn up somewhere with some adventurous tale to tell. Then he headed for the door.

'Could I have a word with you in private?' Nicky blurted. Clifton looked back impatiently.

The WPC whispered something in his hear. She had been around earlier when some of the other officers had been talking to Nicky, and knew who he was. Clifton nodded, then waved Nicky towards the door. Nicky heard the whispers behind him as they left the room and went out into the hall.

'Well?'

'Russell Jones knows something – more than he's telling,' Nicky said explosively, allowing all his frustration and animosity for Jones to boil over. 'It's because of him Chris left the Colts –'

'We know,' said Clifton. 'Iain Walsh told us. We know that you're not a big fan of his either.'

'Chris and I have been checking up on him. There's been some stuff nicked, and me and Chris thought –'

'This would be the "stuff" nicked from Mr Priest's car, and Mr Walsh's Honda, yes?'

Nicky stalled. 'That's right . . .' he said, less certainly.

'We know about that, Nicky. We may not have arrested anybody, but that doesn't mean we're completely ignorant.'

'Me and Chris thought Jones –'

'– was responsible, yes, I know that too. PC Pennington, on the other hand, thinks that you and Chris were involved somehow. He says he caught Chris acting suspiciously on the day that Mr Priest's car was broken into, and that he has found you both lurking around in the Church Hill area. Obviously, Chris was there on the day the car got stolen too . . .'

Nicky's jaw flapped as he struggled to cope with the way this conversation was going. 'B-but . . .'

Clifton smiled and put his hand on Nicky's shoulder. 'It's all right, son. I don't think you were involved, you or Chris. Both Mr Walsh and Mr Priest have told us they know you wouldn't be involved in something like that. What you need to realise is that they have both said the same thing about Russell Jones.' He stood up again and stretched his back. 'So, apart from the fact that we don't know that there's any real connection between Chris going missing and these crimes, your theories about Russell Jones just don't hold water. In fact, I'd go further than that. Instead of working against Jones, why don't you work with him? I bet that if you two put your heads together, you'd be able to be a lot more help to us than either of you are being on your own.'

Clifton left Nicky with that alarming suggestion to deal with, and went off along the hall with the WPC. At first, Nicky was convinced that the DS had got it all wrong. By the time he had turned back towards the classroom door, however, he was already wondering if perhaps he ought to take the sergeant's suggestion a little bit more seriously.

By Saturday, the police were dragging the river.

Nicky and Jazz walked along the towpath, having gone to see what was going on. The police were searching the area where the river curved round the corner of the school and the new road.

'Do you think he's killed himself?' asked Javinder suddenly, in a low, nervous voice.

'Whatever for?' replied Nicky.

'Over the football and things...' Jazz explained. He'd obviously been giving it a lot of thought.

Nicky considered the idea for less than a second. 'Don't be daft. Chris wouldn't kill himself over Russell flamin' Jones or the Colts. He might have killed Jones, but that's different. No, there's something else going on, something we haven't thought of –'

'What had you got in mind?' came a third voice. Nicky spun round, instinctively hostile at the sound of that voice.

'You've got some front coming here, Jones!' he spat.

'Look – I feel just the same as you. I want Chris to turn up, and for all this to be finished.'

'Yeah, right. It must be really cutting you up that Chris isn't around to help me expose you for the fraud you are!' Jones recoiled as if he'd been slapped. Nicky stepped closer. 'You know a lot more about what's going on than you're letting on,' he said, and his hands clenched threateningly into fists. 'I'd like to beat it out of you!'

'Nicky!' cried Jazz, trying to put himself between them.

'You're way off-line, Fiorentini,' said Jones in a low, defensive voice. 'I don't know where Stephens is –'

'I don't believe you!' Nicky growled. He had backed Jones almost to the water's edge, and was flashing white teeth in a harsh snarl of anger. Jazz was taller than either of them, but he was clearly aware just how close he was to becoming the meat in a very unsavoury sandwich. 'I'll get you, Jones. I mean it. I've got my eye on you!'

Those words broke through Russell's armour better than any blows could have. His mouth opened wide – for a moment, he found it hard to breathe. Nicky slowly backed away.

'Wait!' gasped Russell. Nicky paused, caught slightly off guard. 'What did you just say?' Russell continued.

Nicky watched him carefully. 'I said I'd be watching you . . .'

Tears stung Russell's eyes. 'Nicky . . . you're right, I haven't been honest with you . . . not with any of you . . .' Now he was the one with his fists clenched and his teeth set determinedly. 'But I'm going to put that right . . .'

⚽

'No, you've lost me,' said Nicky. 'Tell me that last part again.'

'My brother Mick has been behind all the thefts, everything, all along. He's been making it look like I was involved to force me to stay at home and do what he wants. That's how I found the stuff from Sean's car; he hid the stuff he couldn't sell in the bathtub, but I knew he'd keep the best stuff at home. So I took it back.'

The three of them were over by the old depot, sitting on the window ledge of one of the old factories in Gladstone Street. Behind them, the site was an area of complete destruction, JCBs and sledgehammers having long since reduced the place to a heap of bricks and smashed flooring.

'Is that why you left home?' Nicky asked.

'Yes. I love my family, I really do – but not Mick. We've

142

always had to duck and dive a bit to make ends meet – me dad's had more fiddles going than an orchestra – but Mick's different, he's out of control. If I stayed, I only had two choices. Do what he said, or rat on him to the police.'

'So now he's making certain you don't have the second option,' Jazz said, clearly quite horrified at the picture he was starting to get of the way Mick Jones operated.

'That's right. He told me that I either go back home or he'll make sure the police put all the evidence together and come looking for me.'

'But what has this got to do with Chris?' asked Jazz despairingly.

'I don't know.'

Nicky considered everything he'd heard carefully, unable to draw on any similar experience in the Fiorentini household. 'Why don't you have a word with your mum and dad; get them to make Mick leave you alone?'

'My dad's just a tired old man – he hasn't stood up to Mick for years. And my mum can't do anything either . . . Mick's been running the family for the last two years. It's his fault we've become criminals.'

'My mum would have beaten the whatsits out of him,' Nicky muttered.

'No-one in my family would dare disobey my father in the first place,' Jazz added.

They sat in silence for a moment, each considering their family situations.

'Families, eh?' said Nicky, grinning.

That much they could agree on.

Russell continued to think about what Mick might be working on. 'Mick won't have given up yet. He'll have some plan to stack up even more evidence against me – something that will make everyone believe I've been the thief all along.'

'So have you seen him over the last couple of days?' asked Jazz.

'My brother?' asked Russell. 'No, I don't think so . . . Why?'

Jazz propped his chin on his fist and stared out across the street. 'You said he threatened to keep a close eye on you. But there's been no sign of him at all, right?'

'I know what you're thinking,' Russell said, knowing how

143

hard it was to make them understand how dangerous Mick could be. 'He never shows himself... so I never know when he's watching me and when he's not.'

'I bet he's hardly ever watching you, except when he's got some specific plan in mind,' Nicky said. 'The rest of the time he just relies on you being frightened.'

Jazz agreed. 'He just wants you to think you're in his power. But you're not! All we have to do is to find a way to turn the tables on him...'

Russell felt there was probably some truth in their argument, and he could see the attractiveness of Jazz's idea. However, he couldn't help but think of Mick as this menacing, hidden presence that had blighted his life for the last two or three years, and who would make things even worse unless...

'He has to be planning to frame me for another crime. Sean's stuff has been recovered; Iain has told the police that it wasn't me who took his car. That doesn't leave very much.' He recalled guiltily that Whistler had told the police he was responsible for breaking into Stonebridge's clubhouse. He knew he was innocent of everything except taking the goalkeeper's shirt, but there was no easy way to prove it. So far, at least, no-one had come looking for him, but Mick could easily show them where he was 'hiding'. 'He'll try and fit me up, somehow,' he said. 'And soon.'

'But how?' asked Nicky.

'I don't know!' Russell exclaimed.

'Perhaps he's going to frame you for kidnapping?' said Jazz vacantly. He was still staring across the street, at where some small kids were playing on the flattened ground opposite. His mind had wandered a long way from the point, which Nicky was quick to point out.

'What are you talking about, Jazz?!' cried Nicky.

'Well, we don't know what's happened to Chris, do we? Maybe Mick kidnapped him and is holding him hostage somewhere.'

'You watch far too many American cop shows...' muttered Nicky, who probably watched more than anyone on the planet.

'It's not likely Mick took Chris,' said Russell, even though he had a nagging fear that he might be wrong. 'On the evening he disappeared, we know where my brother was . . . he was right here!' He gestured to the area at the end of the road, where the bollards blocked off the street from the footpath and the abandoned depot. 'The last anyone saw of Chris, he was almost half a mile away.'

'But coming this way . . .' observed Nicky.

'Not along the footpath – we'd have seen him. The same if he'd been coming down here while we were at the bottom . . .'

Russell gestured up Gladstone Street. There was nowhere at all to hide for all of the bottom half.

'So where was he going?' asked Nicky in some exasperation. It was the same question they had asked themselves over and over again.

'You said you and Chris had a plan to keep an eye on me,' Russell thought out loud. 'Chris would have wanted to make sure I was at the practice, right? So he must have been going to the university field. He didn't come along the river, because he knew we'd walk that way. So, he followed the New Road round, and went up the main road to the university gates. From there, he'd have gone to Mac's place. And then . . .' He stopped. The trouble was, they didn't know for sure what Chris had done. Even if he had followed the plan Nicky and he had cooked up, they had no idea how far he had followed it.

Nicky levered himself off the window ledge and strode quickly across the street to the other side. 'This is stupid!' he yelled. 'It's one thing your brother trying to blackmail you into going home, but kidnapping Chris doesn't make sense!' He paused on the far pavement and then turned back. The others lapsed into silence. For a moment, they felt completely helpless. Nicky's frustration was close to boiling point. 'OK. Let's forget Chris for a moment,' he said. His voice became calm again. 'We can't figure that out, so let's try something else – like Walsh's car. The police have never found that. Now, you say that when Mick stole the stuff from Sean Priest, he kept the decent stuff at home, right?'

'Right.'

'What did he do with the car?'

'I don't know. I don't think he took it home.'

'Is that what he'd normally do?'

Russell hesitated for a moment, not wanting to show just how familiar he was with the details of car theft. Years of natural caution had left him reluctant to just blurt out the truth. On the other hand, Jazz and Nicky knew a great deal of the truth about him already.

'Sure. There's a shed by the house – that's where I found the medals and the other stuff. Mick repaints the cars, gives them some new plates, and then sells them to one of his contacts.'

'But not this time?'

'Like I said, I don't think so.'

Nicky paced up and down along the pavement, scratching his head. 'Then he had somewhere else where he could hide the car. Where?' Russell had no answer. Nicky looked at him closely for several seconds until he shrugged. Nicky scowled and turned his attention to Jazz, whose eyes were still fixed across the road. 'Feel free to help any time you're ready,' he mocked, bumping Jazz with his shoulder.

'I was just wondering . . .' said Jazz. He was still peering off into the distance.

'What?'

'That little girl over there. What is she doing with that bag?'

The other two turned to face the same direction as he was pointing. Several dusty-clothed kids were taking part in a complicated game which involved a doll being placed in a black bag and then being taken out again and passed round to someone else while the bag was moved from one spot to another. There was a great deal of laughing and screaming.

'It'll be some housey/doctory/baby game,' he explained. He shielded his eyes to look across the street, avoiding all eye contact with his mates.

Jazz wasn't paying any attention to Nicky at all. 'It's not the game I'm interested in,' he muttered, and he dropped down from the window ledge. 'It's the bag.'

He trotted across the road and through the broken doorway of the old factory unit opposite, clambering over piles of weed-covered earth and bricks. Nicky threw his hands up in despair as he watched him go. Then Russell walked over that way as well, so Nicky followed them slowly, obviously making sure he would be the last to arrive so that he could raise their sanity as an issue . . .

He recognised the bag as he went through the door. He put on a burst of speed which took him past both the others and into the middle of the small group of six-year-olds, raising up clouds of brick dust as he stumbled into the little patch of cleared ground where they were playing.

'It's Chris's bag!' he yelled triumphantly, reaching out towards the handles.

Most of the little kids had scattered at his mad approach or when he had shouted out about his find. One small blonde girl with a face that looked as if it could fold inside out was glaring back at him with her lips trembling.

'It's my bag!' she insisted, bending over to grab it in her tiny hands.

'Yeah, sure!' scoffed Nicky. 'An Oldcester United sports bag, almost new. Just the kind of thing your mum would buy for you to play dolls with!'

'She didn't buy it!' the child insisted, with the kind of logic small kids reserve for when they're sure they're right, and that you're stupid.

'Where did you get it?' Nicky demanded.

'It's mine!' the girl replied.

By now Jazz was on to the scene as well.

'Did you find it?' he asked. The girl settled for frowning and poking out her tongue. Nicky growled angrily beside him. 'Were there some books inside?' he said quickly. Caught off-guard, the girl looked over her shoulder towards a small heap of rubbish to one side. Jazz went past her to take a look. Among the weeds, he saw the bright covers of two ring-binders, a notepad and three textbooks, including a history book. Damp after two nights of inclement weather, they were still easily identified.

'It's Chris's stuff.'

'There weren't any colouring pens though,' insisted a little boy. Jazz could see the red and green streaks on his fingers even through the dirt.

'That's a shame,' said Jazz. 'I bet you like colouring pens.' The boy nodded. Jazz reached into his pocket, where he had a brand new Berol fine tip. 'Tell you what, you can have this one if you show me where you guys found the bag.'

The kid was delighted with this deal, and scampered off back towards the road. The little girl was furious.

'He never found it — I did!'

The whole pack of them were now racing towards the road. Jazz grinned and ambled off after them. Nicky shot him a dirty look and bent to pick up the abandoned bag.

It looked the worse for wear, and not just because Chris shared the universal belief that new kit bags were things you saw in shops but were not to be tolerated in normal life. In addition to normal wear and tear, there was a lot of more localised damage. Nicky looked it over and showed it to Russell as he arrived.

'It looks to me as if it's been run over by a car,' he said.

'More like a bus,' was Russell's assessment.

'So what do we reckon?' Nicky asked him directly. His own thoughts on the matter were pretty clear.

'He was here . . .' Russell said, and he took a moment to look around the site. 'I don't know what he was doing, but he came here Wednesday night. What happened to him then, who knows?'

'You said your brother had a van here —'

'A pick-up, yes.'

They all stopped talking at once, as if someone had zapped them with the mute button on a TV remote control.

Jazz was the first one to voice their growing fears. 'Do you think he ran Chris over?'

Russell's eyes opened wide as he considered the horrible possibility that his brother might have stepped over one final line, but he quickly pulled himself together. 'There'd have to be blood . . .' he said.

Jazz was out in the street again, near the bollards. The others picked their way through the debris to join him, and were forced to share in the costs of rewarding the infants with pens.

'They came up here to play, and saw a white van driving back up the street. The girl found the bag over there, by the kerb.'

Jazz and Russell quickly exchanged glances. Nicky was too observant to miss it.

'What?'

'My brother drives a white pick-up.'

Nicky's eyes shone brightly. It was all starting to come together. 'No blood, so he didn't run Chris down . . .' He ignored Jazz's open-mouthed look of horror and continued. 'So maybe he just grabbed him, pulled him into the van and drove off with him?'

Russell didn't look comfortable about that idea. 'Wait a minute . . . we're starting to get really paranoid here. Why would Mick kidnap Chris? It's a crazy idea.'

'Your brother is crazy,' Nicky said quietly. He realised that this wasn't enough proof on its own. 'Look, Chris isn't going to have gone off with him voluntarily.'

'But you think Mick could have snatched him?' mocked Russell. 'In broad daylight? Wouldn't someone have seen Chris struggle? And where could he have taken him? The only way out of here is on to the main road. Surely Chris could have called for help?'

'Maybe,' Nicky snapped, unhappy at being contradicted when he was on a roll. 'But it's the only thing that makes sense. I mean, he can't have hidden Chris around here, can he? I mean, there isn't anywhere . . .'

At the same moment, they both turned round and looked at the high-walled depot.

'Are you thinking . . .?' said Russell quietly.

'The door's got a flamin' great padlock on it. There's no way in.'

'Russell can get in!' cried Jazz, and when Nicky looked doubtful, he added, 'I've seen him. Well, not actually seen him, but . . .'

The other two were already walking over towards the depot's huge green wooden gates.

'Is this true?' asked Nicky.

'Sure,' muttered Russell. 'But not through here . . .' He checked the padlock to make sure it was solid. It was brand new and very strong. He gave it an experimental tug to make sure it was locked.

'Where then?' asked Nicky.

Russell led the way around the side of the depot, at the end nearest the university campus, almost walking all the way to the river. There wasn't so much as a drainpipe to shin up, and the top of the wall was capped with razor wire and broken glass.

As they reached the furthest riverside corner, there didn't appear to be much more scope for getting in. The path went right to the river's edge, fenced off by a low railing. About a half a metre from the wall there was a board on a wooden post, on which hung a life-saving ring.

Russell climbed up the railing, on to the top of the board. Nicky winced as he watched. It looked a pretty precarious post to rely on. What's more, Russell then lent towards the corner buttress of the wall, bracing his left hand on it while he groped around the corner with his right, leaning further and further out over the river.

'Are you sure you know what you're doing?' asked Nicky, dubiously.

Russell was straining, stretching further and further around the corner above the cold, grey waters of the river. Nicky read the instructions on the life-saving ring.

Finally Jones found what he was looking for. He pulled back a length of old rope, which was looped over the wall. He flipped it up a few times until it was over the buttress and dangling down the wall on their side. Then he took hold with both hands, jumped across the narrow gap and shinned quickly up the wall to the top.

'How did you find that out?' asked Nicky.

'I put it there! First time out, I was coming the other way – it's easier getting out than in. I rigged this up to give me a secret exit.'

'You're a complete nutter,' Nicky said, clearly in admiration.

Grunting with the effort of the climb, Russell had almost reached the top of the wall. He threw out a hand to grab part of the cornice where there was neither wire nor glass, then lifted his right knee up on to the corner as well. Slowly he heaved himself up. Nicky watched in amazement.

'Damn!' called Jones. He was sitting astride the wall and looking down inside the depot.

'What is it?'

'The pile of crates and stuff I used to climb up inside has disappeared – it's just a clear space down here now.'

'Don't go in, then!' called Jazz urgently. 'You might not be able to get back out!'

'I can always get out along the pipe over the river,' said Russell, looking out over the water. There was a strong wind stirring grey waves on the surface. He decided that maybe that wasn't an option after all.

'What can you see from up there?' asked Jazz.

'Not much.' It was gone 4.30pm, and under grim, grey skies, the depot was dark. Much of the interior structure had been dismantled or demolished years before, but there were still small sheds and other buildings, their doors and windows broken or removed; rusting metal storage tanks; twisting webs of pipes and lots of worthless scrap, some of it covered by tarpaulin sheets, but most exposed to the weather.

He looked down at the foot of the wall. He had piled a stack of palettes and crates on top of each other there when he had first explored the depot, but it was all gone now. He could see the cracked concrete floor, darkened with puddles and —

'Oh my god . . .' he whispered, leaning over to take a slightly closer look.

'What is it?' cried Jazz, as Russell almost disappeared over the wall. There was no reply at first, and Jazz and Nicky looked at each other in alarm. After another moment, though, Jones reappeared, looking back down at them with an apologetic smile on his face.

'Sorry, for a moment there I thought there was a massive puddle of blood on the floor. It's just red paint though . . .'

'You berk!' yelled Nicky. 'Can you see anywhere Chris might be?'

'Now who's the berk?' snapped Jones, twisting so that he could see them properly. 'Have you seen how big this place is? There are dozens of places to hide. It'd take ages to search it properly . . .'

'Well, at least shout for him. See if he can hear you.'

Russell shrugged, indicating that he thought this was about as likely to be any use as putting an ad in the paper, but he turned back and cupped his hands about his mouth to amplify his voice.

'Chris! Chris Stephens! Can you hear me?' He paused, then

151

called again. 'CHRIS!!!' Nothing. It was perfectly quiet, save for the wind whistling round his ears and the lapping of the water down below. 'Nothing,' he said, turning back to face the others.

'You might as well come down. It was a daft idea anyway. I mean, there's no way your brother could have carried Chris over the wall, is there?'

Russell lifted his leg back over the wall and let himself carefully back down on the rope. Once on the floor, he had to climb back on to the lifebelt holder so that he could flick the rope back out of sight. Finally, he dropped down on to the wharf beside Nicky and Jazz.

'How many times have you done that?' asked Nicky.

'Three or four.'

'You must be bonkers,' Nicky observed.

'That's the easy bit . . . you ought to try climbing over the river on that pipe . . .' said Russell, grinning.

Having twisted and turned his body, Chris finally managed to place his feet on the side of the old boiler. He bent his knees and kicked out, hitting the side of his metal jail with a solid blow. He continued to thump on the side of the boiler until he was exhausted and breathing heavily around the gag in his mouth.

In the enclosed darkness, the noise sounded like an explosion. He could only hope that whoever had been shouting could hear it too.

'At least we have the bag,' said Nicky, as they walked up Gladstone Street. He turned up to face the sky, thinking he could hear thunder, but though the skies were dark and miserable, it wasn't actually raining. 'We ought to take it to the police and tell them where we found it.'

'That's right,' said Jazz. 'If nothing else, it means they'll know Chris came this far up the towpath . . .'

'It's better than that,' said Nicky, triumphantly. 'It puts your brother firmly in the frame, Russell.'

'You don't *know* that, Nicky.'

'Come on, Jones! Face the facts!'

'I am! It doesn't make sense! What would be the point?'

No-one had an answer to that. They walked along in a sullen, nervous silence.

'You really used to climb over the river on that pipe, and then shin over the wall?' asked Nicky after a while. That was proving much more of a problem for him to believe than Mick being a kidnapper.

'Sometimes Mick used to get me to climb into places for him and unlock the door,' Jones confessed uneasily. 'I've got used to heights.'

Jazz had suddenly perked up. 'Maybe that's what he's going to make Chris do! Help him break in somewhere!'

'That doesn't make sense!' insisted Nicky. 'As soon as he was inside, Chris could just call the police or run away.' Jazz fell back into a defeated silence. Nicky watched him for a moment, then lifted the bag up by the handles for a closer look. 'This is all we have,' he said. 'Let's take it to the police and –'

'Wait,' said Russell. They all halted, and the other two faced him, obviously wondering what new surprise he was going to spring on them.

'Look, I don't really think Mick would go that far . . . you know . . . abducting Chris . . . but if he has, there's no way he would have left the bag here accidentally.'

'Now who's being paranoid?' mocked Nicky.

Jones shook his head. 'Look, I'm not saying I know what's happened one way or the other, but if Mick is involved in whatever's happened to Chris, well . . . finding the bag and that . . . it's too easy! What if it's some kind of test? To see if I run to the police?'

'Would he do that?' asked Nicky.

Russell shrugged. 'I know it sounds stupid, but he watches me. He'd *know* if I tried to dob him in, and then he'd do the same to me.'

A simple idea occurred to Nicky. 'Well, then *we'll* take it. You needn't be involved.'

Russell was still unconvinced – it sounded too easy a solution for Mick not to have had the same idea too.

He looked through the gaping windows of the last of the

empty and partly demolished factories they were passing. Heaps of rubble and half-demolished walls were strewn all over the place. He could almost feel Mick watching him. He started to feel a cold shiver running up his spine.

'He'd have thought of that,' he said, shaking his head. 'If he's watching, he'll know we found the bag together.'

Jones and Nicky pondered that for a while. Without anything being said, they started walking again, heading for the top end of Gladstone Street. Nicky was becoming as nervous about Mick as his brother was.

'We're only safe so long as he knows we still have the bag,' he muttered. Even though he knew this was getting unreal, he couldn't control his growing sense of unease.

'We can't *not* take it to the police!' Jazz cried. 'It's important. They have to know that Chris was following Russell at least this far up the river.'

Nicky agreed with that too. Even though he wanted to complete his work as a great detective by nabbing Russell's brother, there was still a possibility that Chris's disappearance was wholly unconnected with the Jones Affair (as Nicky thought of it in his head). The police were wasting time and effort dragging the river near the school. Chris had at least got this far up the river. They couldn't keep that a secret.

But how could they manage to both hand the bag to the police *and* make Mick Jones think they hadn't?

'I've got it . . .' said Russell. He stopped and faced the others, gesturing for them to draw closer so that he could whisper his plan. They stepped up, keen to see how he was going to sort out the problem. 'As far as Mick's concerned, the key thing is the bag. So long as I have that, he'll believe I haven't spoken with the police. So, Jazz, when you get home, ring that Sergeant Clifton and tell him you've *remembered* seeing someone who might have been Chris coming down Gladstone Street. Tell them you weren't sure before, but that you've thought it over and now you are.'

'You want me to lie to the police?' wailed Jazz. He looked quickly across to Nicky for support.

'Oh, get real . . .' snapped Nicky, all the same very glad that it wasn't going to be him.

'It's not for long. I'll bring the bag with me to the match

tomorrow. In the meantime, the police will still be looking in the right place – the last place any of us know Chris was.' He paused, knowing that Jazz was still very unhappy with the plan. 'It's not really lying, Jazz. We *do* know that Chris was here, after all.'

Jazz looked quite ill at the prospect of misleading DS Clifton.

'I don't understand why we're doing this!' he moaned.

'Because I think I know what Mick's plan is,' Jones answered, with a look of new determination in his eyes. 'I think I've figured out how he intends to make sure the police think it's me who's been stealing everything. If I'm right, he'll be at the game tomorrow. And that's where we're going to turn the tables on him at last.'

# Sixteen

Russell and Mac walked to the match the following morning. They descended Church Hill to the lights, followed the long, winding trail of the new road through the retail park, round the back of the school and then on to the river bank. This part of the route was even more familiar than the first, and they soon reached the end of Gladstone Street and the old depot.

The police had shifted the focus of their activity since the day before. Frogmen were out in the river beyond the depot, and there were uniformed officers outside the gates of the depot, and others combing the waste ground of the old factories.

Jazz had clearly done his bit. Russell wondered how he was feeling this morning. Knowing Javinder, he had probably volunteered for extra housework as a penance for his sins. Russell could hardly blame him – he'd done the washing-up last night without being asked (it wasn't even his turn, but Mac hadn't complained). Mrs MacIntyre was worried that he might be sickening for something.

Russell felt a little self-conscious carrying Chris's bag at his side. No-one in the MacIntyre household had questioned the story he had told about there being a mix-up at school in which he'd ended up with another boy's bag instead of his own. After all, he now had a slightly scruffy Oldcester United bag, while his own bag was brand new.

Mac had looked at it as if he was about to blurt out that he knew who it really belonged to, but he hadn't said anything until they left the house.

'Is that Nicky's?' he asked. Russell had nodded. Of course, Nicky was just as big an Oldcester nut as Chris. 'I'm not going to ask how you got it,' Mac said, obviously keenly aware just how much Nicky had blamed Russell for everything that had gone wrong lately. That was the end of the subject for now, which suited Russell fine. He hadn't let Mac in on the plan at all.

The policemen at the depot gates watched as they approached. Russell was hoping they'd be able to avoid any questions. He felt as uncomfortable as Jazz at the prospect of lying to the police, and the last thing he wanted was to complicate his own position any further. Besides, he'd spent too much time hiding from policemen and security guards to feel comfortable around them now. As they got closer to the depot entrance, Russell started to breathe a sigh of relief – the two constables didn't appear to have any desire to challenge them . . .

'Excuse me, officers,' said Mac. 'We're friends of Chris Stephens from school. Has there been any news?'

'A little,' said the younger of the two coppers. 'One of your mates rang the station last night to tell us that he saw Chris up here. We searched in here last night –' He gestured with his head to the depot behind him. '– and now we're searching over the waste ground. I think they might have found some school books.'

Russell almost slapped himself for being so stupid as to have forgotten the books. In the end, they weren't a problem, but it was the kind of slip he couldn't afford to make if he was going to get one over on Mick.

'Anything in the depot?' he asked, trying to be casual.

'Nothing certain,' the policeman said. 'Someone's been in there. We found fresh paint on the floor, and various bits and pieces have been moved around recently. It might just be some kids like you mucking around!'

'I've never been in there!' cried Mac indignantly, and Russell decided that denial could stand for both of them.

'Aye, well, forensics will tell us what's been going on soon enough,' said the policeman smugly.

The boys turned away and carried on up the footpath to where it turned the corner. Russell heard the policeman chuckle to himself, having clearly enjoyed passing 30 seconds of his morning in baiting Mac.

'I wish I knew what had happened,' said Mac, almost to

himself. Russell looked on ahead towards the dark-watered river beyond the railings. There were no divers on this side of the depot, he noticed. Perhaps they'd searched there already.

There were more coppers at the university, over by the science block and the administration building. Mac spotted flashing blue lights in the distance as they went through the gates. Now what?

Iain Walsh, a few of the other members of the team and a couple of parents were over by the clubhouse, watching the police coming and going. As they approached, Russell heard Stamp observe that it would be a good morning to go burgling on the other side of town.

'What's going on?' asked Russell, although he already had a familiar sinking feeling that he knew what it was.

'There's been a break-in at the university – looks like someone was trying to steal computers from the science block. They gave up when they couldn't get past the alarms and the security cameras, and broke into the main building through an air conditioning vent instead. The police reckon they were looking for the receipts from the student bar; there was a disco there last night.'

Russell nodded. That sounded like the sort of job he and Mick had pulled in the past. Had Jazz been right when he guessed that Mick was using Chris to take his place?

He realised Walsh was addressing the rest of the team, and tried to pull his concentration back to the present. 'I know it's not easy, but you've got to ignore all that as much as you can,' he said, waving in the direction of the police cars. 'Concentrate on the game. Get your kit on and get warmed up. Polly! I'm glad you could finally make it! Do you think you could turn up on time just once for a change?'

While Walsh remained outside to harry late arrivals, the rest of the Colts team went into the clubhouse. Russell took a long look around, but there was no sign of anyone watching him. He muttered a silent prayer to himself and climbed the short flight of stairs towards the door.

The changing rooms were upstairs, above the small pavilion room the cricket team used during the summer. Excited chatter and laughter drifted down to meet Russell as he made his way up; the Kettering team had already arrived and were in high spirits.

The last few of the Colts arrived, and Walsh hurried everyone into getting changed so that they could warm up properly and receive some last-minute advice on members of the opposition team. Studs clattered on the floor as they made their way downstairs and ran out on to the field. Even though he was only a sub, Russell went through the same stretching and limbering-up exercises as the others, then gave Mac a hand by firing some shots at him.

He also took a few moments to size up the opposition as best he could. Kettering looked fit and well organised. They had a left winger who looked strong and busy, and a big, tall striker who made Rory Blackstone look like a midget. They played a sweeper at the back, and three players in midfield who seemed a lot bigger than Jazz, Stamp and Polly. This was going to be tough.

There was one bit of good news. The opposition goal-keeper seemed very stiff and slow, as if he was nursing a bit of a sore leg or a bad back. Twice he ignored shots that needed him to dive if he was going to reach them.

Russell trotted over to Rory Blackstone and pointed it out to the big striker. 'It might be worth having a few shots from range against this bloke – he doesn't look very agile to me.'

Rory squinted upfield. 'Do you think so? Hmmm . . . maybe I'll give it a try.'

Iain Walsh called them all together shortly afterwards. They huddled against the raw December wind and listened carefully. The Colts had never played such an important game before.

'Look, I know this will be difficult, but you have to put all the distractions out of your mind and concentrate on the game. This is a good team and they're used to this level of competition. Several of them have been looked at by League clubs, so you'll need to be on your best form. They play it very tight in midfield, so use the flanks and use your pace. Jazz, Stewart, I want to see you getting wide to support the front two.' Continuing to identify Kettering's strengths and weaknesses, he tried to get his young team to focus on the job in hand. However, they still had that undirected, restless quality about them he had seen in practice. Jazz looked very much out of sorts. 'Listen,' he concluded. 'I want Chris to turn up safe and well as much as any of you. And when he does, I'm going to get him to change his mind about the team if it kills me.' There were a couple of nervous laughs. 'But he isn't going to forgive us if we get knocked out in the first round of the Cup, so you have to win today. Win for Chris, OK?'

A little bit of steel seemed to come back into them after that, and they ran out on to the field looking a little more like their old selves.

'Did you believe that; what you said about Chris coming back safe and sound?' asked Russell.

'Yes,' said Iain Walsh, although he didn't sound as certain as he wanted to. 'I'm sure he'll be back.'

'Good. Because so am I,' said Russell.

Chris heard a whistle blow and the cheers as the game kicked off. He was bound tight, gagged and blindfolded. He felt as if he was in a tight space. He was tired and hungry.

Worse than that, though, the fear that had gripped him since Mick Jones had first taken hold of his arm had never gone away.

The sound of the ref's whistle was quite comforting. Chris listened carefully as the game got underway, and tried to work out what was going on from the individual bits of sound. It sounded as if the home team had quite a bit of support, and he could hear other voices urging the two teams on from the touchline, or calling for the ball out on the field.

For the last few days, except for that one moment when he had heard someone calling his name, the only voice he had heard had been Mick's. Hearing ordinary voices, calling and shouting as the game unwound, made him realise there was still a world outside. He held on to that thought closely.

He wanted to play football again. Whatever it took, he wanted to play again really soon.

Riverside weren't the only ones who had taken a look at the opposition goalkeeper and made their plans accordingly. Kettering had taken one look at Mac and decided to fire a succession of crosses towards their tall centre forward. Mac managed to palm a few crosses away, and disrupted other attacks by challenging hard, but the striker set up a couple of half-chances for his team mates in the first few minutes.

'It's only a matter of time . . .' Russell whispered to himself.

At the other end, Rory Blackstone took Jones's advice early on and unleashed a shot from 25 metres, which the Kettering goalkeeper made a very unconvincing attempt to get to. Unfortunately, the shot shaved the outside of the post.

Iain Walsh grimaced as he saw that chance go begging – there weren't going to be many clear opportunities. His eyes were fixed on the game, ignoring everything else around him. He didn't even notice when Sean Priest arrived twenty minutes into the half.

Russell got up and stretched his legs. Watching a game like this was worse than playing, in some ways. He felt really nervous for Mac as Kettering turned up the pressure, firing more and more crosses towards their tall striker. After half an hour, a fierce header smacked against the bar; five minutes later, the centre forward had another great chance, but was flagged offside.

'Tighten up, Riverside!' Walsh yelled, looking worried.

Russell walked slowly back through the group of parents clustered along the touchline. Mr MacIntyre was standing on the steps of the clubhouse, talking to someone. Russell drifted towards the side of the building, half-listening to the conversation. It took him a moment or two to realise who Mac's father was talking to, but when he figured it out, it made him feel quite cold inside – it was Mr Stephens, Chris's father.

He paused at the corner of the building, near to some rubbish neatly stacked in bin bags, and paused there to listen.

'I'm sure this will all turn out for the best,' Mac's father was saying.

'That's what I keep telling myself,' said Chris's father, sounding very tired and close to despair. 'I can't help but wish that one day soon I can come here and watch him playing for the Colts again – that everything will be just as it used to be.'

Mac's father nodded and tried to offer a comforting smile. They were both looking out over the field, to where the game was getting close to half-time. Russell stepped a little further back into the cover offered by the clubhouse, slipping stealthily out of sight.

There was no sound, no warning. One moment he was alone, the next there was a hand gripping his shoulder and a looming figure emerging from behind the pile of rubbish.

'Hello, again, Russo,' came a familiar voice. Even though Russell had expected to hear it, it still caught him by surprise.

'Mick! What are you doing here?'

'Just enjoying a little morning air, and keeping a close eye on my kid brother.' Mick was grinning, his face twisted in an evil leer of enjoyment. 'Just like I promised.'

'What for? You don't have to worry about me – I'm not going to squeal. You've made sure of that.'

Mick removed his hand from Russell's shoulder and used it to rub his chin. 'Now, have I? That's what I have to ask myself. Can I trust you?'

'You know I don't have any choice.'

The grin returned, broader than ever. 'Well now, as it happens, you may be right. I've taken out a little extra insurance, you see.'

Russell pushed a lock of hair away from his forehead and lifted his head to meet Mick's harsh stare defiantly. 'Have you got Chris Stephens?'

'Who would that be? One of your little friends gone missing, has he?'

'You know he has . . .'

'I don't know – you boys, eh? Always getting into one scrape or another. Is he another little troublemaker like you, Russo?'

Russell found himself getting annoyed at the way Mick kept dodging the question. His brother clearly wasn't going to tell him anything specific. Instead, he was going to tease Russell, to show him how clever he had been, and to make Russell believe there was nothing he could do to harm Mick without getting himself into even greater trouble.

'Where did you keep him? In the old depot?'

'That old place down by the river? The place the police were crawling all over?' Mick's eyes were glistening with anger and spite. 'Did you tell them I was there?'

'No! I haven't said anything to the police! They found Chris's books on the waste ground!'

'Is that right? That was lucky, wasn't it? Are you sure they didn't have any help, Russo?'

'Not from me!' Russell protested with all his might. Mick searched his face. It was Russell's good fortune that he was actually telling the truth.

'Hmmmm . . .'

Mick took a moment to look around the corner towards the field and the distant university buildings. The flickering red and blue lights were reflecting off the glass like Christmas decorations. The thought occurred to Russell that it looked as if the buildings were decked out in the Colts' colours.

'Well, maybe I believe you and maybe I don't,' Mick continued. 'It doesn't matter. I'd moved everything beforehand. It's a shame to have lost that little hiding place, mind. I was mighty glad to find it when I was keeping my eye on you – it's been a fine place for keeping cars and stuff.'

The words struck Russell like a slap in the face. 'You were keeping stolen cars in there! Respraying them! That's where you kept Iain Walsh's car after you stole it.'

Mick grinned once more, always happy when someone recognised how clever he had been. 'Like I said, that was a little Aladdin's cave you found for me. I had to cut the old padlock, of course, and fit a new one. Same with those bollards in Gladstone Street.'

The new padlocks. Russell should have realised. 'What about Chris?' he asked.

'Your mate helped me with a little job, Russo. A little insurance.'

Russell wondered what he meant. Out of the corner of his eye, he could see the police lights flashing against the windows of the university buildings. It came to him at once.

'You got Chris to help you break into the university?'

Mick's teeth showed as he grinned wider than ever. 'You're a smart lad, figuring it out so fast. Smarter than your mate. He set off the alarm in that there science building, thinking he could get the police to come and rescue him. He didn't know that that was what I wanted all along. It was him the security camera saw, not me.'

163

'You wanted the police to come?'

'Of course. I told you, I've arranged a little insurance, to make sure you keep quiet. You see, the police are going to think you were the one who tried to break into the science building. When the cameras saw him, your mate was wearing that old coat of yours...'

Russell was completely surprised. 'My old coat? But that got thrown out!' It was one of the first things that Mrs MacIntyre had insisted on when he had moved into the spare room.

'I know. Interesting what you can find in rubbish bins, now isn't it?' Mick was clearly delighted with himself. 'The coppers may not be that bright, but they'll remember they were looking for someone after that sports shop job who wore a coat just like it, especially if they get a little reminder. And them fellows who run the football team, they'll remember how you wore that coat when they saw you. It'll all fit together like a jigsaw puzzle. And if they ever find the coat...'

Russell felt a moment of panic and his voice became a little louder. 'They'll never believe it was me! I was at home last night – in bed!'

Mick scratched his chin. 'Not much of an alibi, is it? Easy enough to slip out in the dead of night.'

'What do you want?' Russell asked, his voice low.

In that moment of triumph, Mick looked unbearably pleased with himself. He clearly thought he had everything covered. His grip tightened on Russell's shoulder.

'You're starting to see sense, then, Russo?'

'Do I have any choice?'

'Not really. In addition to some stuff I managed to get last night, I still have the keys to that Walsh fellow's car... I can't sell the damn thing, so I might as well get some use from it, eh?'

Russell didn't answer. Instead, he repeated the same question he had asked before.

'What do you want, Mick?'

His brother's face twisted cruelly. He took a moment to look around, making sure that there was no-one likely to disturb them. Then he leaned very close so that he could whisper in Russell's ear.

'If you come home with me now,' he explained, 'we'll forget

this unpleasantness ever happened. You can carry on working for me, just like before. With the added bonus that – if the police ever need to be thrown a small fish to throw them off the scent – I'll have you to take the blame.'

Russell didn't answer for some time. His brother looked confident that he held all the cards and that Russell would have to obey him, just as he had always had to in the past. The only secret Russell had ever been able to keep had been his dream of playing football. Mick had unmasked that secret and taken the dream away. What point was there in defying him?

'If I do, will you let Chris go?' he said, at last, lowering his eyes.

'What does that matter to you?'

'You can't just keep him locked up somewhere, Mick! You have to let him go!'

Mick snarled, obviously angry that Russell still thought he could defy him. 'Don't tell me what to do!' he snapped. 'You obey me! Understand?' Russell nodded quickly. Mick slowly calmed down, and adopted his sickening self-assured smirk. 'If I let him go, what's to stop him talking to the police? What's to stop you changing your mind and coming back to your new friends?' Russell had no answer, but he knew Mick wouldn't have come this far without knowing the solution. All he had to do was wait.

'I know,' said Mick brightly, as if the idea had just come to him. 'We'll have to make sure that when you leave here, you burn all your bridges behind you.' He laughed then, as if he had made some hilariously funny joke. Russell didn't get it.

Moments later he did, and really wished he hadn't.

Mick pulled him back a few steps, behind the pile of rubbish where he had been hiding. He nodded down towards the ground, to where there were four large plastic containers with screw tops, a milk bottle and some rag. Russell's brow creased for a moment as he tried to work out what it was, and then he caught the sharp tang of petrol vapour in his nose and mouth.

Mick was still laughing.

'Boom!' he said.

165

Chris tried to stretch his legs, but he was jammed in too tight. He had no idea of time passing, but the distant sounds of the game were giving him something to fix on. He'd played so often, the natural rhythm of the game was something he could feel in his bones. It would soon be half-time.

Russell stared in horror at the cans of petrol and his brother's maniacal grin.

'I can't!'

Mick's smile disappeared, to be replaced by a fierce glare of anger. 'I told you, you do what I say or –'

'It's pointless! It doesn't achieve anything!'

'It makes certain you can't come back, Russo. You won't be able to play any of your little tricks or try to worm your way back. When this place burns down and you've run off, your new friends will write you off for good.'

Russell stepped back, away from the wall of the building.

'No,' he said, his voice trembling.

Mick's face was twisted in a look of pure fury. Slowly, like a diver rising to the surface through dark water, the mocking smile returned. 'Don't forget, Russo. I have your little friend.'

Russell hesitated. It was the one thing he couldn't do anything about. 'Let him go, Mick. I swear I'll never say anything to anyone. Just let Chris go . . . let me go . . .'

Mick's eyes glittered like snow. His fists were clenched and his knees were slightly bent as if he was preparing to spring at Russell. Slowly, though, he relaxed. 'You just made a big mistake,' he whispered. 'A very big mistake. You're on your own now.'

'No . . . I've got friends . . . they'll help.'

'What? You think they'll be able to stop me? A bunch of kids, some old men and an ex-football player? Not likely, Russo. You've lost.'

There was a sudden yell from around the corner. Russell knew instinctively from the groans of disappointment among the onlookers that Kettering had scored.

'We're not beaten yet,' Russell said out loud.

'Oh, I think you are,' said Mick, smirking.

Russell turned to face his brother. He remembered the

security guard, lying on the floor; he recalled the way Chris and Nicky had mistrusted and despised him; he could picture Chris now, imprisoned somewhere.

He wasn't going to let Mick beat him.

'Take this stuff with you when you go,' he said as calmly as he could, gesturing down at the large bottles of petrol. 'Get away from here. And you'd better let Chris go, or all bets are off. I'll tell the police everything.'

'You'll be dropping yourself into trouble, not me!'

'I'll take my chances.'

Mick took a half-step towards Russell, but the younger Jones brother had moved back into the open, where he would be visible to the players on the field. At last, the mocking, cruel smile vanished. Mick bent over and picked up the bottles, two in each hand.

'This isn't over . . .' he said, and then turned away, quickly disappearing round the back of the building. Russell watched, not certain if he shouldn't follow. Then he heard a sharp blast on the ref's whistle, and Iain Walsh's voice calling everyone together. Slowly, he backed away and went to join the others.

# Seventeen

Mac was more downhearted than anyone had ever seen him before. Russell sat on the ground beside him and tried to catch his eye, but Mac stared broodily at the grass, only looking up to take a drink and a banana when Walsh handed them round.

Eventually, Russell got back up and left him to it. Jazz was prowling around at the other end of the group, looking agitated and uncomfortable.

'What's up?' Russell asked.

'We could have this lot!' Jazz replied instantly, obviously very fired up. 'They're good, but we could beat them.'

'So why aren't we?' asked Russell, and it struck him how easy it was to put his other problems to one side and get back to football. The energy and excitement of the match was sparking around the team like a fireworks display.

'We're playing as well as we can,' replied Jazz. 'But Polly is carrying a bit of a knock, and we're starting to lose the midfield battle . . . Also, Rory's not getting the kind of service he's been used to with Chris alongside him.'

Russell saw him shoot a quick look at where Mac was sitting. He knew there was more to come, but that Jazz wasn't going to say any more without a little nudge.

'How did they score?' he asked.

'A fluke. They broke down the right. Mac came off his line a little to cover the cross, but it looped off Tollie's foot and went over his head. You remember that goal that Germany scored against England in the '90 World Cup? It was just like that.'

Russell nodded in agreement, even though they'd never had a TV in the ramshackle hovel that was the Jones household.

Jazz was watching his face carefully. He answered the question Russell hadn't even asked.

'No . . . you wouldn't have reached it either. Anyway, a minute later Mac pulled off a blinding save – and got a whack in the face for his trouble.'

Russell nodded. Small wonder Mac looked out of sorts.

Iain Walsh was talking to them in small groups, trying to energise the team to go out in the second half and get the equaliser. Russell saw Sean Priest have a quiet word with Mac. He remembered that he hadn't really had much of a chance to talk with Priest since the time he had overheard him talking with Whistler outside the Stonebridge clubhouse after the stuff had been taken from his car. Between them, Chris, Nicky and Russell had returned the stolen items, but whereas the other two had been fêted as heroes, Russell had no idea what Priest thought about him now. All he knew for sure was that Priest had told the police to forget about the theft – did that mean he had forgotten it as well? Or did Priest still believe Russell was involved, or that he had stolen the money from Stonebridge's clubhouse, as Whistler had said?

Did anyone *really trust* him?

Instinctively, he looked back to the pavilion, as if needing to see Mick standing there, watching. There was no sign of his brother. Mac's father and Mr Stephens were still standing on the steps, in front of the window into the ground floor room the cricketers used, backlit by a flickering amber light from inside. Russell felt a deep pit in the bottom of his stomach. He hoped that Mick would see sense and let Chris go.

There was no sign of anyone else hanging around.

His attention was brought back to the game. Iain Walsh had finished the pep talk and was looking concernedly at Polly's calf, which was starting to show a vivid bruise from the whack he had taken.

'I've got some cream in the dressing room which might take the heat out of that,' he said.

'It's getting really stiff,' Polly groaned.

'We'll give it five minutes to see if you can still run,' Walsh told the tall midfielder. 'If not, I'll give Jones a run out.'

Russell almost jumped when he heard his name. He quickly stepped over to where Walsh was now standing up, leaving

169

Polly to pull his sock back up his battered leg.

'Let me go in goal,' he said without introduction. Walsh turned to face him. 'Mac can replace Polly better than I can.'

'You're not ready,' Walsh replied.

Russell plucked at his sleeve as he turned away. Walsh shook him off and jogged towards the changing rooms, head down. When Russell looked away, he could see Mac staring up at him.

'Want my boots while you're at it?'

'What?'

'A bit keen to get my place, aren't you?'

Russell could scarcely believe his ears. 'I thought that was what you wanted!'

Mac's face had hardened into a determined scowl. 'I'm not going to get whipped off in the middle of the game, as if everything's my fault. I'm going back out there and I'll hold up my end. You just concentrate on making sure we don't lose out if Polly has to come off.'

Russell sighed and looked up once more. Nothing was settled, it seemed. Even Mac didn't believe in him.

He found himself staring at Mac's father once more, still earnestly engaged in conversation with Chris Stephens' dad. It was hard to see the expressions on their faces now because the light behind them had grown even brighter, throwing them into shadow. They were facing his way, looking into the distance at nothing in particular, hands thrust into their coat pockets to ward off the chill. Mr Stephens' fair hair was almost like a halo in the light —

'Oh my God!' wailed Russell, and he started to run towards the clubhouse. It was only about fifteen metres to the short flight of steps and the porch outside the pavilion window, through which the light was growing ever brighter. Other people had turned round as he called out, and saw the growing glare through the window.

Mr MacIntyre saw him rushing up. His face started to open into a smile, then took on a slightly bemused expression as Russell closed in rapidly. He opened his mouth to speak just before the window exploded.

Glass flew out all over the porch and the steps, and there was a huge gust of hot air that bowled the two men over and knocked Russell back a step. A huge tongue of livid orange flame sprang out, licking at the top of the window frame and tasting the underside of the upper balcony. Paintwork blistered and peeled, while a cloud of oily black smoke bloomed around the stricken clubhouse like a cloak.

Having tasted freedom, the flame seemed to recede back into the pavilion, which Russell could see was already well aflame. The hot air was roaring and flowing out of the window, driving out a plume of acrid smoke.

Russell stepped back, looking up at the upper floors. They didn't seem to be alight yet, but the wooden building was going up quickly.

Mac and Chris's fathers were picking themselves off the floor. Mr MacIntyre swore when he saw the blaze. They were both covered in tiny shards of broken glass.

'How could that have happened so fast?' gasped Mr Stephens.

'Is anyone inside?' asked Mac's father.

All three of them remembered at once, crying out: 'Walsh!'

Russell remembered the coach striding up the stairs, concentrating on Polly's injury. With luck, he would have noticed something, or perhaps the fire wouldn't have taken so much upstairs.

Mr Stephens raced for the stairs while Mr MacIntyre cried out that he would call the fire brigade and ran for his car. Russell was left standing at the front of the building wondering what to do. An impulse carried him around to the side of the clubhouse, sprinting as fast as he could. He passed the spot where he had been talking to Mick, and noticed that the rags and milk bottles were gone. He continued to the rear of the building.

There was a back door. The wooden panels were broken in and the door sagged on its hinges. It was already on fire, and through the opening all Russell could see was an inferno of heat and light. Even the upper floor appeared to be gushing smoke, and Russell could see orange flames flickering through the upper windows.

Russell almost screamed in fury. He should have realised that Mick was giving in too easily. Instead of leaving any loose ends, Mick had smashed the door in and used the petrol to fire the heart of the building. He probably hoped Russell would get the blame anyhow – but even if that didn't work, Mick would still have had his revenge.

He whirled round, wondering if his brother was anywhere in sight. There were some trees along the edge of the campus on this side, close to the back of the clubhouse. Then along on one side there was the car park and the road leading to the campus entrance, while in the other direction there was the footpath through the gate which led on to the riverside path.

No sign of Mick. But he couldn't have gone far.

He turned back to the clubhouse and completed his run round the outside, going back round to the front where there was now a group of adults and footballers watching in horror as the building was consumed by the raging, fuel-fed fire. Police officers were rushing over from the science block, and a few were starting to form a cordon to hold people back. At the other end of the façade, Russell could see Mr Stephens staggering back down the stairs, coughing and choking. Smoke was billowing from the doorway.

He was alone.

'No!' yelled Russell.

A policeman was gesturing at him to get away. Russell remained frozen to the spot.

That was when he heard a familiar voice calling his name. He turned quickly and saw Nicky in the grasp of a uniformed officer, struggling to break free.

'Russell!' yelled Nicky again, his voice almost lost in the roaring noise from the building. Russell concentrated, ignoring all the distractions.

Nicky was waving his hands, pointing towards the back of the building. Odd fragments of what he was saying were swamped by the sounds of the building starting to break apart, but Russell heard his final words distinctly.

'Your brother – he said he was going to get rid of Chris!'

# Eighteen

Russell looked back at the blazing building. Nicky's words had seized him, almost choking him as if a strong hand had closed around his throat. Mick hadn't just set fire to the building to get Russell into even more trouble – he was trying to murder Chris!

He couldn't believe Mick would go that far, but nothing else made sense. Mick must have hidden Chris in the clubhouse. He wouldn't have wanted to take him very far after he removed him from the depot; not if he was going to get Chris to stage the robbery here at the university. So he would have left him in the clubhouse overnight, tied up in one of the rooms. And if he was right, Chris was still inside, trapped in that fire . . .

Russell realised, as he thought it through, just what that meant. Mick had been trying to get him to set fire to the building. *He* would have murdered Chris Stephens!

He couldn't allow Mick to succeed, not even partially. If Chris was inside, he had to get him out.

The downstairs was a shambles, the single large room filled with flames. That only left the changing rooms upstairs.

Russell looked up. The balcony was scorched but it wasn't burning. He knew at once what he had to do.

He shinned up one of the supporting pillars, hearing the policemen telling him to come back. The paintwork was hot, but Russell was quickly able to reach the balcony and vault over the rail.

There were two tiny windows, narrow apertures about five feet up. The one nearer the stairs looked in on the away dressing room, and Russell stretched up to take a look through. It was empty, but Russell could see flames in the passageway beyond.

The window to the left was in the home dressing room. Once again, he took hold of the sill and pulled himself up. The room was dark and there were clouds of smoke near the ceiling. Even so, Russell could see a shape huddled on the floor. It was barely moving, just a slight rising and falling in the centre.

It had to be Walsh, out on the floor but still alive.

Russell took off his boot to smash the window. It needed several heavy blows before the glass gave and he could reach inside to release the catch. In his hurry, Russell snagged his left hand on a small shard, and felt its bite. He ignored the pain and the feeling of blood starting to flow, and levered the window open.

He hauled himself up and through the narrow space, feeling loose glass falling on his back. The air in the room was hot and foul with thick smoke, but as he dropped to the floor he found he could breathe a little easier.

He crawled over the floor and reached the heap on the floor. Walsh was stunned but unharmed, except for a gash on his head. His eyes were a little unfocused, but he was slowly shaking off the fog now that Russell was there to help him.

'What . . .?' he mumbled, unable to finish the sentence.

'The building's on fire!' said Russell, with some urgency.

Walsh seemed to recover a little more, and shook his head. He touched the wound over his right eye with trembling fingers. 'It felt like a bomb had gone off! The medicine box fell off the top of the locker and cracked me on the head.'

'It doesn't look too bad,' said Russell. 'We'd better get out of here.'

'You'll get no argument from me,' muttered Walsh, pulling himself up on to his knees. At once he tasted the billowing smoke and coughed. 'How did it get this bad so fast?' he wondered aloud.

Russell decided not to answer right now. Walsh lowered himself back to the ground and started to crawl towards the door, using the thin layer of breathable air near the floor.

'Not that way! The passage is full of flames!'

'It's the only way out!' Walsh choked.

'We'll have to go out through the window.'

Walsh managed a short laugh. 'That tiny thing?'

They soaked some cloths in bottled water and tied them over their mouths to make it a little easier to breathe. Then they crawled over the floor to the window. The floorboards were getting hot.

Reaching up to the window, they found a little cooler air coming through the window, but not much. Walsh stripped off his coat while Russell levered himself through the gap. Once on the far side, he turned back to help Walsh through. The coach heaved himself up, using a bench as a step, and pushed his head and shoulders into the gap. It was soon really obvious that he wasn't going to get through.

'Maybe we can take it off at the hinges . . .' Russell offered. Walsh's face suggested they'd need to take the whole wall down to get him out. Even so, they attacked the old frame as best they could. The wood was rotten in places, and without the glass the whole window was weak. Russell managed to snap the bottom spar, and then they attacked the rest of the frame. Russell saw that his hand was bleeding quite badly; it was ripped across the back from the base of his thumb to the middle of his wrist.

It was desperate work. Walsh was finding it hard to cope with the smoke. In less than a minute, he was sweating hard and his breathing had became very ragged. He slumped against the wall, coughing and wheezing.

'Don't give up!' yelled Russell. He grabbed Walsh's shoulders and – with all his strength – pulled the coach's head and shoulders into the enlarged space once more.

The extra inch or so they had made was making all the difference, but Walsh was too weak to lift himself into the space. Cursing and yelling, Russell pulled at his arms, dragging him inch by painful inch through the shattered window. Twice he almost lost him, and twice more Walsh's body seemed to snag on the broken wood. Russell adjusted his grip, ignoring the pain in his hand, and pulled on Walsh's arms again.

Finally, Walsh's chest and stomach were through, and as his weight tipped over, he crashed out on to the balcony, carrying Russell to the floor with him.

Breathing hard, Russell peered through the railings at the crowd below. People were running towards them. Someone had found a ladder, and two policemen were propping it against the pavilion, precariously balanced on the steps, as far from the fire's heart as they could manage. Moments later, one of the coppers poked his head over the rails and started to pull himself over on to the balcony.

'Well done, son!' he said, grinning.

'I think there's someone else inside!' Russell cried.

The policeman's smile vanished.

'What? We were told there was only one!'

'There might be a boy too!' Russell gasped. He pulled himself to his feet as the policeman rolled over the rail by Walsh's side. Just along from where they were standing, the fire was licking at the edge of the balcony once more, and the timber was starting to blacken.

Russell looked out into the crowd of onlookers. He found Nicky's face looking up at him in alarm.

'Where is he?!' Russell shouted. 'Nicky – where's Chris?'

It was hard to make out Nicky's reply above the roar of the flames and the hubbub below. He seemed to be telling Russell to go down. As Russell watched, Nicky waved again and pointed towards where the path disappeared through the old metal gate.

He lowered himself over the railing after a second policeman had climbed up to help Iain Walsh. He slid down the ladder's rail, hitting the ground quickly, and sprinted away from the heat of the fire. Nicky was at the edge of the crowd.

'You're completely mad!' gasped Nicky.

'What?!'

'Climbing in there like that!'

'You said Chris was inside!'

'I thought he was . . .' Nicky said hesitantly.

Russell was suddenly struck by a glimmer of hope. 'Tell me everything!' he said.

It started with the plan he had cooked up to turn the tables on Mick. Instead of Mick watching Russell all the time, they had arranged to find a way to catch Mick in the act.

Gainsbury didn't have a Cup game that weekend, so Nicky had ducked out of the friendly match they were supposed to be playing and had hung around in the bushes at the back of the clubhouse, keeping an eye out for Mick. After all, it made sense that he would have to find somewhere from where he could spy on Russell.

'I never saw him arrive . . .' Nicky explained quickly. 'Then I heard a bumping noise, like two plastic bottles bumping together, and there he was, running along the back of the clubhouse. He hid the stuff among the piles of rubbish, and then he waited there for you.'

'Go on!' urged Russell impatiently.

'I caught a bit of what you said to each other, then you went back, and he came to the back door and kicked it in. He went inside, and then when he came out he said, "Now for that other brat".'

'He said that *after* he came out from the clubhouse?'

Nicky nodded. They both looked at the spreading fire.

'OK, what then?' asked Russell.

'That's what I was trying to tell you. He ran off down the footpath, towards the gate.'

Russell's mind was racing as he thought it all through. Mick must have spilled the petrol around downstairs after he broke in through the back door. He would have used one of the milk bottles with a lighted rag to start the fire, throwing it into the middle of the room where it could ignite the furniture.

And then he had come out and said –

'Chris isn't in there!' he gasped, and then he shouted it again: 'Chris isn't in there!!' Of course he wasn't. Mick would have known that the dressing rooms would be used before the game, while the big downstairs room was too easy to see into. Not here, then.

'Then where?' asked Nicky.

Mick had left the campus through the back gate. Perhaps he had left the pick-up in the old depot? No, not with the police crawling all over Gladstone Street. He'd never get out unobserved.

'Of course!' he yelled, and at once he started running towards the gate. 'Stonebridge! Tell the police Chris is in the clubhouse at Stonebridge!'

Stonebridge was a bigger building, with more places to hide something . . .

And Mick knew how to get in there, because Russell had shown him! It really did make sense!

He could hear policemen calling at him to come back as he rushed away. There were sirens in the distance; fast-approaching fire engines. He ignored them, just as he ignored the throbbing pain in his hand and the uncomfortable tightness in his chest.

Russell thundered along the path and through the gate on to the river bank. As always on a Sunday, it was quiet along this stretch of the river, with just a few students off in the distance. Russell was heading in the other direction, towards the gaunt brick walls of the old depot.

How much of a start did Mick have on him? A few minutes, he guessed, although he knew time could have passed very quickly while he was inside the clubhouse, hauling Iain Walsh through that window.

He looked along the pipe, trying to see if he could see his brother, but he couldn't. Several of the policemen who had been searching the old factories were rounding the corner, heading on to the river bank. Instinctively, Russell slowed his frantic pace so it looked less as if he was running away from something. Even so, one of the coppers called on Russell to halt.

'There's a fire!' Russell blurted. 'At the university sports field!'

'So much we'd figured out,' said the policeman. His colleagues were running past, their boots crunching solidly on the path. 'Why are you running away?'

'I'm scared of fires!' Russell answered quickly. 'I was playing football on the field right by the building – I almost got burned!'

The desperation in his voice must have made him sound almost convincing because the policeman relaxed a little. They were about twenty metres from the depot wall. Russell noticed the green fibre rope was hanging over – not out of sight. Mick must have gone that way! He scanned the pipe once again. Nothing.

Curiously though, one of the boats the police divers had been using was making its way across the river towards the far side. Had they seen Mick?

The fire engines must have arrived at the university now. Their sirens were louder than ever. The policeman looked up, away from Russell, and in that moment the boy ducked under his arm and took off towards the wall.

'HEY!' the copper yelled, obviously realising that he was being deceived. Russell didn't look back. He covered those twenty metres in less than five seconds from a standing start, and launched himself at the rope.

It was like stretching for a cross that was almost too high for him to reach. He took off from his right foot, kicked at the air with his left as if he was climbing an invisible stair, then threw up his right hand to grab the rope. He caught it, felt the fibres sting his palm, then held on with his left hand as well. More pain, as the injured flesh split wider apart and the muscle screamed. Then his feet hit the wall and his boot studs scraped against the brickwork as he pulled himself up to the top and on to the cornice.

'Get down from there!' the copper yelled. Russell looked back for a moment so that he could twitch the rope away from the constable's hands and draw it over the top of the wall. Then he stood up, measured his balance, and started to walk along the riverside wall to the pipe.

'Don't be stupid, son!' he heard the policeman yell, and Russell knew he must be leaning out over the rail below, watching his progress. The top of the wall was narrow, just the width of a brick apart. Russell moved along it quickly, arms outstretched. The wind was plucking at his track suit jacket, but he didn't fall. Moments later he reached the cross struts of the frame that surrounded the end of the pipe.

He looked along the length of the black metal tube as it climbed up and then spanned the river in a straight, horizontal line. He had hoped Mick would be just ahead of him, but his brother was nowhere in sight. Had Mick been able to cross the river so quickly, or was Russell's guess wrong?

Either way, the situation was making Russell panic. Some sixth sense was telling him that this was wrong; that Mick couldn't have got so far away in such a short time. At that same moment he heard something scrape on the metal below him, and felt a vibration through his hands.

He looked down and saw Mick looking up at him, his face

twisted in fury. He had his hands and one foot on a ladder that led up to where Russell was holding on to the pipe's supporting frame. His face was blackened with smoke and oil.

'What are you doing here?' he roared.

'I came after you – I wanted to stop you from hurting Chris Stephens!'

'So . . . you've figured out where he is, have you? You always were too clever for your own good, Russo!'

'Please, Mick . . . can't you just leave it now?'

'Leave it, he says? You idiot, I bet you've half the police in Oldcester behind you! You want to give up worrying about your mate and start worrying about yourself!'

With those words, Mick pulled himself up on to the ladder and started moving quickly up towards Russell. He wondered for a moment if he should turn back along the wall, but that would have left Mick with a clear run towards Chris. In the mood he was in, Mick was going to take his revenge on somebody – better it was Russell himself.

Reaching over his head, he clambered up the frame to where the pipe bent over the wall and started its flat trajectory across the river.

The metal was cold and damp, and the wind gusted and flicked at him as he started to cross the river. He passed by the spiked metal collar, out over the black water. The copper called again. Russell looked behind to his right and saw the officer leaning out over the rail. He was using his radio; calling to his mates. Several of them were on the path, turning back from the fire. They gathered in a clump by the life-saver, shouting and pointing. Russell ignored them and started crawling along the top of the pipe.

An inflatable appeared from underneath, cutting out ahead and to his left. It was the police divers' boat, following them across the river, bouncing across the waves the breeze lifted from the water's surface. It was slowing down.

Russell forced himself to concentrate on his grip as he crawled along the pipe on his hands and knees. The track suit didn't grip as well as his old jeans, so he pulled the leg cuffs up to his knees so that his flesh could get a better purchase. The black metal pipe felt like an ice box to the touch.

He ignored the discomfort and moved as quickly as he

dared, faster than ever before. That momentary pause had allowed Mick to reach the top of the frame as well, and his brother was now venturing out on to the pipe, balancing at first on his feet, but then copying Russell's ungainly crawl once he realised how slick the pipe was.

Mick had always been dangerous, but now he was unhinged. You had to be mad to cross the river like this – Russell knew that better than anyone. Seeing Mick behind him made Russell move even faster. He wasn't sure what his brother intended to do to him – or to Chris, if he got to him first – but he feared the worst.

He moved on, praying that he would reach the second collar soon and know that he was across. Though he'd done this crazy stunt a few times, it had never been under such conditions as this. He felt sick with anxiety. He didn't want to fall, but he didn't have time to be careful. He could hear Mick behind him, his hands slapping against the pipe and his cowboy boots making the metal ring like a gong.

Even though he was moving quickly, it seemed the journey would last for ever. Mick was very close. Russell thought he could feel his brother's breath on the back of his neck. He could certainly hear it; Mick was muttering curses with each gulp of air he took.

At last, the second collar appeared in front of him. Almost there now! Russell stretched through the narrow gap, looking back over his shoulder as he did so. To his horror, Mick was almost up with him, stretching out towards his feet.

He felt Mick's fingers clutching at his foot as he dived through the collar, slithering down the pipe as it angled towards the ground. He heard a loud clang as something hit the pipe hard, then Mick's loud cry. Somehow, he managed to halt himself before he plunged off the side. He gripped the pipe with his elbows and knees, holding on for dear life and waiting for the inevitable moment when Mick would reach out and grab him.

After what seemed like a lifetime, he realised someone was shouting. He opened his eyes and realised that one of the police divers in the small boat below was calling to him. The pipe was about eight or nine metres above the water, and the two wet-suited officers were peering up at him, yelling at him to be careful. Russell looked around. He was lying across one of the joins between two lengths of pipes. It was the protruding metal and the large bolts that he had managed to hang on to. To his amazement, he realised that he couldn't see Mick at all.

Then he heard the second voice.

'Russo!!! Help me!!!!'

Russell looked back. He was just a few metres beyond the spiked collar. He could see the gap where he had snapped away two of the metal bars. It was a slender gap – perhaps Mick hadn't been able to get through? But then he realised that he couldn't see Mick at all.

He crawled back up the slope. As he neared the collar, he noticed a scrap of brown leather, a torn length which was speared through by one of the broken spikes. As he came closer, he could see it trailed over the edge of the pipe. He looked over the side and saw Mick, dangling down towards the water, held fast by his leather jacket.

'Mick! What happened?'

'I got caught, you idiot!' snapped Mick, his face more frightened than angry. 'I can't believe it! I felt something tug, and then I slipped. Next thing I know, I'm hanging over the side here.'

The police boat was just underneath Mick now, but the policemen couldn't reach Mick from where they were. All they could offer was advice of the 'don't touch anything' variety.

Russell could barely believe his good fortune. In reaching for him, Mick had lost his balance and slipped off the side! For once, Mick was helpless.

'Mick, listen to me! Where's Chris Stephens?'

Mick tried to turn his head, but as he struggled the leather ripped a little more. There were only a few centimetres left before it ripped clean through.

'Don't be bloody stupid, Russo! I'm stuck here!' He gestured down at the boat with his eyes, as if to say 'and there's coppers listening'.

'I know. I'll get you down. But first, you have to tell me. Chris is in the clubhouse at Stonebridge, right?'

'RUSSELL!'

'Right?'

Mick's face was purple with rage as he finally realised his brother meant business.

'Yes! Yes! In one of the cupboards in the stock room!' He looked down at the policemen with what might have been an innocent look on any other face. 'He's all right! No harm has come to the boy!'

Russell climbed slowly up to the collar so that he was right above his brother, making sure Mick couldn't reach up with his hands and grab him.

'I didn't think you'd really hurt him,' said Russell, trying to convince himself that it was true. Somehow, it was hard to remember why he was frightened before. 'And the fire was just a distraction, right?'

'Russo!!!' Mick pleaded.

'You might as well tell them, Mick. You see, my mate Nicky saw you start the fire. We guessed you'd turn up today, so instead of you watching me, we were watching you.' Russell heard Mick stifle an anguished moan, and knew he almost had him. 'Nicky had a camera, Mick,' he said.

'Get me down!' Mick yelled.

Russell edged further along the pipe, then turned and faced back towards the collar. The coat had torn a little further. The policemen were urging Mick to keep still.

'There was someone inside the clubhouse, Mick . . .' Russell continued.

His brother's face looked up in alarm. 'Jeez, I never meant for no-one to get hurt!' he blurted. As he realised what he'd said, his eyes shut tight and he bit his lip.

'And the rest, Mick . . .'

'You little . . .' Mick cursed, and he tried to reach up with one hand to grab at Russell's foot. Russell quickly jerked it away, his own hold on the metal collar now quite secure. The jacket tore to within a centimetre or two of the edge. The hem looked as if it might hold for a moment longer . . .

'Tell them.'

'All right! All right!' Mick looked down at the policemen in the boat. 'This is my little brother, Russell Jones. I told some of your lads that he nicked some stuff from a car – it's not true, I took it. They also think he might be involved with another car

183

that got nicked. That's not true either. The car's at a breakers on the other side of town. I tried to sell it, but no-one wanted the pile of old junk, so I got what I could for scrap. There's other stuff too . . . that break-in at the university last night –'

'And the fire,' said Russell, nodding over towards the plume of smoke on the other side of the river.

'And the fire . . .' hissed Mick through gritted teeth. He looked up at Russell. 'That's enough – now haul me up.'

Russell considered this for a moment. It could still be some time before the police from the university managed the long trip along the main road, over the bridge, and then on foot along the river bank to this end of the pipe. Once Mick was safe, what then? Russell realised that he didn't much fancy the idea of being alone on top of the pipe with his brother.

'I can't do that, Mick,' he said. He held out his hand to show the deep wound. 'You're too heavy anyway.'

Mick swayed a little as he tried in vain to get some purchase on the pipe's smooth side.

'So you're just going to let me get caught?'

That was certainly an option Russell was prepared to consider, but he knew that Mick still had the means to make life difficult for him. He might well be innocent of anything since he had hooked up with the Colts, but there was a long history before that.

'Mick,' he whispered. 'If I help you escape, will you promise to go right away? Will you leave all of us alone?'

'Are you trying to make a deal?' Mick squealed angrily, struggling to turn so that he could reach up with his hands. He sounded desperate. Sooner or later, there would be dozens of police swarming around, and there he was pinned to the pipe like a butterfly in a collector's case.

'I just want all this to finish . . .' sighed Russell.

Mick managed to turn far enough that he could see Russell's face. 'No deals!' he hissed. 'Remember, I'm your brother. You'll do what I say. Haven't I always kept me eye on you? Do you think I'm just going to turn me back and ignore you now?'

Russell looked down at the river. The two policemen in the inflatable were looking back at him, puzzled.

He turned back to his brother. 'You're right,' he said. 'I knew you'd never leave us alone.' He reached down with his hand. Mick grinned as he twisted his body round, trying to turn so that he could grab Russell's arm. 'I hope you're still a good swimmer,' said Russell.

Mick clearly realised what his brother was about to do. 'Don't you dare, Russo! Without me, you'll have to look after Ma and Pa all by yourself!'

'We'll manage,' said Russell, and he grinned as he said it. A grin anyone who knew the Jones boys would recognise. And he pulled at the scrap of leather.

# Nineteen

Almost an hour late, the ref agreed to start the second half. Kettering's manager was pretty unhappy with the idea of starting the game again at all, and the ref said his wife would kill him if he was late for Sunday lunch again, but everyone agreed that it really wouldn't be fair if Riverside were knocked out of the Cup because of all that had happened, and that would have been the result if they had abandoned the game there and then. There was no way they could have arranged a replay.

The Riverside Colts were gathered in a small clump behind one of the goals, full of nervous chatter about everything that had happened, and watching the fire brigade damping down the ruined clubhouse. The pitch on that side of the field was a bit damp after the fire brigade had done their bit, and the size of the crowd had grown appreciably as 30 policemen hung around to watch, along with about 300 people who'd arrived to watch the fire. They had all heard the story of the dramatic rescue, the recovery of the missing schoolboy and the capture of a cunning and resourceful crook who had almost evaded the police until he fell into the river.

The local paper had managed to find a photographer close by, and he was snapping away. The word was that BBC Radio Oldcester was sending a radio car, and that they might even make the evening national news.

'I don't see how we can just pack up and go home,' said the ref.

Reluctantly, the Kettering boss agreed to delay their return, and to play the second half. While he called a few parents on Mr MacIntyre's mobile phone, Sean Priest lined up the Colts.

'Will Mr Walsh be all right?' asked Jazz.

'Sure. They're just playing safe, taking him into hospital. Smoke can get on the lungs in a fire like that, and he was in there for quite a while before Jones got him out.'

Russell grinned sheepishly. He had been told what a hero he was so often he was beginning to wish he'd gone into the river instead of Mick.

He'd had a few moments to speak with Mr MacIntyre and explain that he was moving back in with his family. Mac's father understood, of course, and said he'd do what he could to find his father some honest work. Maybe they could get Marie and Davey back into school too.

'OK,' said Sean. 'I don't have much to say about the second half. After everything else that has happened, a game of football isn't all that important. So go out there and have fun.'

'What about Polly?' asked Stamp, reminding Priest of the whack the midfielder had taken. After an hour of standing around in the cold, his leg had stiffened up even more. There was no way he could play.

'OK. I suppose we'll have to play a sub . . .' He looked around and started laughing. His eyes fell on Russell. 'I don't think your fans would ever forgive me if I didn't put you on. Go on, super-sub, show them what you're made of . . .'

'In goal?'

Priest was almost overcome with amazement. 'Don't you ever give up? You've got a split hand, Russell!!'

'Yes, but Mac's had a whack in the face . . .' said Jazz.

'And Russ can hardly be expected to run around in midfield after everything else he's done.'

'All right, all right! I know when I'm beaten. Anything else? Should I ring the FA and tell him you're available for the next England game?'

'No, I'm happy . . .' said Russell, and the grin all across his face showed that he was. He pulled off his track suit and found his goalkeeper's gloves. Mac pulled off his goalkeeper's jersey but it was too small for Russell to wear, so Jones dived into his bag and pulled out a worn old yellow and black shirt, and tugged that over his head.

'Actually, there is another substitution you could consider . . .' came a voice from the back of the group.

'You can't play, Nicky! You're registered for another team!'

187

'Not me,' said Nicky, shaking his head as if he was astonished that Priest didn't know what he was talking about. He stretched out his arm in the direction of the car park, where a man and a boy were talking with some of the police officers and a doctor. They were all laughing and joking.

'Now, you really are joking this time, aren't you?' asked Priest.

'And was he?' asked Griff.

Chris waggled his hand in a maybe/maybe not gesture. 'Sort of. I was still pretty stiff after being tied up on and off for three days, but the doctor said he couldn't see anything wrong with me that a few days' rest wouldn't cure. That and a solid meal. I was so glad to be out of that cupboard, I was ready for anything.'

'You should have seen him!' said Nicky. 'This copper had some biscuits in his car, and Chris ate the lot in about three mouthfuls.'

'What did you expect?' demanded Chris. 'Mick had kept me locked up in different places for days, and he only fed me McDonalds every now and again. I was dying for some real food.'

'Weren't you frightened all that time?' asked one of the girls who had bravely tacked themselves on to the edge of the group.

'Some of the time. But Mick never got really nasty – not like on TV, or something. I was a bit worried when he dragged me out to help him stage that break-in at the university, because I was sure we'd get caught. I'm not cut out for a life of crime. Then, when I could hear someone playing football outside, all the fear went away. I just wanted to get out there and play.'

'So it was the game at Stonebridge you could hear?' asked Griff.

Chris nodded.

'So what happened then?' asked Fuller, who was deeply sceptical about the details of the story even though he knew the substance of it was true. The kids at school had been talking about nothing else for days.

'I came on for the last ten minutes.'

'And he scored!' laughed Nicky.

Fuller fell back against the back of the bench, looking around at the crowd that had gathered to hear the story. 'You don't believe all this, do you?' He scoffed. He jabbed a finger at Russell. 'I suppose you saved a penalty, right? And Chris's goal was a last-minute winner; a fifty yard thunderbolt the keeper couldn't reach?'

Griff put him in a headlock. 'Don't you read the papers?' he asked.

Russell cleaned up the story before Fuller was strangled. 'They got a penalty just after the restart. Mac said he thought their bloke would blast it up the middle. I was sure he'd place it, and I went right so that I could use my good hand.'

'And?'

'And he blasted it up the middle,' Russell admitted.

Everyone laughed. Fuller managed to utter a sour 'Some hero you are' amidst the ruckus, but even he was finding it hard to be cynical in the face of such a brilliant tale.

'And Chris got the winner, right?' asked Griff.

'You're as bad as Fuller!' mocked Nicky. 'This isn't Children's BBC, you know. The Colts lost three-one, and Chris got a three inch tap-in your mother could have scored,' explained Nicky. 'He was about three miles offside, but who cared?'

No-one had, except for the TV news crew who arrived just in time for the final whistle. For everyone else, it had been the perfect end to the game. Three or four hundred people had applauded the two teams off the field at the end, and Mr Stephens had virtually had to prise Chris away from the others to go home and get some rest.

'How's the hand?' Mac asked Russell.

'Fine. Sean's patch-up did the trick.' He flexed it a bit to test the wound. 'It's still a bit sore, but I'll be fit for next week.'

'So, everyone's happy ever after, eh?' asked Fuller. 'You're going to be the goalkeeper for the school team and the Colts. Mac gets to play midfield, and Chris gets his face in more newspapers than Cantona. God, it's enough to make you sick.'

Russell nudged Chris and tried to keep his face straight as he replied. 'Well, there's still the matter of my brother Davey.

189

It seems he's got the bug now — fancies himself as a bit of a midfield player . . . you know, working just in front of the back four.'

'What?' howled Fuller. 'That's my place!!'

'You're only as good as your last game, Fuller,' said Chris, grinning.

The bell was ringing for the end of lunch, and they started to troop to their different classrooms.

'Brilliant,' laughed Nicky. 'Did you see his face? What a sucker . . .'

'Don't get too clever about it,' said Russell. 'There's my sister as well.'

'Oh, right!' scoffed Nicky. 'And she wants to play right wing, does she?'

'No,' said Russell. 'She just fancies the bloke who does . . .'

Chris and Jazz were weeping with laughter as they staggered into the hall behind the other two. As far as they were concerned, that was the moment that Russell really did become one of their team mates . . .

Now you've read *The Keeper*, why not catch up with Chris and Nicky in the other exciting books in the TEAM MATES series?

OVERLAP

Top-scoring striker Chris Stephens and fiery midfield dynamo Nicky Fiorentino are the stars of their school team – best mates off the pitch and an awesome combination on it. They sweep all before them in the battle for the County Schools Cup, and the two lads celebrate one victory after another. It seems nothing can stop them lifting the cup – until the day a talent scout turns up to watch them play, and the best of friends become bitter enemies . . .

ISBN 0 7535 0080 9

FOUL!

Football-crazy Chris Stephens can't believe it when he's offered a place on a soccer exchange scheme with some American players. It's the opportunity of a lifetime. But when Jace Goodman arrives from Miami, it soon becomes clear that he's never played football in his life. Who is he? How did he manage to get a place on the scheme? And just who is the scar-faced man who comes looking for him . . .?

ISBN 0 7535 0070 1